EMISSARY

EMISSARY

MICHAEL LEON

ISBN: 978-0-9944209-2-3
eISBN: 978-0-9944209-3-0

Typeset and cover design by BookPOD Pty Ltd

For all the special El's who have touched my life.

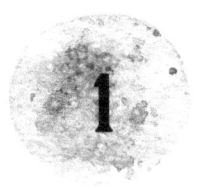

EARLY VISITATIONS

VINCENT FELT THE COMFORT of the approaching morning light more than most, for he alone knew the dark harboured another world.

He had felt its strange entanglement that morning, arriving for the next day's lecture, the last for the year. The campus grounds were free of the normal car fume and students rushing. Cool pre-dawn light heightened the forest-lined shapes of eucalypt and pine, drawing darker memories from the recesses of his mind. The dark had many forms; you could feel it even in light and in the wind as it swept through narrow corridors funnelling cold whispers, as if short of breath. Vincent walked through the tunnels. Concrete walls filled with posters old and new; a torn kaleidoscope of student advertising flapped in the breeze. He mistook its sounds for footsteps.

He quickened his step, passing through the darkness without incident, approaching a tree-lined pathway to his office. But footsteps remained in his mind, echoing in the silence like shade encroaching the light. A real noise invaded his space, a shuffle in the forest leaves, perhaps a small feral cat. He gazed out to the dense eucalypt forest, hoping to catch a glimpse of the scampering animal but instead silence, bar the sound of his own heart beat.

Vincent stood still in the dawn light, a trickle of sweat formed from his brow, his muscles tightened. He stretched, seeking relief, chuckling unconvincingly at his imagined fear.

Light began to filter through, evoking the sounds of life waking. Amongst the sounds of sparrows singing and cats scurrying, he thought he heard a voice, distant yet directed toward him alone.

"I see you," he thought, before the words repeated. "I see you."

And then the shadows returned, the shadows that had haunted him all his young life, buried deep and swarming through his mind. They re-ignited deep fears and a forgotten pain.

It captured him, like a black hole captures stars.

His mind raced over long buried memories of adolescence. Crawling insects he had called them, but the invading form had been something else entirely. He never saw it but he had felt it, swarming, enveloping his skin, suffocating him, but when he dared look - nothing.

Just ten years earlier, he was told often by those who should know that the insects didn't exist. They were hallucinations brought on by drug abuse. But the doctor's reassurances didn't help. Even worse, he had faced the darkness without his parents. Both had been taken by a single vehicle collision, leaving him to face adolescence alone, a state ward his home. Ultimately he was diagnosed with depression and paranoia, brought on, they said, by his parents' deaths, leaving him too traumatised to face the truth. Drugs minimised his hallucinations, but were replaced by a greater evil - addiction to those very drugs, lasting throughout his teens. They were Vincent's loneliest years.

Vincent blocked the painful memories as he turned the door lock to enter his cramped, book-filled office. He scrimmaged in the semi-dark for the light switch, hitting his shin in the process. A figure startled him, before he recognised his own reflection in the office window. Laughing at his reaction, he stood gazing at his image. He peered down to his arms for sores, as if he were that frightened teenager again, before turning away, disappointed at his reaction.

Time had passed since his affliction, filled by hard work, allowing him to almost forget and move on. He opened the file drawer of his desk, casting his eye over five years of study – Einstein, Galileo, Kepler, the Reformation – each file containing pre-prepared lecture notes. He removed an envelope labelled *Higgs Theory* and placed it in a well-worn note pad he always carried in his coat pocket. His trusty note pad was like an old friend that he called on when needed, this time as a reminder for his next day's lecture. He had no time to prepare any further this morning, given he was meeting his friends, Constantine and Ella about a 'project proposal' on offer. Vincent checked his watch and cursed to himself, realising he was late. He hurriedly closed and locked his file drawer, switched off lights and headed for the university's bus depot, where they'd arranged to meet.

He arrived at the bus stop, short of breath, and found Ella parked nearby, waiting.

"You're late," she said, more with a smile than annoyance. She was calm and happy in her own space, which was her way.

Vincent always found her smile reassuring, as if she understood his curious ways. She was different from most people he knew, quirky and mysterious, as if she too held secrets. Over the last year they formed a bond of sorts. The truth was he wanted more than a friendship, but she'd shown little interest in him beyond their shared fascination for history and science. He had ventured many 'passes' subtle and otherwise, to no avail. Over time he resigned himself to a one-sided attraction, accepting their friendship and hoping she might eventually warm to him.

"Sorry, slept in," Vincent lied, as he settled into the passenger seat. Ella brushed her long auburn hair across her shoulders, before turning the ignition to the car to set out for Constantine's home.

They drove for some time, saying little, both at ease with their silence, a comfort developed from their year-long habit of sharing a morning coffee and conversation. Then Vincent spoke.

"So what's this mysterious project all about?"

Ella held back her response as she negotiated the snake-like curves of the road leading up to Constantine's hilltop home.

"We're nearly there, so I'll let Constantine tell you."

Vincent was disappointed with Ella's reluctance, for in truth, he was uncomfortable around Constantine. He had known him a lot longer than Ella, but had shared very few conversations, beyond polite banter. But despite his discomfort, Vincent remained intrigued by Constantine. He always prodded Ella to tell him more about him, for there was something about his manner. He had the familiarity of a long lost uncle.

"Give me something," he pleaded in a joking manner.

"It's related to Jean's work," said Ella, her mind clearly more on the road than their conversation.

Vincent's intrigue grew, for he had first learnt of Constantine's work through his Uncle Jean, who worked with Constantine on many projects. Vincent had developed a strong bond with Jean during those years, whereas Constantine remained a mystery. So it surprised him that Constantine should want to seek his help.

"Jean's work? In what way?"

Ella slowed the car to a crawl and turned to him, beaming one of her smiles, "I'll tell you more later, but for now it's better Constantine tells you directly."

Her smile always reassured Vincent. He remembered being immediately drawn to her, smitten by her attractive flowing auburn hair and calm demeanour. She acted like someone older than her twenty-eight years, blessed also with a wealth of scientific knowledge. She didn't much believe in small talk. She often gazed blankly through such conversations, seemingly bored, always returning to her favourite topic - science. Their friendship was the antithesis of the darkness he felt in his adolescence. It brought a joy to his life that had been missing – his chance at happiness. Ella had never known the young man plagued by mental illness, and he never wanted her to know.

"I'm nervous about meeting him. He has hardly spoken to me these last few years. Why would he want me to work for him?"

"He thinks highly of you, Vincent. He often speaks about your dedication to research and tutoring future scientists."

Vincent looked directly at Ella. He was surprised by her remark. He felt Constantine had little interest in him, like a father who had been disappointed in his choices.

"He's never said that to me. I know he must have some interest as he was good friends with Jean, but beyond that, we have little rapport," said Vincent, fishing for more information. The truth was he had wanted Constantine to notice him. Vincent admired his brilliance. Constantine was a scientist gifted with the rare capacity to understand the many strands of science, from quantum physics to astronomy. Vincent wanted to be like him, but his youth was lost to his demons. Those were valuable years where he could have built an expansive overview of scientific knowledge, instead of the highly specialised view he possessed. But instead they had been taken up by his fear of the shadows, drugs and the death of his parents.

"I've not told you this before. I feel as if he reminds me of someone, but I can never figure out who," said Vincent.

"Perhaps you have met him before, in another life or another universe?" asked Ella, winking, as she regularly did when she wished to change the subject of the discussion. But Vincent was in no mood to talk about current scientific conjecture. He rolled his eyes in frustration at Ella for not telling him more about Constantine.

"We're almost there," said Ella, indicating and turning into a long straight drive-way leading to the entrance of Constantine's home.

It was a small cottage, almost hidden by an encroaching forest. Nevertheless it had a natural charm, blending in with the dense growth. Its location surprised Vincent as he always imagined Constantine lived close to an airport to accommodate his frequent travel abroad. His home felt welcoming, a natural retreat high in the hills, which lifted Vincent's spirits – it was his first real chance to spend time with Constantine, on his own territory. He hoped he'd be more relaxed and open than he'd been in previous exchanges, but Vincent's hopes were dashed as they pulled up to the columned entry. Constantine stood at the open door, offering no greeting. He looked to be in fear, eager to move inside, hastening them to follow.

"Close the door," he said, staring icily at Vincent until he did as asked.

Vincent followed both into a small, cluttered lounge room that opened to a deck area with views of the surrounding forest. Books were chaotically strewn across the floor, seemingly tossed to where they now rested.

"Please, sit," said Constantine, clearly in no mood for small talk. Vincent stepped over a pile of scattered files, sitting at the end of a rectangular pine table. A single file filled with papers, neatly laid in the middle, provided the only semblance of order in the cluttered room.

Constantine's agitation remained, even inside. *No wonder*, Vincent thought. His life was a whirlpool of travel and meetings. He was an enigma to Vincent, sometimes an intense quiet man, other times verbose and passionate. He was no doubt worldly. Vincent had heard so many tales of his travels to the continents of the world from his uncle, but little about the man. He only learnt more about Constantine after Jean's tragic death a year earlier. It was not long after, Constantine hired Ella to do research for him at the university.

"Sorry, I'm having a busy day," said Constantine apologetically, before sitting down.

Saying no more, he shuffled among the papers on the table, selecting a single page and handing it to Ella. She read it in silence as Constantine sat back and observed her.

Their relationship intrigued Vincent. He at times treated her more like a daughter than a work colleague – as if they had a bond going back many years. They clearly understood each other, sharing knowing glances.

"Why didn't you call me about this?" she said, concerned and sounding more like an equal partner than Constantine's assistant.

For any other person, Vincent would have thought nothing of the reaction. (Problems with their business, health concerns, financial worries, any number of issues that would upset people in their day to day lives.) But Ella rarely reacted in that way.

"We have to finish our project soon. There's no other way," he replied. Ella agreed.

She appeared to want to say more but sat back instead, waiting for Constantine to speak. Vincent's intrigue grew as he patiently waited for inclusion. Soothing music played in the background, at odds with the tense mood building around the table. A nervous silence ensued before Constantine finally acknowledged him.

"Vincent, we've known each other a year now and I know I've told you precious little about our work, but there has been good reason."

"You and Jean were busy and constantly travelling," said Vincent.

"You're so much like Jean. I didn't get to talk to you on the day of the funeral. I'm sorry for that."

"Don't be. There were a lot of people. The whole day was a haze. It's still hard to believe he's gone," said Vincent, politely. The truth was he remembered Constantine well that day. He'd spent little time before leaving, as if he had more important matters to attend to. But that was his way, self-absorbed, too busy to talk any longer than was necessary. If it had been anyone else he would have dismissed them as rude and had little to do with them. But for reasons he could not understand, Vincent felt a connection with him that he needed to understand.

"He was a brave man and dedicated to his work. Did he tell you much about his research?"

"Not really. But he spoke often of his travels with you to Europe. His face lit up every time he reminisced. He held you in high regard."

Constantine smiled for the first time, only half listening. His mind seemed distant, perhaps reliving his exploits with Jean.

"He cared for you, Vincent. More than you know."

"Yes, if not for Jean..." Vincent began, but paused. It was Jean's support that aided his recovery. He provided lodgings, insisted he get an education and ultimately cured him. *New experimental drugs...worth a try*, he remembered Jean advising him. Not that Vincent cared. He'd have tried anything to end his hallucinations. Miraculously the drugs worked. A reflective pause filled the room and it was Ella who broke the silence.

"I forgot to bring last week's research papers." She politely excused herself and left the room for her car. Constantine waited till he heard Ella close the front door before speaking. His mood turned more serious.

"There's something you didn't know about your Uncle," he said, removing a small container of pills from his coat pocket and throwing it to the middle of the table.

"Recognise these?"

Vincent knew the contents well. He had taken the medication daily for five years. They had cured him of his affliction and released him from the nightmares that haunted his young life.

"Yes, Jean supplied these for me. You knew about my condition?" Vincent said, concern in his tone, not because he cared if Constantine knew, but more the thought that Ella too knew of his dark history.

"I've always known," said Constantine, picking up the tablets and studying them. "You see, the doctor who developed your medication...was me."

Vincent sat quietly, but his rage built within. Why would Jean keep that from him? Why would they both not tell him the simple truth? What had they to hide?

"It doesn't make sense."

"I'm sure very little made sense to you in those years, but the important thing was you were protected."

"Protected from myself, you mean. I was delusional. The pills cured me and saved me from a complete breakdown."

"No. Your demon was very real."

"Real. How could you know what I faced? It's worse than any demon you could imagine," said Vincent, emotions charged and eyes welling from the memory.

"Jean and I knew it...because we faced it too." Constantine looked at the pills for a time.

"But there's another demon now. It's coming for you Vincent and those pills won't help you anymore..." But Vincent refused to listen cutting him short.

"I'm cured. I've not had the nightmares for five years," he said, desperation growing in his voice, like the small sweat beads forming on his forehead.

"You know that's not true. This morning you felt its presence, didn't you?" Vincent thought back to the shadows that taunted his mind on campus.

"How did you know?" he asked, wanting to deny Constantine's claim, but unable to, "I imagined a noise. It was nothing."

Constantine stood up, walked across to Vincent and leaned forward on the chair beside him. He was a tall man and intense, which could be disarming.

"You know that's not true. You could never mistake the feeling that you experienced as a boy. That same feeling brushed close to you this morning, didn't it?"

Vincent couldn't deny the coldness he felt that morning. He was confused now, about to deny such feelings, when he felt a surge of energy emanating from somewhere in the house. He glanced to all corners of the room, before he saw a shadow dart across the doorway of an adjoining room. His fear heightened. They weren't alone.

He felt an intense pressure start to weigh down on him. He looked for answers from Constantine but none were offered. *Was it happening again?* He nearly passed out from the force bearing down and yet Constantine appeared unaffected.

"Please help me," he gasped.

He heard Ella re-enter the room, walking toward them. To his surprise, she walked to the deck to look out across the forest, looking for something. The oppressive humidity soaked up the room's air, thick pressure seemingly turning in on Vincent only.

"Please help...the weight...too much..." Vincent cried, staggering up from his seat, quickly drawing Ella back to his side.

"Sit down," she said, concern etched on her youthful pale face, before looking to Constantine for guidance.

"It's too late. The invasion has already begun," he said, removing a small transparent orb from his briefcase. Vincent's gaze was drawn to the object. It was a perfectly rounded orb, filled with a swirling viscous substance that looked un-earthly.

"Vincent should not have come today. We've exposed him to great danger."

"Better here with us than alone. It's aware of him now."

It was true Vincent sensed a force, that same uneasiness he experienced as a young boy. A heaviness, like an impending storm was about to engulf him, yet Constantine and Ella stood unaffected, without fear.

"We have to leave," he cried, but his friends remained unmoved.

It was then, for the first time, Vincent saw a light emanate from Constantine's arm. Soft rays swirled like a moonlit ocean, as he waved it over the orb he held. The light from his hand appeared to interact with the viscous substance, changing its swirling colours to a luminescent gold. He laid the orb on Vincent's open palm.

"Grip it tightly."

Vincent did as asked, squeezing it tight. His fear intensified when a pale green mist wafted toward the orb, as if drawn to it.

"What is that? What's happening?" he asked, thick mist tightly wrapped round his fist. Ella sat close.

"I will explain, but for now, you must not let go," she said, urging him to hold it tightly.

Vincent would have fled, but a force of a hundred gravities now weighed him down. All feeling drained from his body, except from the hand clasping the orb which grew cold as ice.

"Hold fast. It's your only protection," said Constantine, his manner controlled but his eyes wide and full of urgency.

"Cold. Too cold," said Vincent, chilled pain burning his palm. He turned to Ella for comfort.

"The cold will soon pass. It's counteracting the heat given off from the invading force. Let the immersant repel it."

Vincent's head throbbed, from the heat building around his fist. He looked down and saw sweat pouring down his arm into the blur of swirling mist that had engulfed his hand. He was certain he'd lose it to the acid-like mist. He fell into shock, disappearing deep into the recesses of his mind. Traumatic times in his life sprung forth – his parents' death, emotions of despair and vulnerability and the loneliness and depression that followed his drug dependency. A blur of emotions raced by, encircling his mind like the mist that had captured his hand. But then like an electric jolt, the physical pain brought him back. He saw a shadow that terrified him.

"Must go. It's coming for me," he cried, as old demons returned, more vivid than he'd ever experienced.

"Don't resist, Vincent. Let the immersant do its work. It will save you," said Ella, holding his cheek gently, staring deeply into his eyes and trying to reassure him. Vincent's mind was filled with a montage of the demons that had destroyed his young life, but Ella's gaze made him want to believe her. She had strangely beautiful eyes, like no other woman he had ever met. For the first time he felt she harboured feelings for him. He couldn't speak, but he willed his head to move in the affirmative, holding the orb with a strength that surprised him.

Then he felt a pain like no other, as if lashed by a dozen snake bites as it moved. It felt like a spider crawling on his back. Fear magnified in him, from the unknown attacker.

It continued to move, playing with him, offering only jagged glimpses in the corner of his eye. Something was near. He felt its vibrations around his body, a feeling he knew. It pierced him at the base of the neck, now moving as easily through his body as around, as if it was taunting Vincent. To his horror, mist seeped from pores in his skin, forming into a shape before his eyes and holding his gaze – as if contemplating. He wanted to let go of the orb and Ella sensed it, lowering her hand into the swirling mist, clasping his fist tight.

"This thing. It's alive. It thinks!" cried Vincent, trying to let go of the orb, but unable to break Ella's grip.

"Nearly done. Feel my power and focus on that," she said.

As he did, the floating mist returned to his hand and the swirling substance in the orb grew in intensity, shaking his hand violently.

"What have you done to me?"

The substance tightened further, like an ominous storm that had them locked in a deadly embrace. The pain grew. Vincent closed his eyes, too terrified to look, convinced his arm was about to be torn from him by the barbs of the circling substance. His mind was a seething movement of fear and light-headedness, before the pain passed. The immersant worked, freeing him. Sweet movement returned to Vincent giving him the sensation that he was floating.

It was some time before he dared open his eyes. Ella had let go her grip and the mist had dissipated. Just his bare hand remained, shaking uncontrollably, not from the invader, but from his own fear. The life he thought he'd left half a decade ago had returned. He wept uncontrollably, his deepest fears exposed before the very person he had never wanted to know his secret.

"You're safe now," said Ella, holding him close, trying to console and reassure him.

But Vincent wasn't reassured; he knew the insidious effect the crawling shadows had on his life back then – hope and happiness all impossible. He stood, looking around the room, before turning to them both.

"How do you know of this evil? Why weren't you affected?"

Ella approached Vincent, holding his arm gently, seeking the trust that was now wavering in him.

"We can't tell you. Not yet. But I promise you will know soon."

Vincent wiped the last of his tears away, knowing their friendship had changed forever. Ella had kept secrets from him, secrets about him. He would not share his thoughts with her.

Constantine approached him.

"The immersant has given you immunity for a time. But like a virus, this shadowy force will quickly overcome it. In a few days, perhaps a week, it will return. It sees you now as it soon will see us all," he said.

"What do you mean by immersants and virus? You owe me explanations!"

Constantine gave the briefest of smiles, about to reply, before a sound outside stopped him.

"We have no time to convince you what we say is true. It must not see us. From this point on you'll have to rely on your instincts," he said, before turning to Ella.

"Are you sure the immunity took hold?"

Ella nodded in the affirmative as she too studied a bright light emanating from her arm.

"You will meet us in London in two days. Come there and we will find you," said Constantine as if his instruction a mere formality.

"England in two days? Not likely," said Vincent. His body movement returned to normal.

A noise approached the room, a shuffle, like an infant crawling along the floor. Constantine and Ella studied Vincent, both waving their torch-like lights over him, before Ella spoke.

"You'll experience many sensations. Some you'll recognise, some not. Vincent, you must meet us in London. Your life depends on it. I'll explain everything then," she said, with the dart of a brief but warm smile. Vincent wanted to hold her close, but his life changed in that instant, as Ella than Constantine revealed the first of their secrets to him.

They vanished before his eyes as if a holograph had been suddenly turned off.

Vincent blinked his eyes, convinced the drugs had played tricks on his mind, but they had vanished. He cried out to Ella, waving his hands wildly around the room, in the vain attempt that he could touch her. *Was his mind playing tricks again as it had in his youth?*

"Ella!" He cried forlornly, but all he heard now was the faint sound of something approaching. His fear returned. In no mood to stay any longer than he needed, Vincent ran to Ella's car, intent on escape, but there were no keys in the ignition. Ready to flee on foot, he remembered his youth and how fear controlled him, so much so he'd hide for weeks on end terrified of the shadows. In adult life he'd learned to cope – to confront his fears.

Had he imagined everything? Vincent had to be sure, so he walked back into the house, repeatedly saying *face my fears* as he made tentative steps into the lounge room. All was quiet - as if nothing had happened.

"Ella!" he cried, all silent bar the echo of his voice. *It'd been an elaborate joke,* he thought, before a rustling noise from the outside deck made him think otherwise.

"Ella, this isn't funny." No reply.

He crept toward the deck, relieved it was empty. Then he looked out to the forest, not believing his eyes. A moving smoke-grey mass glistened in the early sunlight, like a fine spider web stretched across one large tree, hovering like a space craft, as if it were watching him. But then it suddenly tracked snake-like deep into the forest undergrowth. He watched in disbelief, alarm building in him. His arm began to ache again. It was real and dangerous. Vincent was intent on escaping.

A force gripped him. It was no trick of the mind as it wrapped vice-like around his right hand, scorching his skin. He tried to shake free from the web-like mist, but was unable. His hand vibrated violently, controlled by the invader. His struggles futile, the force lifted him from the ground and threw him across the deck with the strength of a dozen men, leaving him stunned and defenceless to its advance. Its hissing sound grew in intensity as it clasped tighter, squeezing the life from his hand. Vincent cried out, but he was alone, at its mercy. The dragon shadows had reclaimed him, returning Vincent to a life he thought he had forever left behind.

Vincent woke not on the ground where he'd been attacked, but in Ella's car, with no memory of how he got there. He cared little. His instinct was to flee the danger. Miraculously, her car keys were in the ignition. He clenched the keys, right hand still shaking uncontrollably, left hand trying to steady it. The experience shook him to the core, but he managed to start the vehicle, relieved when the engine kicked over allowing his escape.

By the time he arrived home he'd settled sufficiently to consider his next move - misty webs that controlled his body, two friends who vanished before his eyes. What would the police make of such a tale? What would they make of him? He had a history of depression, numerous stints in psychiatric wards and documentation of psychotic episodes. The past was behind him and as far as he was concerned, that's where it would remain.

He stayed home for the remainder of the day, door locks secured, constantly listening for any noise and looking at every shadow, but normality returned to him in his home. Late in the night he anonymously reported suspicious behaviour at Constantine's home to the police but only after consuming much whisky. He didn't want to sleep that night, remembering the black dreams of his youth, but in the small hours of the morning, Vincent finally surrendered to the alcohol, falling into a fitful sleep.

Vincent woke to early morning light and his alarm ringing loud, exacerbating his hangover. He thought about staying home, barricading himself in, before choosing to go about his activities with some degree of normality, in the hope that the memories of the previous strange day would fade. At the university, Vincent tried to act as if nothing happened, preparing his lecture as he would on any other day. But that changed mid-morning, as the Faculties Dean, Peter Shrimpton requested a meeting. This was far from normal. Peter was a very busy man and had called on him only once since he joined the university over a family's complaint about his teaching methods. So Vincent entered his office with feelings of trepidation.

"Vincent, great news about the consultancy. I wasn't aware of your efforts to attract external funding," said Peter, happy with the news on his desk. Vincent played along as if he himself was aware. "I don't blame you of course, businesses are so damned unreliable, but this is resoundingly clear. Congratulations!" Peter stood and shook his hand vigorously, before handing Vincent the letter.

Vincent thanked him, quickly reading the offer. Its letterhead displayed Constantine's company logo and its contents expressed his gratitude for the work carried out by Vincent, accepting his business proposal to assist them in an urgent project. Attached was a cheque to Vincent's faculty to cover all costs associated with the project as well as a handsome reimbursement for stand-in lecturers required in his absence. Also attached was a return ticket to London – he was to commence work with Constantine and Ella by week's end.

Vincent wanted to refuse the offer, but for what reason?

"They spoke about it, but I didn't expect it to be so soon. This is too much a burden for you, Peter."

"Don't think that, Vincent. We have built up a good list of stand-in lecturers, just for occasions like this. If anything, the money is a godsend for our budget." Vincent nodded, unconvincingly and Peter must have seen his indecision.

"Look, I don't want to push you into this project. Think it over and get back to me. Okay?" Vincent smiled and nodded again, unable to say anything.

"Take the ticket with you as you would be leaving tomorrow." Vincent nodded before shaking Peter's hand and leaving.

His mind raced as he left the room. He buried himself in his work, ignoring the decision he would have to make. But his restlessness built all day. Even the comfort of the lecture hall failed to stem the wave of fear taking him over. *Should I go to London?* he wondered, until the rising sound of students' murmurs and half laughs brought him back to the job at hand.

"Sorry, could you repeat the question."

"Surely the great discoveries have been made. There's little more to search for. Our place in the cosmos, the standard model has been discovered and explained. It's just the 'devil in the detail' now," said David, a new student, confident beyond his years, eager to speak his mind and less eager to listen.

Vincent's gaze roamed to the clock mounted on the back of the lecture hall, his mind struggling to engage the young man's inquisitive nature. He forced a learned reply.

"Man's discoveries have been impressive, but even with all the gains over the last millennium, our best scientists can only describe four percent of the universe. So there'd appear to be a few more hills to climb, David. Somewhere, someone in the future will make another new discovery to rival Galileo, Newton or Einstein. Enquiry, rigorous pursuit of the truth about our place in the cosmos will never end. Our greatest scientists and philosophers showed us this."

"But there are limitations to our discoveries, physical limitations. You can only prove what you can see. No more," said David, eager to debate and certain in his convictions.

The clock showed the lecture was near ended, and David's fellow students didn't share his enthusiasm for a drawn out discussion, but the new boy showed an interest beyond his years.

"Perhaps we are only limited by our minds. Past civilisations believed the Earth was flat, so how can we be sure that current perceptions about our place in the cosmos aren't also flawed?"

"Maybe it's better that some things are left undiscovered?" asked David. His gaze was suddenly threatening.

Vincent's hand throbbed again and the familiar weight bore down on him, as if the lecture hall were folding in and around him. The tightness around his hand slivered up his arm to the throat, making him struggle to speak. David had a steely gaze. The slightest of grins formed in the corners of his mouth, as if he controlled the force over him. Vincent forced words out quickly, fearful he would collapse from the pressure.

"Perhaps...perhaps...we'll discuss this further...at the next lecture...thank you all," said Vincent, bringing the lecture to an end. He stood behind the lectern, as composed as he could be, although he was certain he would fall to the ground any minute.

The lecture theatre slowly emptied. Conversation echoed loudly across the hall, most about his strained performance. Vincent faked a smile to those students that passed a concerned glance his way. He politely nodded, signalling he was fine. David filed out of the lecture room with the other students, but not before shooting Vincent one last intense glare, blending hostility and satisfaction. As David walked through the exit doors, the tightness around Vincent disappeared.

The students had gone, leaving Vincent alone in the room. The eerie quiet chilled him, like the rising damp that penetrated the wooden floor boards. Vincent's gaze was drawn to the three small easterly windows where the sun's warm rays streamed through on to the floor. He walked there to warm in its rays and to watch David leave with the other students. But he could not see David among them. To his horror, Vincent saw another familiar figure. A man stood in the distance who looked remarkably like his uncle Jean. But his gaze directed at Vincent burnt like a furnace. He knew then it wasn't Jean. The man grinned and shook his head as if there were an inevitability that he'd claim Vincent. In that instant, Vincent knew that the force that had claimed his early life had returned. And it came in many shapes now, an entity of unknown origin. The Entity wanted Vincent. Vincent pressed his hand to his top pocket, where he'd placed the ticket to London. In that moment, the paper it was printed on seemed a visceral and certain lifeline, a passage towards answers.

Brighton Pier

VINCENT WALKED THE NARROW cream corridors from his plane to immigration, the relative quiet of the lengthy walk-way giving way to the chaos and bustle of passengers queuing with passports in hand to enter England. Confusing signs didn't help his mood. He was unsure which of the dozen or so queues he should choose. He'd already wasted ten minutes in a line, before realising he hadn't filled in the required immigration declarations.

Large groups of people made him nervous at the best of times, but the unsettling events of the last few days had left him agitated. Any one of the faces that filled the room could mean him harm. He sensed someone or something was watching him, but in this crowd he had little hope of discerning the danger. By the time Vincent left customs, he was convinced of being followed. Either his life was in danger or his fear of shadows – his disease of the mind – was creeping back. After half a decade of normality, even success, his world had suddenly been flipped into chaos and uncertainty. Shadowy enemies returned, waiting for him to succumb to their taunts.

Vincent opted to line up for the ticketing booth rather than grapple with the many self-serve machines.

"Here is your rail ticket, sir. One single ticket to Victoria Station."

"Thank you," said Vincent absently, so self-absorbed had he become in the events of the last week in his life. He was also tired from the flight. He'd been unable to sleep on the plane, half watching the endless movies screened and re-screened on his personal television, as his mind replayed the events that led him to this.

It was a brisk early morning at Heathrow station and the tube train to London was already busy as he boarded it. Vincent was lucky enough to claim a corner window seat and placed his travel case beside him. He sat in an empty corner of the carriage for three quarters of the journey, but once it neared inner London and the underground, the crowds started to flow on and off the carriage. The effects of the long flight started to take hold as he fell in and out of his fitful light slumber.

He woke with a start from his micro sleep to the sound of loud music. A heavily tattooed youth stood in the middle of the carriage, seemingly oblivious to the disturbance he had created. The young man reminded Vincent of his own tumultuous youth. Fear had stopped him from leading a normal adolescent life. He stumbled through his teens, unsure whether he ran from real devils or his drug addled mind. Drug addiction took over his life until it became more powerful than anything else, trapping him in a numb oblivion that allowed him to ignore the shadows.

He peered out the window as the train pulled up at Earls Court station. A crowd of commuters scurried past, heading for the exit as Vincent's train slowly accelerated in the opposite direction. People herded toward the crowded single exit – except one. A lone man caught his eye – was it Jean? The stranger leant against the wall allowing the impatient crowd to pass him by, seemingly waiting for another train. For that brief moment their eyes met. A familiar look shocked Vincent. It wasn't Jean, it was David. But he couldn't be certain. He strained his neck to look back, but the young man fell out of sight.

Vincent's pulse raced at the thought of it being David - he was being followed. *But how did the young student find me? What are the chances of us crossing paths? Am I walking into a trap?* Endless permutations crowded his mind.

The train arrived at Vincent's destination. Suitcase in tow, he walked toward the wide open spaces of Victoria Station where commuters scurried in all directions filling the large expanse with a sea of movement, except those gathered around the electronic board, studying arrival and departure times. Vincent chose to wait in the forecourt of the busy hub at a small open cafe. He sat only for a few minutes, before Ella approached from the far side of the forecourt. His heart skipped at the sight of her graceful movement. She was dressed in jeans and a jade green shirt accentuating her flashing sea-blue eyes and auburn hair. Tall and lithe, she looked more like a model than a scientist. Her presence drew many admiring eyes. He smiled as she approached him, hoping she too would greet him excitedly, but to his disappointment, she was formal and business-like. Vincent hid his disappointment by pulling a chair out from the table and offering her a seat, before sitting down, too.

"So, you got your way. I'm here."

"It wasn't my way," she said dismissively.

"Well, Constantine's then."

"Partly," she said briefly, offering little more solace.

"Ella, I'm tired and fear for my life from something I don't recognise or understand.

And now I've learnt I don't even know you. So who, or should I say what, are you? I don't even know your business that well."

"We have no business. The company is merely our cover. We have no need for money. We create what we need, but the rest of our time is used to study your world."

"You worked at the university for a year. You're saying you did nothing?"

"I learnt about you. I kept an eye out for your safety. And I was always in communication with Constantine. We have special powers. We can always speak with each other, any time."

"Then tell me more about your special powers, so I understand how I can help."

"I will tell you much more soon, but not now. It's too dangerous."

"Ella, if you want me to help you, I have to know what's happening. You don't know how much I struggled as a young boy. It's important I know what I'm seeing is real. It's more important than you could ever realise," he said, opening his hand as a gesture of faith. Surprisingly, for the first time, Ella took his hand in hers.

"It is very real, but it's safer that you don't know too much for now. It could save your life. You face great danger, but for now the immersant protects you."

"Protects me!"

"Keep your voice down," said Ella, flashing a concerned gaze around the people in earshot of them.

"I nearly died back there! You left me at the hands of some invisible force, and now you tell me nothing. I knew it was a mistake, I'm leaving," whispered Vincent, about to get up. Ella held his hand tighter, willing him to stay.

"You can't escape your destiny, Vincent. You must confront it or die."

"Is that a threat?" he said.

"I'm trying to save you."

"Give me one reason, one piece of evidence. For all I know, I've gone insane again," he said, before immediately regretting his admission.

"You've never been insane," she said, with an assurance that unnerved him.

"How would you know what pain I endured? You know nothing of those years," he said, frustration building, unable to control his emotions and drawing concerned looks from people in the vicinity. Ella smiled back at them, to ease their concerns.

"Give me your other hand, too."

Vincent's hurt remained but he wanted to listen to Ella, having spent the last year trying to get closer to her with no success. Now she showed warmth he had not felt before. His feelings for her overcame any doubts. He extended both palms. Ella gently slid both her open palms over his, a delicate caress filled with warmth. The faintest of lights radiated from her hands to his, a mist like cloud formed around their hands, just as quickly evaporating, leaving a sensation that alarmed him. The crawling barbs of the shadows that haunted his life as a young man returned, that unmistakeable horror that ruled his life for half a decade.

Vincent flinched, wanting to withdraw his hands and escape the memories of the sorrow, but Ella willed him to remain still, breathing deeply, guiding him to do the same. In one slow movement of her hands the shadows disappeared.

"I know of your past life," she said. Her gaze was knowing but warm, as if she had witnessed it firsthand.

What strange powers does Ella possess? Vincent thought. With a wave of her hand she had created the disease that tormented him in his youth and with no more than her will made it disappear. He sat before her like an open book, his past life fully revealed; the despair, the torment, and the shadows.

"How could you know?" he whispered, half to himself.

"I will tell you more, but we have little time. Have you had other unusual experiences this week?"

"Yes, you both vanished at Constantine's home."

"We were always there. We just couldn't allow you to see us in its presence."

"Presence? What do you mean?"

"I'll tell you soon, but not here. Please, it's very important. Have you had any other unusual experiences?"

"The force grasped me just after you vanished and threw me to the ground. I thought I'd die."

"Yes I know. After that?"

"You saw that and did nothing?" said Vincent, angry at the thought. He realised then, why the car keys were in the ignition, whereas they previously were not.

"Please, we have little time," said Ella, agitated.

"I met a boy, David, tall, thin. I thought I had met him before. He was new to my class, that day. He threatened me. Do you know him?" Vincent asked.

"Yes and no. What did he want?"

"Nothing. He debated with me, before l felt that same pressure around my hand...then throat. I looked for him as the students left the lecture hall but he disappeared in the crowd, before..."

"Before?"

"I thought I saw Jean."

"Anything else?"

"Well, I'm not certain of this, but I thought I saw David again. Today. Standing at Earl's Court. I'd been dozing off to sleep, so it could have been a dream. I don't..." Ella cut his words short.

"It's no dream. You're in its sight now and its power is building. We have to keep moving."

"It? What do you mean it? Who or what is this boy? Why is he following me? How can he follow me? Please Ella, give me a reason to trust you."

"You'll learn more, when we meet Constantine. We are going to Brighton where it is safer," she said. Her gaze had turned from Vincent toward the Victoria Station departures and arrivals electronic board. The crowd gathered there were studying arrival and departure times – all but one. A young man was gazing their way, with an angry stare, like a leopard about to be unleashed on its helpless prey. But something held him back, like an invisible collar.

"We must go now. Platform eight to Brighton leaves in five minutes. I'll meet you on the train," said Ella as they both hurried for the platform.

"Which carriage? How will you know...?" Vincent, turned back to finish his question, but Ella had vanished. His heart beat faster as did his footsteps. Then the crowds squashed to a crawl as they forced through the single entry to platform eight. For one terrifying moment, Vincent felt a force settle on his right hand – unmistakeable - but the slithering noose just as quickly left him as he boarded the train.

He finally relaxed five minutes out from Victoria Station. The threat had passed and his spirits lifted when Ella walked from the adjoining carriage to sit opposite him. Her anxiety seemed to diminish as she too sat back in the blue velvet seat and gazed out at the passing scenery.

"I love trains, the way they glide. They almost float," she said, admiring the view for a time, before closing her eyes.

Vincent wanted to ask her if they were being followed, but he let her rest, instead studying the contours on her smooth face, her beauty accentuated by the morning light. He imagined kissing her tender cheeks as he had done so often before, his feelings intense, sparked by the earlier soft caress of her hands at Victoria Station. What strange powers did she and Constantine possess? Were they friends or frauds playing on his frailties? If his visions were real, then the truth was he'd never been ill, but if that were the case, could he ever rid himself of the deadly force?

The only certainty he felt was that Ella's smooth touch excited him, like no other woman he had met. He fantasised that when she caressed his hands at the station, she was showing her true feelings -

but he knew that not to be true. Somehow he had to break through Ella's guard and show his true feelings for her. Even in danger his desire for her remained. As Vincent studied her, Ella drifted into a deep sleep, looking still and serene, as if she was a painting on a canvas – a familiar canvas he had seen many times before. He felt the same way about Constantine and now David. He knew he had not met any of them before and yet his instincts stayed with the idea that he had, in another life perhaps - and in that life he was sure he loved Ella deeply and she him. Like a greedy child, Vincent wanted that love again and again. If he could find the courage to face the shadows, he might yet convince her of his love and unlock her mystery. He wanted to wake her, tell her how he felt, but dared not, so he left her to sleep all the way to Brighton. The train slowed as it glided into the open, seaside station, waking Ella.

"Have we arrived?" she asked, stretching her arms, regaining her bearings. Her first instinct was to study the platform and the many people now on it.

"Who's following us, Ella? Is it David?"

"I was looking for Constantine. He said he'd meet us here, either on the platform or just outside."

They exited the train and the crowded platform. People scurried in all directions, seeking taxis, buses, food or their next train. Ella and Vincent stepped out into Brighton City proper, but not into the usual line-up for double-decker buses and taxis. A line of police officers in full riot gear ringed the station. Queens Road was cordoned off with chequered coloured ribbon and sounds of people chanting in the distance.

"What's happening?" Ella asked of a nearby officer.

"A crowd of demonstrators are heading up Queens Road and will continue round to North Road to assemble in Victoria Gardens that could get unruly. No buses in or out for the next few hours I'm afraid," he said, before turning back to his place in the 'front line'.

"Constantine may be caught in the crowds. We'll meet him at Brighton Pier," said Ella.

At that they headed down side lanes for the ocean shores of Brighton, toward the demonstrators. The chants grew louder with every step. Three blocks from the ocean, the crowd of demonstrators began to fill all roads in front of them. They carried placards demanding 'free education' as they chanted their anti-government choruses. With no way through, Ella changed course.

"We have to head right, toward the lanes. I don't think the crowds will be there. Too narrow," said Ella, signalling for Vincent to follow her into a maze of winding narrow cobbled lanes, disorienting him. Ella appeared to know Brighton well.

He kept pace with her until the crowd blocked his view and he lost sight of Ella. The lane forked, leaving him to guess the direction, ultimately veering right. Decision made, Vincent ran quickly to catch her, only to face a dead end. He doubled back, annoyed by his error. But an eerie silence suddenly blanketed the area, as if he stood in another world. The narrow lane, already dim from the enclosed three storey buildings, turned dark as midnight, apart from a narrow band of sky directly above.

Vincent cast his gaze to the small slit of pale blue sky, still as a spotlight. Then it shimmered. A thin translucent force began to peel from its rays, sliding down the surface of the surrounding terraces, an opaque landslide of energy, dripping like blood to the ground, shimmering across buildings and cobblestone road, before locking Vincent inside the dark lane. A mist formed, rising two metres. The familiar hissing noise reverberated as if in a snake's lair, until a single human shape formed – one he knew.

David stared with a still, satisfied purpose, like a lion stalking its prey, his face fully formed but body blurred, as it slowly developed structure. David had changed somehow. He was taller and older, no longer the gangly teen, more a young man, his strength more defined, his presence more threatening.

"Who...what are you?"

"I'm your only friend, Vincent. I can help," he said, moving back a pace.

"Help? I'll tell you how you can help. Stop stalking me."

"You believe you're running from danger, yet you know nothing about your supposed friends."

"I know less about you. Let me go," said Vincent, trying to break free. But David clapped his wrist firmer, drawing him closer.

"They're not who you believe them to be. You'll find that out soon enough."

His grasp tightened until a mist formed around Vincent's arm. Nausea gripped him, a stifling pressure, as if a hundred gravities pushed down. Had the immersant failed to protect him? The mist burned, with acid-like pain, as the crawling shadows burnt through his skin. Vincent felt the savage pain ripple through his body as he fell to the ground, believing the force would finally take him.

The intense pain reminded him of another place he had long locked away in his memory – the pain of withdrawal from his drug addiction. He'd endured what felt endless nights bathed in a cold sweat as the creeping shadows of pain tortured him. The tidal wave of pain screamed like a cyclone, engulfing him, suffocating life until he wanted no more. He felt the same way now, trapped in the Entity's tentacles, before he heard a familiar voice from behind.

"Vincent, come with me now!" said Constantine, his hand firmly grasped around Vincent's arm, jolting him from the Entity's deadly grasp.

"I can't stop it much longer. Take my hand. Now!"

Vincent was overwhelmed by pain, gripped by its force, but somehow drew his arm from the deadly web toward Constantine. A bolt of energy surged through him, releasing him from the danger. Vincent was free. He ran, slow at first. But soon he was moving faster than he had ever run before. He fled from that place, for in it contained a darkness he had been hiding from all his life. If he returned to such a place he would surely die.

Through winding narrow cobbled lanes he wove, voices in his head calling him back. *You go toward danger. Do not trust them,* came the words of David then Jean, repeatedly willing his return. But he blocked their pleas, following Constantine through the maze to an underpass that opened to the pebbled ocean shore. The day was bright. Salty head winds buffeted the shore turning the clear day chilly. Small choppy waves, snowcapped, swirled in parallel lines to the shore, drowning out most sounds, even the traffic noise that ran beside Brighton beach.

"The pier is in that direction," said Vincent, pointing to his left, drawing a wry smile from Constantine.

"We're meeting at the old pier," he replied, pointing to a derelict square shaped framework, its connections to the beach long ago destroyed. Sunset rust foundation posts stood where once was a walkway. The iron skeleton rose out of the water, an eerie reminder of nature's ability to slowly destroy man's structures if left untended. The original pier had been some hundred metres out in the ocean, a mere shell of its former glory - defiantly standing, a ghost-like reminder of its heyday as a meeting place at the turn of the twentieth century. A time when gentlemen with top hats strolled with women dressed in fine lace on sunset evenings. Just a kilometre to the left, stood the 'new pier', a ready reminder of how the old pier must have looked.

The scenic view broke Vincent's mind free from the claustrophobic encounter, but did not erase the danger of his situation. A powerful entity meant them harm.

"Why here at a beach?"

"Not on the beach," as Constantine pointed toward a long line of catamarans. Their empty masts rattled melodically in the ocean breeze, like door chimes. Fifty catamarans laid in want, for the coming summer rush. But today business was slow. The breeze was too cold to entice any sailors, except Ella who was paying the owner for hire of a double hulled blue catamaran, ten metres high to the mast, its sails unfurled, ready to launch.

"Great, we're going to sail our way out of trouble," said Vincent sarcastically.

"We're buying time...and it's a perfect day for sailing," said Constantine, looking out to the strong breeze, seemingly unconcerned about the earlier threats.

They cast off from the shore, slowly at first as they sailed directly into the strong head wind. Fifty metres out, Constantine tacked the catamaran hard right. They now sailed with the full breeze behind them. Its strength accelerated their speed as they quickly gathered pace. The sails tied into position, all three sat for a time enjoying the refreshing ride as sea water sprayed across the bow, all the while eyeing Brighton's changing coastline. Both Constantine and Ella seemed entranced by the forest green sea and the accompanying gulls racing them across surf green waters.

The sleek cat glided effortlessly through choppy seas, before Constantine changed tack to head back toward the old pier, now some distance from them. Their speed slowed to a crawl as the blue and white sails of their boat laboured against the headwind. Seemingly bored with the slow pace, Constantine sat beside Vincent in the centre net between the two large fibre hulls. Vincent broke the silence first.

"This apparition, it warned me about you. Why would it do that?"

Constantine looked first to Ella, a knowing look that they often shared, which annoyed Vincent further. Ella started to speak but Constantine spoke over her.

"Listen. Can you hear it? Not the breeze, another sound." All went silent, noticing the breeze had dropped. Constantine drew the sails down and dropped anchor, leaving the boat to drift forward until the anchor took up the slack. An eerie calm followed. *The force is returning?* Vincent thought, his eyes rapidly scanning all directions, searching for the tell-tale signs. He saw only seagull flocks swirling high above.

Constantine sat still at the front of the catamaran, studying a light emanating from his arm as he scanned across the ocean. Minutes passed before he spoke.

"It can't reach us here. The entropy is too great and this boat too small to house its energy. We are safe," said Constantine, seeking to reassure but failing.

"Its energy? What is it?"

"It's a force we know little about. It appears to be growing in strength and capability. It has taken human form quickly. Much quicker than last time. We call it the Entity for it can take many forms."

"So, we'll just sit on this boat until it attacks us again?"

"We needed time Vincent, and this is the safest place to be right now. It can't merge with the ocean's energy. There's something in the ocean's structure that repels it. This is why we came here," he said, before signalling to Ella. To Vincent's surprise, both dived into the frosty waters, circling the boat for a time, studying it from all angles. They swam effortlessly through the choppy, cold seas, unaffected by the chill, contented as if in their natural state, like two lovers in a tropical lagoon.

Constantine dived deep, and did not return. He looked to Ella. "Where are you going? Why not take the boat? What if the Entity returns?" said Vincent, firing questions machine gun like in his panic.

"The answer is deep below. We'll return soon. It cannot penetrate the waters. If you see it, immerse part of your body in the ocean and it will not be able to harm you," said Ella, before she too disappeared under the rolling seas.

Vincent moved to all sides of the boat expecting them to re-appear from the depths for breath. Many minutes had passed and they still had not re-emerged. The breeze had dropped off all together. Even the choppy waves had subsided leaving an ominous quiet he did not care for. But then he heard a low hissing sound in the distance. A sound he was now familiar with. He looked in all directions for a sign of the Entity. *Come on, where are you? Don't make me jump in the water. Where are you?* He repeated under his breath. All the while the hissing sound grew in intensity.

He was now sure that the Entity was somewhere near. The sound felt to be coming from where they hired the boats, but there was no one there. He scanned across the shoreline until he saw a familiar shape – David, standing atop the old pier, on a large square frame at its highest point. He climbed restlessly along the blood rusted steel frames, holding his gaze on him – a deadly intent in his eyes. He looked more like a caged tiger, as he effortlessly leapt around and through the relics of the once famous pier. Only this cage had no high perimeter fences to secure its beast. Open water was the only barrier between the pursuer and the pursued. Fear overtook Vincent as he removed his shoes and socks, and lowered his feet into the ocean. It was cold but he did not care. *If you see him keep part of your body in the water,* he said to himself repeatedly, trying to reassure himself but failing.

Vincent considered diving into the water, when he saw the Entity squat low to the steel structure as if preparing to leap toward him. But something held the Entity back. Instead David leapt to the lowest iron girder, low to the ocean, studying the waters as if he were about to dive in.

SET SAIL

THE CALM ELLA AND Constantine felt in the Earth's ocean belied the storm that was brewing above. The ocean's cool waters were like the lakes of their own moon, Ontario Lacus. Swimming in its swirling oceans exhilarated them. It was spring below the waves and the fauna and flora were as dynamic as its land cousins. Predator and prey alike filled this underwater world, boldly encircling its currents in a daily ritual of life and death.

Any other time they would have basked in the ocean's natural beauty. But a force of immense power would soon sweep the ocean depths, quickly adapting to its environment. Then there would be nowhere for them to hide.

Constantine signalled Ella to follow him to the caves, several kilometres off shore from where the boat lay, using effortless dolphin-like strokes to reach the cathedral shaped caves in short time. Both entered the caverns, pitch black to all who swam there – but them. The cavern lit up like a stage as they opened their arms and activated a radiant light connected to them like a second skin. The cave, as big as Notre Dame, housed a deep-sea creature known as the vampire squid. It had features not dissimilar to squid-like creatures that roamed the pitch black depths of Ontario Lacus.

"What are we looking for?" Ella asked, telepathically.

"We are looking for components similar to the *sembas* of Lacus Sound, but with important molecular differences that will be harder for the Entity to counteract."

Constantine showed Ella the structure of the creature's molecules by spanning his arms. The molecular structure was displayed on his light web as if on a computer screen. Once identified, he pointed for Ella to swim west, before he searched the east side of the cave. Both glided effortlessly as they searched, guided by web light, performing experiments in the hidden cavern unlike any undertaken by scientists before them, to fight an enemy from a universe unknown.

Vincent sat forlornly on the deserted vessel, unsure whether to wait or set sail. An hour had passed. They could have drowned for all he knew, but the last week taught him to expect the unexpected. His gaze shifted regularly from the ocean surface to the old pier where David remained atop the cast iron frame, pacing impatiently. He seemed to be searching for a way to cross the ocean divide. But to Vincent's relief he was unable. *But for how long?* Vincent wondered. It was adapting to its environment, taking human form – what next? It effortlessly 'morphed' from the mist like substance to many shapes. Why not water? Endless questions raised fears in him. Should he set sail and escape? Where should he sail to? No, he must wait for Ella and Constantine, even though the Entity's words haunted him and created doubt in him. Then the Entity's voice filled his mind.

"You will soon find out that I speak only the truth, human."

The Entity's words were as if he was standing in front of Vincent, but he was too far away. Was the Entity reading his mind? Could he speak telepathically? Vincent engaged him with his conversation of minds.

"Why would they befriend me, only to betray me? It makes no sense."

"You are mistaken to believe they think like your kind. You know this not to be true," replied the Entity, in a calming almost conciliatory manner.

"Come closer and I will tell you what you want to know."

Vincent knew he should not listen, yet something in his voice made him follow. He unfurled the sails and glided the catamaran within a hundred metres of the old pier, knowing the danger, yet still compelled to confront it. As threatening as its powers were, there was a terrifying familiarity compelling him to face it. He moved to pick up the anchor, when the Entity spoke telepathically again.

"I know you love the female Odorphin."

"What do you know of love?" Vincent asked, hiding his anger that the Entity seemed to be able to read his thoughts.

"I know it can bring you great joy, but also great pain."

Vincent turned from the anchor and looked in the Entity's direction. His words about Ella unsettled him. He needed to see his eyes to sense if he spoke in truth or betrayal.

"I've endured pain for much of my life. Ella says that your kind have been responsible for most of my suffering."

The boat continued to drift closer to the pier. Vincent could see his eyes now. David stood very still, his intense gaze following Vincent's every move. Vincent felt the danger like a steer straying too close, yet his compulsion to learn more took over.

"What is it you want from me?" Vincent asked nervously.

"What does the Sun want from the Earth? It wants nought, it just is."

"Just two hours ago you attacked and tried to kill me. Why? What have I done to anger you? I don't know you," he said, prompting the Entity to glare his way.

"I cannot kill you. You know not what you speak of. I'm here because of what you have done with your life."

The Entity spoke in riddles, drawing Vincent further into a conversational web, eyes engaged, as his boat drifted ever closer. *But didn't all three speak in riddles?* Vincent thought. Maybe he was no more than a pawn in this dangerous game. An unwilling sacrifice for reasons he didn't understand.

"You are the stranger, and yet you tell me not to trust my friends. How do you expect me to react to your presence?"

The Entity drew deep breath, as if summoning all his strength, before jumping from the middle frame of the pier, ten metres down to the narrow steel lower rung, effortlessly maintaining a leopard like balance.

"Think what you like, but I speak the truth, whereas your so called friends deceive you. You'll never hear the truth from them. They, like you, are blinded by their beliefs." Excitement was building in his voice.

Vincent realised he'd drifted too close to the pier and quickly dropped anchor – but an almost instantaneous energy surged from the pier across the still waters, its wave like force engulfing him in a shadowy mist. The anchor made no difference as the force effortlessly drew his boat toward the pier. Vincent tried to dive to freedom but his body was held firm to the boat by an intense paralysing force. He managed only to move his right arm to water before the Entity held him like a statue. *The ocean protects you,* he remembered, but it had no effect. The force encircled him. A vortex of mist gathered. Its energy was so strong it threatened to swallow him, ship and all, into the water's depths.

"Here is your truth. You are at the gateway that you have sought all of your life. Your life's work realised," said the Entity.

"What do you mean?"

"The gateway of the multiverse. Step through and see what you try to understand."

Its appearance slowly faded, blending into the mist which now engulfed Vincent. Its force slithered snake-like, relentless and overpowering, until the shadows finally claimed him. His body drifted closer to the top of a whirlpool of water. Vincent was looking down on a long water-made funnel that seemingly had no bottom. Its power was too strong to resist.

"Here is your life's work. Claim it now," said the Entity. Its body now had fully vanished. Only its voice – first David's then Jean's - echoed in Vincent's mind. Yet something held him from the abyss. It was his hand immersed in water that held his last remaining thread to the real world.

"Let go of the water and feel the peace you crave." Its voice enticed him. Vincent tried to hold, but something in the Entity's hypnotic tone, made him want to let go. Could it be that the answers to his scientific quest lay so close?

Constantine searched the cavern walls in total darkness for a full hour, his web light guiding him to the deep sea squid that inhabited this dark cave, a vampire squid. His light web opened at full stretch, a living, interactive computer, seamlessly controlled by his mind, manipulating complex formulas with apparent ease. Symbols flew across his physical screen at lightning speed, developing the new immersant, based on the creature's rare DNA.

Ella was now at his side. Both analysed the creature in their digital laboratory, not built from technology, but of living tissue, their 'light web'. The living specimen was 3D scanned, recreating a perfect holographic copy, and digitally dissected down to the level of quarks, gluons, pions, protons and neutrons, to find the elusive resistance that would make up their next immersant. Holographic images sprung from their web, intricate detail not before seen on this Earth.

"This immersant should provide resistance for a week, although the Entity's powers are adapting quicker than I hoped," said Constantine, turning to Ella for confirmation and receiving it.

They were about to create the immersant when they felt a force reverberate from afar, a surge carrying the Entity's signature. Ella reacted immediately, signalling to Constantine that she'd investigate. She accelerated from the cave like a missile, the force of her light web vibrating at great speed. In moments the Entity came into her view. Their boat lay beside the old pier and Vincent was helpless in the Entity's clutches. All of them faced great danger now.

Vincent all but let go his grip, before he heard Ella call to him. "Hold my hand, Vincent," she said, floating above the vortex, hand outstretched.

The Entity had drained him of nearly all strength and resistance. Oblivion was close, but his desire for her and the promise of what might be, gave him a strength he believed he had lost. He strained his free hand to hers, breaking the heavy gravity, to feel her soft touch again. In an instant, Ella brought him from the abyss and the mist was gone. Vincent lay with Ella on the boat, now a safe distance from the old pier. The deadly shadows dissipated as tiredness overtook him.

Vincent woke, still lying on the catamaran. Its blue and white canopy glistened in the sunlight, and a gentle breeze wafted over its full sails. He could hear a flock of seagulls flying above and the sound of Ella and Constantine talking behind him. He thought to join them but instead he gazed skyward as majestic gulls hovered into view, their large wingspans held still and wide as they allowed the breezes to take them where they chose. Vincent felt like them, part of a carefree flock hovering above, taken by the winds of fate on a journey he did not understand. But he was a lone bird. There was no flock of like-minded creatures sharing his journey. He felt loneliness.

"How do you feel?" came Ella's voice from behind, breaking Vincent's imaginings.

"I'm still tired. Did it come for me? Did it really happen?" he asked, desperate to believe his delusions had not returned.

"The Entity is very real and it will continue to return until it has you and has us all. Our only defence is the immersant," said Constantine, sitting beside Vincent, holding the familiar orb.

"More drugs," Vincent said, pulling back, wondering whether it might be the cause of his hallucinations.

"I know a lot has happened, but what you are experiencing is very real. This immersant will protect you," said Ella. Vincent was less than convinced and showed his doubts by turning away from Ella toward Constantine.

"You left me alone with that monster!" Vincent shouted.

"We won't make that mistake again," said Constantine.

"That's not exactly reassuring."

"I understand your doubts, Vincent. But you have to believe me when I say that Ella and I have your interests at heart."

"If you want my trust, show me the same," said Vincent, defiantly. Constantine looked to Ella, before giving a look of resolution.

"Very well. Against my better judgement, we will tell you more about our lives. Will that be sufficient to convince you of our good faith?"

"It will go a long way to re-building my trust," Vincent replied, looking Ella's way.

Constantine sat back on the boat, resting against the main mast, looking around at the calm ocean, breathing in the cool fresh air before turning to Ella.

"Ellatine Braccus Max will tell you what you want to know. The Entity has gained great powers, quicker than I anticipated.

I'd explain everything, but I sense you would prefer that Ella told you?"

Vincent nodded his head, holding his gaze her way.

Constantine smiled at Ella, before turning to Vincent. "If that is your wish. But allow me to share one secret with you," he said determinedly. Suddenly a force field cloud hummed like there were a thousand bees hidden in the swirling cumulus. Effortlessly he hovered to the height of the ship mast, appearing to float in mid-air. The humming noise grew in intensity as if a jet were building for takeoff. Yet even in that noise, Vincent could hear Constantine's words clearly, as if sound waves emanated from his own mind.

"Believe what you see - what you've always seen. For that is your future," he said, before the surrounding force turned opaque around him. A second later he vanished, leaving only the sound of water quietly lapping against the boats two long narrow hulls. Ella sat quietly, back against the mast, studying the circling gulls for a time before breaking the silence.

"So, what is it you wish to know?"

Vincent felt a sense of terror and exhilaration at the same time. He'd waited a long time to know Ella's secrets, but he also feared the truth would change their friendship forever.

"Tell me everything about your life and your people."

A week earlier and Vincent would have thought her stories the imaginings of a crazed mind – or of his. But the events of the past few days were real, he was sure of that now, just as he was sure of his love for Ella. He had to believe her, for if he did not, he wouldn't care to live in this strange, dangerous world.

"I will, but not here. Let's set sail."

Ella lowered the mast to set their catamaran out to the open ocean. The sails quickly filled with a strong breeze at their back and powered away from the Brighton shore.

"Shall we go to France?" Ella joked. Her long hair flowed in the breeze like the sails above her and her eyes lit up with excitement for the journey. Vincent could see the natural affinity her kind had for exploration

"Perhaps Paris? It is the lover's city." Vincent teased.

Ella giggled with delight, showing her adventurous mood. "You may need this." She reached into her pocket and drew out an orb, smaller than Constantine's, but unmistakable as its glass marble-like ball ignited into rainbow colours.

"More drugs to defend ourselves?" Questioned Vincent, fearing their journey was being observed.

"No. This immersant will allow you to better understand me. That is what you are after, isn't it?"

Ella extended the orb in her open palm, inviting Vincent to hold her hand. He gently lay his hand over the orb, whilst gently caressing her hand with his thumb.

"I want to know everything about you, Ella."

The orb released a violet mist that encircled them. Unlike the barbs of the Entity's mist, this soothed Vincent. He held his gaze toward Ella's hypnotic eyes, feeling a mixture of desire and light-headedness. He felt disoriented and thought it was the effect of the drug. Ella shook her head, as if she had read his mind and actioned for him to look down. Vincent was shocked to find that he and Ella had risen high above the boat up to the top of the mast. They were literally flying alongside the white main sail.

"Am I dreaming?" Vincent asked. Ella laughed as she went to let go of Vincent's hand.

"No, don't let me go!"

"Trust me. You won't fall."

Vincent had a fear of heights at the best of times. To float a hundred metres high in mid-air was a tall order. He tried not to show fear as he reluctantly tried to let go of Ella's hand. Ella must have sensed his panic, for she very slowly released the pressure of her grasp to allow Vincent the time to get used to his situation, until finally he floated free in the wind.

"Your powers amaze me," said Vincent, surprised he did not fall. Soon his confidence grew and he began to take in his surroundings without any fear at all. "Do you always fly in your homeland?"

"All the time. The people of Titan were born to explore. Our world's sky is like a celestial Everest. We don't have one moon to gaze at. We are greeted by the grandeur and beauty of Saturn and her moons. Its celestial show is like no other. Every angle, junction and shadow is accentuated, like a doting mother revealing her pride to her family. Unlike your moon, my land is tidally-locked to Saturn, so we always see our Saturnine mother in the sky."

Vincent could see the moon in the distance. It was slipping below the horizon and out of sight from the Earth's sky for the evening. Vincent tried to imagine how it would feel to have the sky permanently filled with planets and moons.

"You must miss that. The beauty must inspire your kind?"

"It does. We are born to follow the wonders of the celestial movement, like the arrow hand in a grandfather clock; our rhythms are locked to Saturn."

Vincent's confidence grew as he adjusted to Ella's immersant. He felt as if he floated in the air rather than flew, but when the winds buffeted his body, he lost control.

"Spread your arms as if they are the wings of a seagull," said Ella.

Vincent quickly adjusted to his new capability and soon gracefully hovered in the breezes, affording him time to gaze at the surging oceans below.

"It is so beautiful from up here. I couldn't imagine a world without oceans," said Vincent. Ella breathed in the sea breezes and nodded her agreement.

"It is a wonderful experience that I will never forget. It holds a diversity of aquatic life, too. But we have our lakes."

"Tell me about it."

Ella glided closer to Vincent, so that she could take his hand as she spoke.

"My home is blessed with beauty and surrounded by three natural wonders. To the north are the Great Lakes known as Titan's blood. To the west is the Great Escarpment, one hundred and fifty kilometres of mountains, our largest. And to the east lays the water ice plateau. Known as Titan's Jewel, the frozen expanse stretches all the way to the Dark Terrain, gateway to the dark side of Titan."

"We have sent satellites to Titan and have mapped much of the terrain. The geography is as you describe it, but it appears lifeless. How can this be?" said Vincent, puzzled.

"I am from a very different Titan to the one you know," she replied.

"Are you from the future?"

"Possibly," she said, drawing a reaction from Vincent.

"Riddles. Always riddles. You must know. Your capabilities are far beyond that of our race," said Vincent in a terse manner. Ella reacted by stopping in mid-flight. She reached for Vincent's second hand and held both as they floated in mid-air. She looked directly at Vincent and spoke slowly and purposefully.

"I am telling you what I know. These are not riddles."

"So your Titan is from a different time, you're just not sure whether it is the future?"

"No, I'm not saying that. My best guess is that my Titan and your Titan are one and the same, but they are in different universes."

Vincent did not respond immediately, as he took in what Ella was proposing. If she were telling the truth, she was proof that the universe was not alone and the relatively new science hypothesising that we lived in a multiverse was correct.

"You have travelled from another universe?"

"Yes, we have," Ella replied with conviction. Vincent shook with excitement at the thought of such a possibility. The fact they could fly appeared proof enough that Ella was not of this Earth. He cast his gaze toward the south where a storm was brewing and wondered whether he was hallucinating. The events were too extraordinary for him to accept, yet here he was.

"Tell me of your people and your past. I need to know more."

Ella smiled as she let go his hands and glided away from him. "Come follow me and I'll tell you more."

Vincent willed himself forward and soon caught up with Ella. They flew at speed, away from the catamaran below, further south toward the storm.

"You learn quickly," said Ella, as she invited him to twist and dive through the quickening ocean breezes. The more Vincent showed his skills in flight, the more Ella revealed.

"We are a race not unlike yours. We are filled with curiosity. Most Odorphins are satisfied with exploring our home as inter-solar exploration requires much learning and practice. But the more ambitious of us explore further afield. A select few explore the wonders of our solar system, particularly our mother planet, Saturn, but also our neighbouring moons Tethys, Enceladus, Mimas, Dione and Lapetrus. You see, exploring – or voyaging as we call it – is our most valued life purpose."

"So everyone voyages in your culture? Do they engage in other passions? On Earth, our people have many pursuits. We have farmers of the land, city dwellers and nomads too."

"Your culture remains in an earlier evolutionary phase. You have to work together as a culture to survive. We are born with a light web which feeds, protects and shelters us, allowing our race to pursue what nature intended us to do – voyage and learn about the world in which we live, so that we can find our rightful place in it."

"So you were born with light webs or did you invent and develop them?" Vincent asked. Ella lifted her arms to reveal her light web to him.

It appeared as though a blurred light connected Ella's arm to her upper body. It remained formless, like a thick fog, until she willed a change. A shape formed within the fog, a shape he knew.

It was a three dimensional view of Saturn. Vincent shook his head in disbelief.

"Have you developed a technology to do this?"

"No. We were born with this capability. Where you are made of matter, we are made of two types of matter. We have a light inner skeletal body frame of solid matter, similar to your bodies and an outside frame blurred by the subtle matter light force that surrounds and protects our inner body. This subtle force is a blend of matter and energy, altogether different from the normal matter that makes up your universe. It's responsive to mental rather than physical forces, yet pliable enough to change from photons to the strongest matter discovered in our universe. As far as we know, our shape-shifting capability is unique in our universe and yours. We can change into anything we are able to imagine, allowing us to fly like birds through the thick, low gravity hydrogen atmosphere, or we can be fish shaped allowing us to effortlessly explore the depths of our great lakes. We can even be human, as you can see."

"You are gifted with amazing powers," said Vincent, admiringly.

"That gift is given to us from birth. But, like your brain is underdeveloped at birth, so too is our light web/ brain connection. Much training is required to reach our true capabilities as shape shifters."

"You have family?"

"Yes."

"Do they nurture and train you during your formative years?"

"Not as you know it. We do have child bearers, but they form only a part of our communal circle."

Ella's response made Vincent think about his own family upbringing. Due to tragic circumstances, he was brought up in a communal structure of sorts. He lived in a mix of foster homes and half-way houses after losing both his parents at a young age.

"Tell me about your parents? Did you know them well?"

"I knew them as well as others in my communal family. We learnt from an early age to value the natural world within which we lived more than that of our own kind. We were taught to respect and adhere to the teachings of our family, but our true destiny lay with our mother, Saturn. She had many lessons for us, but the first and most important was to live our lives like her. The rings that surrounded her were known as her light web. Every Odorphin aspired to shine like our mother. Hence our light webs form a connection with our mother planet that remains until our death. That sense of destiny cannot be fruitful unless we train from an early age to perfect the mechanics of our light webs. We learn the skills to voyage, for our first initiation is to circumnavigate our land of light."

"Your initiation sounds akin to our graduation ceremonies from being students to becoming adults."

"Yes, in many ways it is. But where you learn the skills to survive in your world, we learn to explore."

"We are not afforded that luxury. Most students have to choose a calling and specialise in it. It could be in trades, sciences or arts, a whole host of directions. It can be a difficult time," said Vincent, recalling his troubled period of life and the fear he felt, rather than hope.

"We learn the skills necessary to undertake the navigation, so that we may honour our mother's light web. We choose one of her ring's ice rocks and name it in honour of our voyage. Then our challenging voyage begins. It requires that we have mastered the natural skills of our anadels and ardels, no mean feat."

Vincent looked puzzled.

"Look beside you," said Ella, pointing in the direction of a seagull that flew close to them. "Anadels are like your seagulls, only three times larger and more bat-like than bird. Many generations earlier, our culture studied the dynamics of anadels. The laws of aerodynamics understood, our forefathers crafted wings like theirs, a fragile narrow skeletal inner body, allowing them to mimic flight in Titan's dense low gravity atmosphere. Complex respiratory systems were copied and adapted, and allowed hydrogen to partly bypass our lungs into special air sacs filling our outer bodies with air which assisted strong pectorals and forelimbs to engine our sleek flight through the Titan atmosphere."

Vincent nodded and then Ella continued.

"Now, look below you, to the east," she said, pointing to the shadow of a lone shark that circled a sea of fish. "Arlas are predatory, like your sharks, but smaller in size and a cross between your eels and fish. Fuelled by the exhilaration of flight and our wonder for exploration, our forefathers next mimicked the great arlas, the largest lake-faring mammals on Titan. Gill-bearing filaments were developed allowing the exchange of methane moisture for hydrogen. Chemo-receptors allowed higher senses of taste and smell, so as to better detect the currents and vibrations of our aquatic world. Suitable muscles on either side of the back were also adapted, giving S-shape curves for more rhythm as well as the streamlined shape to decrease friction and increase our speed through the helium lakes."

"Do they hunt anything that enters your lakes? Sharks have attacked humans as well as our sea creatures."

They attack anything they consider food – the basic animal instinct of survival. If we entered our waters without the protection of our light web, we would surely perish. But we are never permitted beyond our communal families until we are well versed in the use of our light webs and have faced many challenges. Like you, we have to overcome our youthful fears before our communal family decides we are ready."

A clap of thunder surged past them, making both look toward the storm they were approaching. Ella studied the storm for a time before speaking.

"Would you like to ride this storm with me?" Ella asked, holding her gaze, waiting for a reply. Vincent felt she was challenging him, so he responded in the affirmative in a nonchalant manner, hiding underlying reservations. But, his confidence was high as he seemed to take to flying with ease and his fear of heights had subsided.

"Absolutely. I think I was born to fly," he said, brazenly.

At that, Ella turned north east, straight toward the darkest cloud.

"Follow close behind me and mimic my actions, for we will fly through the centre of the storm."

Vincent replied but Ella didn't hear him. She accelerated away from him, expecting him to follow. Vincent was given little time to think about his situation, so he accelerated also and soon caught up. They flew below the gathering cumulus that was steadily darkening to the ominous colour of the deep ocean below them. Vincent was surrounded by two walls of water, above and below. Intermittent lightning and thunder added to the sense of danger. Vincent wanted to return to the safety of the ship, but feared losing site of Ella more, so he focused his mind on copying her every movement. They glided further into savage winds, exhilarating and terrifying Vincent, equally. The largest of lightning bolts blasted jaggedly down to the ocean just a hundred metres in front of them. Ella reacted by soaring upward away from the lightning blast and in the direction of the darkest formations of clouds.

Savage winds buffeted them from all directions, making it impossible to glide. Ella responded with speed rather than agility. She moved her arms closer to her body, like a ski jumper and powered through the dangerous winds. Vincent could not turn from the danger. Instead he focused solely on copying every movement Ella made and willing ever greater speeds. The icy winds stung his body. Science had told him that he should have perished in the chilly upper atmosphere by now. Yet even though his body felt the pain of the extreme conditions, his mind was unaffected, almost apart from his dire position, like a vivid dream.

He continued to fly forward, doggedly determined to stay with Ella, almost as if he were trying to prove himself to her. He was beginning to fly through the eye of the storm with confidence until one large thunderbolt cracked and reverberated around him, like a hundred horn blowing trucks were converging on him from every direction.

The sound froze him, like the water crystals that filled the storm cloud. Vincent was suddenly paralysed and at the mercy of the howling winds. He gave no resistance to the conditions as gravity pulled him down to the ocean below. Vincent was spinning out of control as his line of sight switched rapidly from the storm clouds to the ocean and finally darkness, before hitting the cold dark ocean waters.

Vincent woke disoriented. He was surrounded by a huge expanse of blue. He sat up quickly to get his bearings. Had he died? The last thing he remembered was falling. He wondered where he was as his senses slowly started to engage his surroundings. He looked around and realised he was back on the catamaran. To his relief, Ella sat at the other end of the boat, looking at him.

"What happened?"

"You fell into the ocean."

Vincent quickly recalled, "I should have died. I was too high to survive that."

"I wouldn't let that happen to you," said Ella. She stood up and walked over to Vincent and sat beside him. "There is too much for you to do..." she said, smiling and putting a comforting arm around him, drawing him close. "...and you have so much more to learn."

Vincent said nothing more, surprised by Ella's affection, but enjoying her unexpected closeness. They both looked out across the ocean to Brighton shore.

"We're nearly back. How long was I unconscious?"

"A few hours."

"What went wrong? I was flying through the storm, then a thunderbolt exploded close to me. I started falling...that's all I remember. Did the immersant lose its potency?"

"No. It will remain in your system for many days. You lost focus and fear took over."

"I don't understand."

"The immersant may feel as if it changes you physically, but it actually changes the way in which your brain receives information from your body's receptors."

"So, I am imagining all this?"

"No. You are experiencing everything, but in another more subtle dimension where your aura's receptors have a greater influence on your brain's view about reality."

"So it is real?"

"It is very real, but it is in another dimension."

Vincent stroked his hair off his forehead, as if trying to will the information to be less challenging. "Why did you encourage me to do this, if it was dangerous?"

Ella removed her arm from his shoulder and gazed directly into his eyes. "You are going to face far greater dangers from the Entity. You need to be prepared."

"You're training me. But why here, in this place?" Vincent asked, pointing toward Brighton and the old pier.

"This is but a first step. The training you need is close to here. It is the only place on your Earth that can help you. We want to take you there for your ultimate test, but for now you can learn different skills along the way."

"I don't have a light web. I can't manufacture anything out of nothing. How can I face such a challenge? You could train me for years and I still wouldn't be ready."

"You don't have years. It will be more like weeks. But that is not our choice. The Entity has revealed itself to us and it will not operate on any schedule you or I would ever understand."

Vincent looked away from Ella, back out to the storm from where they had come. Anger built in him about the situation they were facing. Why him? Hadn't he faced enough darkness for one lifetime? He watched the storm fade over the distant horizon, before turning to Ella.

"Did your people face such challenges?"

Ella was guiding the boat back to the shore. She lowered the sails and allowed the boats forward momentum to drift them the final hundred metres to their destination, before replying to Vincent.

"We faced many challenges to become adult Odorphins. Our most skilled rigorously trained from an early age, perfecting the mechanics of their light webs for new explorations. We were mentored until we perfected our abilities, so that we could circumnavigate our land of light, but our training was never extended to the Dark Terrain and Dark Land. The Dark Terrain is a sweeping desert making up some one fifth of our world bordering the dark side of Titan. The other side of Titan was destined to be always dark, except for the enticing moments of summer solstice which brought light to the dark. Then, small edges of its plateau were exposed to a brief window of light, where most were doomed to eternal darkness. This was a Titan where most Odorphins never ventured. Exploration of this land remains our individual choice. Only a small percentage of our people have explored it. The barren desert has claimed many lives over the eternal seasons and remains even now enshrouded in many myths."

"It is like our early journeys to the North and South Poles. It is too inhospitable for most, remaining the domain of our most adventurous scientists and the inquisitive. Have you conquered the Dark Lands?"

"Yes, thanks mostly to one courageous Odorphin, Braccus Max, the first explorer of the Dark Terrain. Braccus Max was an outstanding scholar eager to learn. He also had boundless energy for exploration. He was the first to discover the mysteries of its flat desert plains, random craters and fractured tiger stripe plateaus. It was said that Braccus Max returned a different Odorphin as a result of his journeys."

"Did you meet him?"

"Oh yes. He was my grandfather."

The boat slid into the sand embankment, near to the boat hire area. Ella secured the sails, before jumping out of the cat into the water.

"He was a great man, but that story can wait a little longer. We should return to the hotel that Constantine has organised for us and get some valuable rest. I will tell you more, perhaps over dinner." At that, Ella returned to the boat hire operator to pay for their half-day ride. Vincent was tired from the long day but his natural inquisitiveness pushed him to ask another more personal question.

"Do you have someone special...I mean someone you love?" Vincent stammered nervously.

Ella revealed a knowing glance before responding. "No, I don't. But my instincts tell me that I'm on the right path toward finding that someone." Ella brushed Vincent's waist as she walked past him. "Time for dinner, don't you think?" She said, not looking back. Vincent watched her slowly walking along the shore for some time. He had faced so much on this long day and yet all he could think of now, was to have dinner with Ella.

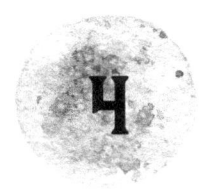

THE KING'S PALACE

ELLA AND VINCENT FOUND their lodgings among one of the many terrace hotels that lined the Brighton foreshore. Accommodation was aplenty, given the summer peak season remained months away. Constantine had picked a small bed and breakfast with ocean views, allowing them to rest before the next day's long journey from England to the European continent. Michael, the owner, was a well-spoken Englishman, amiable and well versed in French and Italian. He offered advice on the best place to dine, both locally and for their next day's destination – Venice.

Vincent showered and freshened up as best he could, given his luggage remained at the Victoria Station locker rooms. He wished he had his finest clothes, given he was about to dine with Ella, but he had to make do. The choice of restaurant was left to Ella and she decided on the Royal Pavilion Restaurant, overlooking Brighton Gardens. It was a former royal residence for the Prince of Wales who later became a king. Brighton was his special retreat between 1787 and the early nineteenth century.

"I wanted to take you through the Royal Pavilion before we dine in their restaurant. I know you love history," she said, as they both strolled across Brighton Gardens to the palace's entry. Vincent did love history. It gave him great strength at times. The romantic stories of the past had motivated him to succeed in life, the opposite in every way from his earlier drug-addled life.

"Why did you choose me? My life's been filled with failure and drug abuse. What could I offer you and Constantine?" Ella paid the tour entry fee before responding.

"You and Jean shared experiences no other humans have. You both faced the Entity. But you faced it alone. Your uncle admired your courage to survive that."

Vincent had developed an inner strength from facing his ordeal, but ultimately he could not have built his career without help from Jean and a mysterious benefactor. Vincent shifted closer to the University where Jean worked. Jean was a busy man, punctual and strict but he offered a hand to Vincent when he most needed it. The first year was a struggle, but Vincent earned his board by keeping his uncle's home clean both inside and out. He was reasonably well paid, fed and clothed but more importantly challenged; for Vincent could only remain in his uncle's home if he studied as well. It was in those months and years that Vincent first gained entry into university and ultimately a post graduate degree in science. His new life had begun.

Vincent was proud of his achievements as both a lecturer and physicist. He desperately wanted to return back to that life. But for now he could momentarily rest and relax as he and Ella wandered through King George IV's 'holiday home', a perfectly refurbished eighteenth century palace – royals lived well, no matter what century. The rich colours, the myriad of rooms, grand chandeliers and silver-lined banquet tables made Vincent fantasise about his future.

"I wish we could share this lifestyle," said Vincent, touching Ella's arm as they drifted through the many palatial rooms.

"Your life could be even grander than this," she replied, with a confidence that disarmed him.

The tour completed, they were guided to the dining hall, their first evening dinner together. Ella's beauty shone regally that night, enhanced by soft candle light and the moon-lit marble balcony that looked out on to the court yard of the palace – Brighton Gardens. All doubts Vincent had about the sincerity of their friendship melted before Ella's radiant beauty. Intoxicated by her delicate, sensual presence, he bravely proposed a toast to express his feelings for her. "To the most beautiful woman in the world, or should I say the most beautiful in two worlds," he said, drawing laughter.

"So you are in love with an alien?"

"How could I not be?"

Ella gazed deeply at him as they sipped on their wine. He wondered if she harboured some love for him or mere curiosity. The quiet relaxed calm of their evening was only broken by the waiter, delivering aromatic food to the table of white linen and 'royal silver'. Small talk continued through the two courses, surprising Vincent, for Ella was not one to engage in such banter. He had not seen her so relaxed before. The setting contributed to the mood. A star-filled sky and a garden below was filled with party lanterns to celebrate the commencement of the annual arts festival. They shared a perfect evening, free from the perils they would soon face, savouring the simple beauty of friendship, indulging their senses – through conversation, hearty food and the serene beauty of their surrounds. The conversation flowed effortlessly, joyfully.

"So, you were going to tell me more about your life. I want to know more about your grandfather."

"He was one of many well regarded explorers that inspired the next generation of voyagers. Braccus Max was one of a handful of voyagers who set the bar higher, exploring new frontiers previously thought inaccessible. Importantly, he passed on new skills gained from his voyages, to willing students."

It sounds like the old tribal customs on Earth. Tribal leaders would share stories of the past with their tribe around campfires."

"It is not too dissimilar. I remember Braccus Max sharing tales with our communal family when our Saturn mother and her moons were at their most visible in the sky. We would learn much from the information he shared through our light webs, but the telling of the voyage brought his experiences wondrously alive."

"Something like a lecture at a university," said Vincent, thinking of how he taught young, willing minds.

"Yes, but in the grandest of settings. He would talk to us positioned high above our Great Lakes, making sure our mother Saturn was in full view. At times, it felt like Saturn was listening to my grandfather and smiling."

"What made him so special?"

"He had a thirst for the unknown. Voyaging over previously explored lands did not interest him. He was always intrigued by the unknown. Unfortunately, his risk taking was admired and ridiculed in equal measure."

"That sounds odd. Why would courage be ridiculed?"

"Braccus Max earned admiration for his voyages to the Dark Terrain, but something happened on those deserts that made his investigations turn even further afield to the Dark Land. Some say he encountered a mysterious force there, while others believed he went mad from the isolation of that exploration. Whatever the truth, he devoted the remainder of his life to understanding the forces that lay beyond the Dark Terrain in the land of eternal darkness."

"Amazing courage."

"Some agreed with you. Fuelled by early success, my grandfather enlisted a few young explorers, adventurous enough to risk the journey deep into the Dark Land, his final and most infamous journey. The group disappeared for two seasons. Most believed they had perished, but Braccus Max alone returned to his Odorphin homeland against the odds, completely changed - many believed mad. His life was consumed by the discoveries of that journey, findings he spent two seasons recording. A few were excited by his findings but most had their suspicions, believing his 'voyage' a fanciful work of his imagination. You see, his work constantly referred to the 'hollow people', mysterious entities encountered on the northern boundaries of Dark Land. Braccus Max believed this his greatest triumph but it was largely ignored as the wanderings of a crazed mind. His work in time was forgotten by all but one."

"Constantine?"

"Yes. Constantine's research revealed dark land matter was not formed of atoms, nor did it interact with Baryon matter. But it did interact with our light web. Both behaved more like a perfect fluid, without viscosity. The particles did not interact. Both moved past each other never colliding. I worked with Constantine to further his theories, discovering new particles – neutrinos and axions, but also non-matter. We successfully recreated holographic replicas of those fundamental particles, on our light webs. To our surprise, we learned that these particles were capable of light speed travel and more. Soon after, Constantine became the first Odorphin to cross to an alternate universe."

"When did Constantine first see the Entity?"

"Constantine studied humans free of any interference for nearly a century of your years. But on befriending Jean, an Entity appeared. It was no different from this Entity. It was a dense vapour-like force. Its interest remained exclusively in Jean. It caused him no physical harm, but over time Jean developed psychological afflictions. He could not see his attacker, but he felt its painful barbs."

"So it has always chosen to attack us, rather than understand or observe us?"

"Unfortunately, yes. Constantine was forced to immediately develop immersants to protect Jean from it and for a time they worked. But the Entity always overcame them. It adapted and bypassed every new and more complex immersants we developed. The Entity itself changed too, taking increasingly complex forms. It had gained the ability to attach to many surfaces, even humans over time."

Vincent realised that he himself had experienced exactly this.

"So, you worked with Constantine, developing the many new immersants?"

Ella nodded her head. "Yes and that is where I should end this account. If you want to know more, talk to Constantine. Fair?"

Vincent wanted to know more, but he was satisfied that Ella had confided many of her secrets. So he nodded in agreement and sat back in his chair to savour more wine.

"Don't you sometimes wish nights like this could go on forever?" said Vincent, hoping she shared his elation.

"Vincent as beautiful as this night is, you must know something very important. It is the truth you want from me?" Ella asked, taking his hand and holding it gently. Her eyes were intense now, as he had never seen them before.

"That's all I ask," he replied.

"The drugs we took today will hold back the Entity's powers for no more than a week, after that I fear Constantine won't be able to develop any more. Do you understand what I'm telling you. We have at best another week."

"Then why are we running to Europe? What will that achieve? We may as well have stayed home," said Vincent, knowing there must be more.

"Because...we leave in a week. Constantine and I leave Earth, probably never to return," she said, holding her gaze, nothing more for her to say. Vincent took in the ramifications of her words; he'd be left to face the Entity alone. He pressed her further, unsure he was hearing all the truth.

"Why must you leave? You have been here for a year. Why not another?"

"We must leave. Trust me. It's the only way for us all. The return to Titan will be of high risk, but to have any chance, we must return to the location of my arrival on Earth."

Vincent withdrew his hand from hers. Feeling Ella was being coy, he reacted. "Why pursue our friendship? What purpose did it have? It seems to me to be all a waste."

"There is a wonderful purpose, but you'll only find out if you take this journey with us. You have to trust me," she said, hoping to convince him. Instead she roused his anger.

"Well one thing is certain, you couldn't ever love me. You've made that clear. Don't you see that is why I came here? I hoped that you would see how I feel for you." Ella sat quietly. Sadness filled her eyes as she spoke.

"That's true. I don't love you, Vincent. Not in the way you want me to. But what you don't realise is that you don't love me. Your love springs from another place, one that will be revealed to you at the right time."

Vincent looked away at the stars and the full moon, now low on the horizon, hiding his deep hurt from her gaze. He wanted to say more, much more, but he waved to the waiter requesting the bill instead.

"Can we go now? Let's walk along the ocean. I really need to clear my head right now," he said, forcing a smile through saddened eyes.

The ocean shore walkway was quieter now. An occasional person or couple passed them, lost in their own thoughts or discussions. Abandoned posters were the only reminder of the morning's rally. The traffic had all but disappeared too, allowing the gentle sound of waves lapping on to the beach to be heard. Vincent's mood matched the subdued lighting of the quiet pathway.

Both stood facing the soft ocean breeze, looking to their right out over to the old pier. Its decaying frames haunted the shimmering waters, dancing before the blood red moon, tantalizingly close to the horizon.

He shook slightly, recalling the events on the old pier that day, fearing that the next time he faced the Entity he could be alone. The thought made him turn away from the pier's ghostly decaying frame. With Ella beside him, he walked on in silence. The new pier was everything the old pier wasn't, lit up like a long birthday cake. Boisterous crowds further livened its gleaming snow white structure. And there at the end of the long walkway stood the brightest light. An explosion of coloured lights and metal swirled and curled against the pit black ocean.

The crowds on the walkway also grew as they came closer to the pier. One particularly colourful character stood out among the night revellers – a dark-skinned man with long black dreadlocks and a distinctly Jamaican appearance. He wore large silver earphones and glided on roller blades, twisting his body in all directions yet still maintaining balance, while his expressive hands communicated as he danced with uninhibited joy. To Vincent's surprise, Ella knew him.

"Dancing divinely tonight, Izzi," said Ella, providing him a warm, knowing greeting that only friends show each other.

"The moon is glidin' tonight my darlin' El...I tink I will sing to de gods tonight. Where has my favourite lady bin...Izzi rasta marn has bin tinkin of you," he said with a devilish smile and hungry eyes, bringing laughter to Ella and a hug before introducing him to Vincent.

"Izzi, I'd like you to meet Vincent."

Izzi held his hand out to Vincent, offering a Caribbean style handshake.

"Eet's a pleasure to meet de lucky marn who accompanies de jool of Brighton...what a purrrfic night too darnce wit my Ellateena...

the gods muz be appy dis evenin," he sung more than spoke. Ella laughed again at Izzi's charm before speaking.

"Vincent, Izzi has a special talent, he can read hands...care to try him?" she asked, Vincent agreeing.

"For a small contrebuuushan my fellow travlarr of de staarz," said Izzi, quickly gathering Vincent's hand before he could change his mind. Izzi stared intently at Vincent's open left palm, a gaze well practiced and convincing.

"Ahhh...de staarz darnce wit you Vinnee my marn...dey arr teezin you cos you don't look at dem...day callin you marn....too darnz wid dem...but dey grow weary wid you coz you don't hear dair calls...ur spell hars to be broken...broke soon marn...mebe dis night," said Izzi, releasing his hand and turning to Ella. "Are you helpin dis Vincent marn, mah beautiful Ella?"

"Yes I am Izzi. What should I do?"

"Ride de wind wit him, mah lovely...da wind blowin down Brighton way, on da edge of de waters...out where its dark...where da wind is true," he said, staring out to the ocean as if he could see their guides, waiting to show them their secrets. But abruptly, he turned to Vincent.

"Dat will be twenty pound, Vincent marn." Hands outstretched, Izzi smiled expectantly. Vincent begrudgingly obliged, before he and Ella bid him farewell. Izzi was a happy sight as he glided away into the night. Vincent believed his good humour was the result of the twenty pounds, but Ella believed otherwise.

"Come hold my hand, let's walk to the pier together," she said, her own mood infected by Izzi's unbound happiness. Vincent too perked up. Believing the twenty pounds a good investment, he took Ella's hand and walked to the shining light that was Brighton's pier, the site of holiday cheer for revellers young and old since 1899. They laughed like young lovers as they walked down the famous wooden floorboards, past games rooms, pubs and cafes to the 'rides area' the furthest point on the five hundred plus metres walkway.

"Let's ride on this one. It'll be fun," said Ella, her eyes lit up like a young school girl about to ride her first pony.

'This one' was 'The Booster' a steel structure standing forty metres tall with a rotating connecting steel pylon spanning thirty metres with protected seating compartments at each end. A three minute ride took those who dared to ride it from standstill to 3.6 G's of force in just under three seconds, turning a full 360 degree rotation every five seconds.

After the day Vincent had, it took some convincing for him to join Ella. Laughing and playing on the pier, Vincent had forgotten his friend was not of this Earth, but strapped in and ready to take off on The Booster, he quickly remembered.

"I suppose this is a play thing compared to your experiences," said Vincent. The machine suddenly sprang into action, imposing a body bending force on them. Ella breathed in the 'G force' as if it were a balmy summer day, before she turned to him, bliss etched across her blushed cheeks.

"Would you like to know what I am experiencing?" said Ella.

Having just been told he was unlikely to survive past the next week, Vincent figured he should experience all life had to offer, "Absolutely!"

Ella revealed her light web. It was something akin to the Entity's misty aura at first, but then a light shone from the swirling smoke like substance that momentarily blinded him.

"Don't look away. Come closer to me and look into the light," said Ella, stretching her arms apart as if to embrace Vincent with her fiery cloak. Vincent's eyes stung at first, burned by the star-like brightness of her light web. But as his eyes adjusted, discomfort turned to pleasure. Enraptured by its hypnotic beauty, Vincent gazed at something no other man had seen. Images danced back and forth and drew Vincent in further to her glowing light web.

Total calm overtook him, soothed by Ella's voice. He could see she sat beside him, but it felt as if she spoke from a distant ocean shore.

"Join me now," she called and he willingly crossed the waters to be with her. The 'G force' swirling his body on the ride's continuous 360 degree arc, suddenly flared and the steel cage protecting them vanished – and then the strangest feeling - his body too vanished. All he could see was the fiery sun and a starry backdrop.

It was as if he were the whole Earth, floating in deep space rotating the Sun. But its 365 day rotation had sped up to that of the Brighton Pier ride. Vincent circled the Sun every five seconds. The feeling was more real than anything he had felt in his life. As he continued to circuit Earth's star, he could see and feel its heat rising from below the corona, gas violently bubbling up to the surface and just as violently collapsing back down into its fiery depths. Solar flares burst out toward him, dangerously close. So too the solar winds, which constantly fired past him, on to the great expanse of the solar system. When he turned to observe the passing solar winds, he no longer was Earth. Instead he was a comet surfing the solar winds past Mars, then Jupiter, finally approaching Saturn.

He and Ella rode the solar winds at light speed, to the Saturn rings, where they were slowed by its gravitational field, at one with its missiles of rock and ice, a cosmic traffic lane a kilometre wide, trapped eternally in orbit. The giant gas planet exuded immeasurable power and intoxicating beauty, mesmerising him with its myriad swirling patterns of tiger-like colours. The surface was mostly of hydrogen gas, forming patterns that reminded him of thinned paint stirred with the colours of tan, gold and clay and the occasional dark splash of charcoal from large hurricane-like gas storms thousands of kilometres wide. The changing textures hypnotised him, like a Salvador Dali painting that had folded in on itself, dancing to the vibrato chorus of its savage dutiful rings.

They circled a quarter of its circumference before parting Saturn's force at a right angle toward Saturn's largest moon and

Ella's home - Titan. Appearing a tiny moon at first, compared to the gas colossus, Titan soon revealed its own grandeur as they approached the sand orange clouds, a thick shroud that hid its surface from all space travellers. They flew through the thick smog laden atmosphere of nitrogen and methane, blinding Vincent momentarily, until they broke through the mist, revealing Titan's landscape in all her beauty. They veered left around the natural columns of Titan's Sierras, to reveal its great lakes, a smooth surface reflecting the light like a shaded mirror.

It was then that Vincent felt Ella's true nature. Her human form was unable to cloak her alien origin. Ella was home, her face lit up, as did her light web, gaining an angelic violet hue. She belonged to its land, and there they slowed, hovering above a particular place in the landscape.

"Where the lakes border the mountains...that's my home," she said, a longing in her eyes telling Vincent she wanted to return.

"But I don't see anyone there. Where are your people?"

"There is no one. Not in your universe. But the lakes shine, don't they?" she said proudly. Vincent nodded in agreement, staring with her at a land awash with gold and orange hues.

"I have two homes. Land and lake," she said, leading Vincent away from the rocky land, deep below the still surface of the methane lake.

He expected water-like texture. Instead he felt a cross between air and water – swimming in a fog made of clay dust. Titan's lakes were dense and claustrophobic. In parts, Saturn's rainbow light diffused and mixed the swirling methane, creating a light show akin to a strobe light and smoke, a swirling blend of rich colour in parts, squid ink black in others. The kaleidoscope of colour and pattern disoriented him after a time. But for Ella, he would never have found his way to the surface, lost in an eerie technicolour maze devoid of gravities and structure. He was relieved when they surfaced. Ella flew through the clouds to Titan's highest peak, nearly two kilometres high, again stopping.

"Our land sits at the base of this mountain. There are natural formed caves here. At one time, the lakes extended all the way to its base, long before our time. The Odorphins have lived in these caverns for many thousand generations. It's a sacred place where we seek refuge in between our journeys. We live to roam our lands and explore its wonders. There are very few lands we return to, but this more than any other is our homeland."

Titan had great beauty but its hostile environment terrified more than excited Vincent. Any thought of living on such a planet horrified him. The thought depressed him, as he realised they could never be together. He had fallen in love with a holograph, an image created to reassure him. Ella's life was a masquerade to survive in a foreign world so that she could live among aliens - humans. And yet, no amount of logic could diminish his feelings for her. Something in her manner drew him closer, wanting him to be with her always.

Then the thought hit him. What must Ella really look like? She lived in a land totally hostile to him, a world of low gravity and no air. Their differences had to be extreme. And what did she make of him? Did she face him every day harbouring thoughts of revulsion to his human form? He laughed to himself at his naivety, a single tear welling in the corner of his eye as he gently took Ella's hand.

Ella was right to fend off his advances. They were no more than naive, fanciful fantasies. Vincent wanted to return home and Ella sensed it. In an instant the Titan backdrop disappeared, replaced by the rotating 'Booster' on Earth. It was as if they never left. Vincent felt great relief to be home – happy – before he realised Ella too must find his Earth unsettling. He knew then what he must do.

"Ella, I want to help you and Constantine to return to your homeland. I don't know how I can help, but I want to do this more than anything I've ever wanted to do in my life."

His tears rolled further down his cheeks, accepting he could never have Ella's love, but he felt happiness also, relieved to know the dark dreams that haunted him all his life were very real. Whether it be in his death or in victory, he would finally face the fear that had so insidiously cast a web through his life. He held Ella close.

"You've taken your first step to a life you were destined to live," said Ella.

"Tell me about my destiny?"

"Hundreds of years ago, one of the many great thinkers in your world measured light. This was an astonishing creative thought, given he had no light web. Our web allows us to see light actually travel on photons, where your people, blind to the universe's beauty still made this discovery."

"Yes, I believe his name was Rohmer, three hundred and fifty years ago. His calculations were close too – three hundred million kilometres a second, quite a triumph of observation," he said, recalling one of his many lectures.

"Constantine has spent these hundred Earth years learning the 'mathmatica', as have I from him. What a grand achievement as a race of people. I wish I could stay for a hundred years also to experience more of your race but it cannot be."

"Why did he come?"

"Simple. Advancement of the voyage," she said, pausing to choose her words carefully.

"We are blessed with more acute vision, unlike your people, but we have become blinded by its power, forgetting to use our intuition," said Ella, holding Vincent's shoulder in admiration for his fellow human's conquests.

"But I'm just one of many million scientists, Ella. Many are far more talented than me and producing outstanding research. I am a long way from producing that level of science" he said, believing he couldn't possibly make a difference.

"Discoveries are discoveries because they are so unexpected. Has any other human experienced what you just have?" Ella gave the briefest of smiles, her eyes lighting up in the fading light, as if she knew something about Vincent. Not of his past, but of what would be.

SOUND WAVES

VINCENT AND ELLA ARRIVED at St Pancreas Station to board the high speed bullet train to the European continent. The station was modern and comfortable, like the sleek speedy engineering marvels it housed. An impressive gothic entry led them to the 'under croft', a former storage basement that once housed beer barrels, but now was the gleaming arrival point for check-in to destinations local and abroad. A silent escalator whisked them to the long worm like sleek machines of steel and painted mirror – a number of them quietly brooding under one glorious roof, the biggest single roof structure in Europe. Sky blue light flooded in from the newly painted dome bringing a spacious peace to what was one of the busiest train terminals in Europe. A tide of people hurried over floors of timber and stone, past gothic carvings and a grand sculptures under the station clock. Vincent's journey started with a journey shared by many millions every year, but ultimately his journey would venture far beyond the rail lines. He didn't know where or how, but Vincent would play his part in helping two extra-terrestrial voyagers transit across two universes.

It was early morning, but already the spacious halls had filled with travellers heading to every corner of Europe. Vincent and Ella re-united with Constantine in front of the 'departure board' as planned. Constantine, clearly relieved, embraced Ella and shook Vincent's hand firmly.

"Ella tells me you're eager to help us," he said, studying Vincent closely for his reaction.

"Let's say I had an out of body experience, that softened my attitude," he replied, making Constantine laugh loudly before they both embraced.

"I'm sorry we couldn't take you fully into our confidence. Even now, we must keep certain details from you, but when the time is right, you'll know more," he said, with conviction.

They proceeded to the platform and the 'Eurostar Javelin' as it had been affectionately nick named for an earlier Olympic Games. Each carried single travel bags, which they quickly offloaded into the compartments at the front of the carriage. There they proceeded to their allotted seats, a four seater plus middle table reserved at the far end of the carriage. Ella sat with Vincent on one side and Constantine faced them.

In no time the eighteen carriage train quietly slid toward its first destination, Paris. Its slow acceleration belied the three hundred kilometres per hour top speed that it would soon reach. Leaving the bustle of central London relaxed Vincent. He quickly settled back into the plush, cream velvet seats and enjoyed the country scenery as it whisked quickly by. The first class ticket afforded them efficient service and a quiet carriage, they being the only occupants. Vincent wondered whether that was a result of the high cost of a ticket or Constantine's doing - either way he didn't care to find out. As they approached Devon, Constantine asked Ella to check all the carriages for any sign of their pursuer. She exited the carriage quietly, leaving Vincent and Constantine alone.

"Has there been any sign of the Entity, since I left you both at the Brighton Hotel?" Constantine asked.

"Nothing, since the new immersant."

"Good, it's worked. We have bought some time," he said, clearly relieved as he relaxed back in his seat. He and Vincent both watched the passing scenery for a time, before Constantine broke the silence.

"You experienced the light web with Ella last night. How did it feel?"

"I was frightened at first, but when I felt there was no danger, I relaxed and enjoyed the experience," said Vincent. His eyes glazed at the thought of the experience. A contented smile spread across Constantine's face. He sat forward in his seat before speaking.

"Ella told you the story of our forefathers. She tells me that you want to know more?"

"Very much so." Vincent's feelings were lifted by the growing trust Ella and Constantine were showing him as they confided more. "Braccus Max was a courageous voyager. How did he influence you?"

"Yes, Braccus Max's work inspired me to follow his research. Unlike most Odorphins, I chose to explore the sandy deserts of the Dark Terrain and further on into the Dark Lands, a five thousand kilometre excursion. I became the first to fully navigate the land of no light, a challenging and strange land devoid of Titan's great helium lakes and mountains. I endured extreme climate and faced many dangerous situations, but I developed new skills as I adapted to changing circumstances."

"Our human race has had to adapt to the challenges of changing climate, also. But it took us more than a single lifetime to do that. How did you adapt so quickly?"

"We have an advantage over your kind."

"Your light webs?"

"Of course. Facing the extreme cold and hostile winds of the Dark Land required that I fly higher than any other Odorphin before me, so that I could survive above the methane filled storms of the lower atmosphere. In that warmer upper atmosphere, I rode the wild winds and massive clouds of the stratosphere from south to north, then conversely its lower altitude winds north to south, voyaging where no others dared. Where the typical Odorphin flew the lower winds, bird-like, I developed new capabilities, spreading my light web wingspan some five metres across. I also developed bat-like radar to map the land below, disseminating vital information about the strange land in just three seasons. These new skills added much to our rapid evolution into space flight. But that was only a small jump compared to what I discovered in my latter voyages."

Constantine stopped his story and rested his head back on to his headrest. He turned his gaze out to the passing scenery, seemingly looking to the morning drenched landscape to help him recall his life-changing voyage.

"On that voyage, I observed Braccus Max's supposed myth, the 'hollow people'.

"Braccus Max was right after all?"

"Yes. I discovered that one of our great voyagers was not mad. Braccus Max suffered the barbs of many, who dismissed his ramblings on the hollow people as fanciful. He had devoted many years of his early research to the area without success or material evidence. Ultimately, it was consigned to folklore. You could imagine my elation when I found evidence of his claims, although I had little chance to celebrate at the time."

"Tell me what happened."

"It was during my third season's voyage of the Dark Lands and the most difficult. I had encountered more extreme wind gusts in the upper atmosphere than ever before. My efforts to navigate through the hostile winds had exhausted me. For the first time, I flew low on the land to see out the great storm. I was completely exhausted having only reached the half way mark of the Dark Land crossing. I sheltered in the hostile land for three orbits, a length of time never endured by any before me. The cold should have killed me but for the appearance of a strange force that somehow countered the deadly cold. It allowed me time to recover for the remainder of my journey."

"You spoke to this hollow entity?"

"No. In my weakened state, I believed I was hallucinating. No words were spoken, but I felt its protective force. The energy remained wrapped around me, an invisible cloak shielding me from the bitter cold for those three long orbits. By the time the great storm cleared, my energy had sufficiently restored to allow me to complete my journey home."

"Did you return to the Dark Land?"

"Not immediately. I had records of this interaction in my light web. After I recovered from my ordeal, I devoted a great deal of my time to studying the mysterious force. It seemed to fit Braccus Max's description of the hollow people. The experience had a profound and motivating effect on me. I soon discovered unique revelations about their world which accelerated our evolutionary capability to voyage the universe and beyond."

"Beyond meaning your voyage to Earth?"

"Yes. Ella and I are the first to travel across different universes. So you see, taking leaps of faith into the unknown can bring big rewards. This is why we are taking you on this journey across Europe," said Constantine. He reached out and lightly held Vincent's shoulder, seemingly wanting to highlight what he was about to say.

"You are here to learn, Vincent."

"Learn what?"

"Many things. But trust me; the skills we are teaching you are not just for the sole purpose of surviving the Entity. We want you to experience new revelations to help your kind to evolve, too. But to do that you are going to have to take a leap into the unknown also."

Vincent wished he had no doubts, but the dramatic series of events had crashed into his life without warning. Mixed emotions pulled him toward an uncertain fate, leaving him fearful and confused. The events he had experienced felt very real, but so too did the ghosts of his past. Were they real events or was he hallucinating? He could never be certain. But he was sure of his feelings for Ella. If she were in danger he would do all he could to help, no matter the risk.

"I want to help, but how? Your's and the Entity's powers are beyond anything I could defend." There was helplessness in his tone.

"Do you think we would bring you here if we believed you had no unique talents?" said Constantine, inviting more questions.

"I had a voyage with Ella beyond anything I had experienced in my life. I have no such powers."

"That's true. You were a passenger on Ella's light web, yet you still experienced something you would not have believed possible. You do hold within you the power to instigate voyages of your own, unassisted. You just need a little help," said Constantine, drawing a small orb from his coat pocket and placing it on the table.

Ella returned and sat quietly, her gaze turning from the immersant to Vincent. Seemingly, both waited for Vincent to respond to the challenge. The uneasy quiet remained before the silence was broken by the sound of an approaching train's horn in the distance. It flashed by in the blink of an eye. The speed and power of their combined force shook the sealed window, startling Vincent.

"Quick aren't they?" he offered meekly, explaining his reaction.

"It's all relative. If you're to help us, you'll have to learn to handle speeds far in excess of that," said Constantine, locking his gaze on him. "Care to try?" He asked as he picked up the orb and displayed it in his open palm.

Vincent's mind raced. He had learnt Constantine wasn't one to offer meek challenges. Fear grew in him. He tried to hide it from Ella, who sat beside him, by saying nothing, and listening intently.

He could feel her willing him to accept Constantine's challenge to show his faith in them and himself. He felt cornered by an unpredictable future he had little control over. But he clung to a vain hope of capturing Ella's admiration and love. He glanced at her briefly, summoning courage from her evocative eyes and replied.

"Yes...yes I'll try," he said finally, drawing the faintest of satisfied sighs from Constantine and a supportive touch from Ella's hand.

"This immersant will enhance your senses, magnifying them to such a degree you'll feel an out of body experience. It will stimulate your own light web, what you identify as your body's aura. Your aura, Vincent, is particularly strong. The visions you had as a young boy growing up were all very real. But instead of using immersants to enhance your perception, you were administered the opposite. Your Earth doctors numbed your aura's powers. So rather than expand awareness, your senses remained firmly locked within your physical body. The drug you are about to experience will reverse that for a short period of time."

Vincent thought to change his mind. The last thing he wanted in his life was to encourage the return of his hallucinations.

"How long?"

"The immersant will take effect within a minute. Its full force lasts just a few seconds," Constantine said reassuringly, before continuing, "but each second will feel longer, much longer. It will be the briefest moment in your life, but it will alter your perception forever. We call it bright radiance."

Vincent knew that Constantine was not prone to exaggeration. The stakes would be high.

"I'm here to help you, not be a passenger," he replied, clasping his fists in a determined manner, before opening them for Constantine.

Constantine laid the now glowing orb on Vincent's open palm, before issuing his last warning.

"If you do this, you do it alone. We cannot help you with this journey. So, the choice is yours." Vincent nodded his acceptance and then grasped the orb. He held his gaze on Constantine's light web which was ablaze with fiery colour, as he repeatedly swept it over Vincent's closed palm.

Vincent shook with fear, he hoped imperceptibly, determined to hide his fear from Ella. Sweat formed on the top of his brow as he clasped the orb tightly and voyaged toward the unknown. In a second it was done.

"Listen to me carefully, Vincent. You should be sensing that another train is fast approaching us from the opposite direction. Its speed, like ours, will be three hundred kilometres an hour. That means the combined speed at the point of passing will be ten kilometres per minute – in other words the whole experience will occur in little more than a sharp breath. But that I'm afraid is not quick enough for our experiment. Out in front, as both trains sound their horns, is the wave of sound, streaming ahead of them on molecules of compressed air. Both sound waves will be heading for impact at twelve hundred kilometres per hour. You must project yourself to be smaller than one of those billions of molecules. Focus on that projection and you will become it. In a way, you will be surfing the stretched vibration wave headlong into the other approaching tsunami. You will stand between two rogue waves in the middle of a vast ocean about to collide."

The chemical began to stream into Vincent's consciousness. He felt an intense cold rush that reminded him of cocaine, but a hundred times more powerful, magnifying his mind and creating clarity for the absolute present. Constantine's words were so clear, Vincent felt he was predicting every word before he heard them. His sharp hearing already turned to the approaching train. He sensed its exact location, as if he stood beside it. Yet the train was many kilometres away.

"You're reaching bright radiance. You have the ability to turn imagination into reality. You must picture yourself balancing inside the sphere of the smallest particle. You are smaller than a quark. In that place, you have no mass. In that cocoon you cannot be harmed. But be warned, you will experience sensations that will make you believe otherwise."

Vincent's clarity for the moment grew at exponential speed. He heard and interpreted Constantine's words at the same time. Each word was a symphony of elaborate sound waves vibrating across his face, like stormy seas battering high cliffs.

"When our train sounds its horn, you will react and catch its first vibration. It will feel like jumping on to a droplet of water from high rains."

Vincent's mind separated from its familiar place, leaping from his body like a freed jaguar. He studied the movement of sight and sound around him, aware of every vibration and photon. The carriage was ablaze with the chaotic movement of light and sound. Then he heard the blast of the train's horn in the distance, and his call to ride the sound storm. More by reflex than by thought, he moved his focus from the inside of the carriage to the unprotected surge of energy building in front of the train like a concentrated pulse of wind.

Vincent had landed on a single molecule of cold air, one small part of a tidal wave of energy accelerating effortlessly from the speeding train. In that first instant he felt no fear as it was more a reaction than a thought. But once on the perilous journey, he felt the power of the force thrash his body. Fear gripped him. *Think of yourself not as a physical body*, he kept repeating to himself, establishing some control over his fear. The journey, which in real time would be less than a second, was slowed in this place of bright radiance. It felt as if he rode not one wave, but many large waves, each stacked atop another toward a wall of energy that alarmed him. A force writ large as if the clouds of the largest storm were about to ram into the wave of energy he rode. His instinct was to dive under the wave like a body surfer, but there was no under or around its malevolent force.

He held on to the surface of the molecule and immediately regretted his reaction. That was a human reaction of fear. He corrected his thoughts, imagining instead that he was the smallest of quarks, sinking into the bubble molecule, allowing its smooth viscous shape to form a perfect orb that protected him.

The two powerful forces struck each other; long before the trains passed, setting Vincent's sphere in a spinning motion that accelerated exponentially like an ice skater spinning on a single spot. They struck at a combined two thousand four hundred kilometre per hour force that accelerated his protective case's movement to many times that speed. Vincent remained centred in his molecular cocoon, observing its wall rotating wildly but holding still. The moment filled him with both wonder and terror equally. Vincent's confidence grew, even though hell raged around him. But this was but a small taste of the fury that was about to engulf him.

Both trains headed toward him, causing a second human reaction. He jumped for safety to the side of the tracks, but in doing so broke his protection, exposing his body to the full force of both trains. He could do no more than cover his face - again a human reaction. Feelings swamped his mind, leaving him vulnerable. He wondered how much room would exist between the two trains when they passed.

Vincent stood paralysed with fear between the tracks, both trains now upon him. He remembered wanting to die quickly as he felt the power of both trains scream past. His senses remained heightened, allowing him to position himself perfectly between the two screaming steel walls that had engulfed him. Balance and counterbalance was all he could think as the force rocked him from all directions. The second it took for the two trains to pass felt more like an eternity as he calculated every minute movement to keep his footing between the tracks. His finely tuned hearing burst with the enormous roar of wheel on steel. He felt the sting of a billion small blows as each wind-blown molecule struck his body.

He summoned all his powers of concentration, as the slightest contact with metal would have shredded his limbs as his body spun uncontrollably against one train than the other. Somehow he held his position until the trains passed, but only just before the prevailing back draft knocked his weary body to the ground.

Vincent lay on the track, in shock at what had just occurred. He had escaped death, expending all his energy and nerves, facing a terror greater than the sum total of all his previous dark horrors. He felt only the cold steel of the rail lines and the rough texture of the ballastless concrete slabs pressed against his body. But in the harsh chill of his surrounds, he felt the warm rhythm of his heart miraculously still beating. He wanted to crawl off the track toward the surrounding shrubs and savour its peaceful natural surrounds. But he was distracted when he heard the soothing sounds of Ella's voice.

"Time to join us," she said, suddenly appearing before him.

Vincent wanted to speak, but he couldn't. He had just escaped death. He knew not how, but he had cheated the trains of their vengeance. His enhanced senses were now dying embers as normality returned - his 'bright radiance' seemingly drained.

"Yes, take me back, must go back," he said, not even realising he was already back in the carriage with Ella and Constantine. He had fallen into shock and needed time to take in what he'd just experienced. Ella wrapped a blanket around him and placed a sandwich and hot chocolate on the table.

"A few human comforts for you. It will help," she said. Vincent immediately sipped on the hot chocolate, which soothed his rattled nerves. Before long he was hungry, quickly finishing his meal. Surprisingly, his energy returned.

"I suddenly feel strong again?"

"It's the immersant," said Ella.

"Residual elements will remain in your system for many more hours," added Constantine.

Vincent's curiosity quickly returned as he recuperated from the shock of his experience. "Tell me more about yourselves. I feel I'm changing, gaining strength. I need to know - from both of you - why you are here on Earth? Why are you training me? Why..."

"Slow down, Vincent. The remnants of the immersant are still fanning your receptor/brain connections, filling you with an urgency to know everything. Sit back and allow us to tell you more, but relax your mind," said Ella.

Vincent begrudgingly sat back. He had never felt more alive in his life. In truth, he wanted to leave the confines of the train and fly with Ella and explore the universe. But his desire to know the truth about his friends took precedence. Constantine held off saying more until Vincent had settled.

"Some of the elements in the immersant you just took came directly from my studies of the Dark Land. For that brief moment you felt what it would be like to be a more evolved sentient being, a stage of evolution your kind will not feel for many thousand years. Similarly, my discovery on the Dark Lands moved the evolution of our race forward in a startlingly quick manner."

"Did it take you long to realise this discovery?"

"It took many of your Earth decades to identify the force that had somehow protected me from the extreme cold of the Dark Land. This unknown force was invisible to the eye, smaller than molecular and atomic level. My research into sub-atomic particles was painstaking and required a quantum leap in comprehension. But our race is gifted with the light web, which allows us to permanently collate information in our memories - our own unique research laboratory. In a quarter Saturn circumference, I successfully recreated Dark Land matter. I was now capable of exploring the extreme conditions of Titan unharmed."

"Did it encourage more Odorphins to follow?"

"Many more followed. The exploration of the Dark Land grew exponentially. Soon many Odorphins explored their solar system, freed from physical restrictions, protected by their light webs. But no amount of development could take them to the levels of inter-galactic flight. But that is another story. We have a few hours before we arrive at our destination. I suggest we rest."

Surprisingly, Vincent agreed. Where his energy abounded before Constantine started to speak, he was suddenly feeling tired. He turned to Ella. "Was there something in the drink?"

"Yes. It simply sped up the process of ridding your system of the immersant. You are better to get some rest now. We will ask a lot of you in the coming days."

He slept all the way to Venice, a sound sleep unlike any he had experienced before, oblivious to the discussions, sometimes heated, between Ella and Constantine.

6

VENICE

EVEN ON DISEMBARKING, THE day remained a blur of incoherent images until they boarded the vessel that took them to the 'island canal city' of Venice. A one hour ride followed across calm early evening waters of the 'Laguna Veneta' to the famous canals of the aquatic city.

Gondoliers stood ready to serve at every small pier, dotted along the intricate maze of canals. Constantine led Ella and Vincent through the intricate web of narrow laneways that linked the waterways. He took them ever deeper into the chaotic city, searching for a particular gondolier, continually enquiring in Italian for his whereabouts and receiving expressive and sometimes entertaining replies. Finally, the right operator – Gianni – took the three through narrow waterways, bridge lined and crammed full of other gondoliers, each trying to guide their passengers across well chartered waters. Gianni pointed out features of the ever changing buildings that lined the canal borders. Occasionally Constantine translated his comments.

"We are heading for the 'Grand Canal'. At its northern border we will be dropped off. From there I'll be taking you to the most famous area of Venice, Piazzo San Marco."

Constantine said very little about their plans that day, preferring to play the tourist guide. Not that Vincent minded. He welcomed the chance to forget their situation even if for only a short time. The scenic tour through the lined streets of water and centuries old architecture relaxed everyone. Vincent sat at the front of the long narrow wooden gondola, his gaze sweeping the wondrous sites of Venice. Constantine and Ella sat at the back of the gondola and Gianni stood behind them, expertly manoeuvring through the many narrow and crowded canals. At times, whole groups of gondolas got caught in the canal confusion. Gondoliers passionately shouted instructions to each other as they unsuccessfully tried to break free from the crowded stone banks. It appeared to amuse Gianni as he effortlessly guided his craft through all kinds of situations, never once slowing.

It reminded Vincent of the previous day's encounter between the trains where he too needed Gianni's confident balance and iron nerve. He wondered how Gianni may have fared, before turning to Constantine.

"How long has Gianni worked as a gondolier?"

"As long as I have known him and I first met Gianni Galermo over thirty years ago. I learnt the hard way, to only travel the canals with his experienced hand."

And indeed, Gianni had the hand of a maestro, standing upright gently guiding his century old gondola with a single three metre oar as if it were a harp string. His dark Mediterranean features instilled a calmness born of a man satisfied with his life. He was the very opposite of typical Italians. Most appeared a passionate yet unorganised people, going about seemingly simple projects in the most difficult manner, preferring to argue over their endless mistakes. However, beneath their chaotic exterior lay a culture capable of the sublime. The design of Venice alone was a human work of art. They soon bid Gianni farewell as he politely assisted them from the gondola. They were now free to explore the maze of narrow lanes that surrounded the water canals of Venice.

Vincent had not ventured overseas before, so Venice was an altogether new experience. He had studied many cultures, including Italy, but to be there among the people, walking the narrow streets, floating on manmade canals, lifted his spirits. Occasionally he sighted a glimpse of the canals as they passed over narrow pedestrian bridges. But over time the water views became a rarity, as they continued deeper into the labyrinth of white and rustic Venetian architecture.

Crowds steadily built as they headed toward 'holy turf'. Here, no maps were needed as the atmosphere of expectation alone acted as a magnet. The rustle of feet across cobblestone and the hum of expectation slowly built as they approached their destination. The open aired narrow lanes turned to underground corridors, as excited tourists filed toward a simple set of archways, belying the grandeur that awaited them.

Vincent heard the gathering crowds long before he entered Piazzo San Marco. Akin to a football crowd, they assembled in various parts of the open expanse, staring in all directions at their holy surrounds. Vincent soon joined them, hypnotised by the aesthetic majesty of the grand piazza. Cobblestone, marble, concrete pillars stretched to the sky, silhouetted by religious cathedrals that filled the landscape in all directions.

The 'Piazza', as it was known by locals, was filled with colour. Every Mediterranean hue was accentuated by tourists' flashing cameras, recording their magical piece of Venice. Vincent walked east across the open Piazza toward the columned entry to the church of St. Mark. Its foundations stretched across the full length of the Piazza. Its facade was lined with great arches and marble decoration. One Romanesque carving of the 'Four Horses' decorated the central doorway presiding over the Piazza, symbolising the pride and power of Venice.

Vincent stood in the centre of the great urban space where people not traffic prevailed. His gaze swept the kaleidoscope of architecture full circle, breathing in the rare view, before Constantine led him to a second grand expanse. They walked north of the church to the Piazzetta, an extension of the Piazza with open views to the lagoon.

"The Piazza forms the social, religious and political centre of Venice," said Constantine, barely heard over the sound of the large excited crowd. "The Piazzetta forms the commercial and financial centre." A Clock tower stood tall over the Piazzetta. It faced out toward the harbour. Vincent admired the beauty of the ship-lined harbour, bathed in pink from the low setting moon and cooled by open sea breezes.

"The tower was built in 1499," said Constantine, shouting now.

Vincent felt its history too, joined in the sea of humanity, who had come to pay homage to their fore-bears, Galileo Galilei, Michelangelo, Leonardo da Vinci. All had walked these pavements in earlier centuries and that history spoke to Vincent that evening.

"The Bell Tower of St. Mark is a significant marker for human history. Do you know why?" Constantine asked.

"Of course. Galileo introduced his telescope to the Senate of Venice and the Doge. Thanks to the demonstration, Galileo was named professor to the University of Padua. He received a favourable commission, too."

"Would you care to see that historic moment?"

"Every historian in the world would give anything for that privilege."

"Yes, they would," said Constantine, looking intently at Vincent before continuing to speak. "Look up to the top of the Bell Tower."

Vincent tilted his head back and gazed up to the famous monument, one of Venice's most recognisable. It was the tallest building in Venice, standing just under a hundred metres high. It was reconstructed in 1912 after the collapse of 1902.

"It's a tragedy that the original was devastated by..." Vincent stopped mid-sentence, for the structure was no longer the reconstruction, but the original form built in 1499. Vincent instinctively looked to the crowd to measure their reaction, but they continued to take photos as if nothing had happened. He turned to Constantine for answers.

"Only we see this."

"Have we travelled back in time?"

"In a way. Yes. But as you can see, only the Bell Tower has been affected."

Vincent gazed in all directions across the large square, verifying what Constantine had said was true. "How do you make this happen?"

"I have created this through my light web."

"No one else sees this?"

"No. They cannot see us either. Look up again."

To Vincent's astonishment, he saw two figures standing at the top of the Bell Tower. Both men were talking, expressively, as they viewed out across St. Marco square. One was dressed in a close-cut padded jacket over a linen shirt with deep cuffs. The other looked more regal, wearing a flowing robe and matching hat, emblazoned in colours of red and gold.

Vincent studied the unfolding scene. "This can't be..."

"Wait," said Constantine, cutting Vincent short.

The first man lifted a telescope to the viewing platform of the tower as he explained to the other how to look through it. Vincent shook his head in disbelief.

"Galileo is showing the Doge the first telescope. Right?"

"It wasn't the first, but it was Galileo's modified and enhanced version of the first."

Vincent watched the two as they conversed enthusiastically and imagined what they were saying. The Doge no doubt, looked out to

Venice with new eyes, as Galileo proudly explained the mechanics of his new invention.

"This was a turning point in human history," said Vincent, genuinely moved by the occasion. "Thank you, I will never forget this moment."

"It shows how a single invention can mean so much to many."

"He was ahead of his time."

"He faced ridicule, scorn, imprisonment and ultimately execution. Yet, he held true to his convictions."

"Did you face similar circumstances, Constantine?"

"In a way. My discovery was certainly met with scorn."

"Tell me about your discovery," said Vincent, eager to hear more about his two friends' lives.

"Multiverse travel evolved slowly, taking me a Saturn year or three Earth decades to fully realise. But it was worth the sacrifice, as my work on the subtle matter light force at the sub-atomic level changed everything. New developments accelerated. Gill bearing filaments were re-constructed to allow deep space breathing capability and the development of inter-planetary voyages. This in turn led to the development of long-distance communication using light waves and with that, fundamental ways in which the universe existed were revealed. I developed 'holographic reconstruction' or the ability to create images of ourselves – avatars, with our consciousness attached. Avatars were lighter than the smallest atom, hence capable of travelling at light speed. Whole new fields of exploration exploded. Inter-planetary exploration turned to inter-galactic. I took it further to inter-universe exploration. No one believed other universes existed, but I would not be swayed."

"Like Galileo."

"Yes. From that point I worked tirelessly on it, assembling a small, loyal team of like-minded 'voyagers', one a very promising young student."

"Ella?"

"Yes. Ellatine Braccus Max, great-granddaughter of our most famous explorer. It was Braccus Max's voyages that gave me the inspiration and courage to become the first Odorphin to reach across the multiverse. Many believed it was likely to be a one-way journey, if I was fortunate enough to survive the experience."

"You did survive it," said Vincent.

"Yes. But at the time, there was a possibility my critics could have been right. Unlike interstellar travel, communication across the multiverse was impossible. It was potentially a life sentence to an unknown world, the prospect of surviving tenuous at best. It took me two Saturn years into the project, to develop a way to communicate from across the universe."

"You would have seen so much. What did you first communicate?"

"It was a detailed communiqué, a mixture of anecdotes of my experiences on a planet called Earth and a larger document detailing some of the discoveries of Earth's great voyagers – I called it 'the mathmatica'. It was a large volume of work, I found indecipherable at first, but bold in its aims, given it was written by a race with no light web capability and an inability to see the 'subtle dimension' as we could. It astounded me to discover how you explored the solar system."

"In space rockets."

"Yes, rockets. But also telescopes. Your discoveries reached beyond some Odorphin discoveries, which was remarkable. Your physical structure is more like the animals of Titan than Odorphins. You lack full sight, seeing only three dimensions, but you have an instinct for the fourth and subtle dimension, using your mathmatica."

"Thanks in a large part to the man in the Bell Tower," said Vincent, still gazing up at Galileo.

"Yes, he uncovered many secrets, just as I have revealed enough Odorphin secrets to you for one day. I will leave Ella to tell you what followed."

Constantine then waved his light web in the direction of the Bell Tower, making the historic Bell Tower and its occupants disappear, replaced again by the modern version. Vincent sighed and shook his head at what he had just witnessed, before he hugged Constantine in appreciation for what he had shared. For the first time, Vincent felt a connection with him was growing, based on trust.

"Looks like Ella wants to show you something," said Constantine. Vincent turned to see Ella in the crowd, waving to them.

"This way," said Ella, signalling them to follow her to an arcade lined with shops and restaurants. The most famous of them all was the Caffe Quadri, situated on the corner of the square, with sweeping views across the Piazzetta, the lagoon and its popular walkway.

"It's customary to enjoy a drink here as a welcome to Venice," said Ella, offering Constantine and Vincent a chair.

Caffe Quadri was famous for good reason. Italian style mahogany furniture in rich red sumptuous surrounds set the scene and the impeccable service complimented it. The three were seated at a table offering sweeping views of the Piazza and Promenade Lagoon. An immaculately dressed waiter promptly served them, ready to entertain or serve them in right measure. Constantine ordered a bottle of 'Vino Nobile di Montepulciano', a well-regarded red wine from the Tuscany region. He joked to the waiter and tipped him before sitting back to take in the breathtaking views.

"Special place, isn't it?" He enquired, before pointing to one of his favourite hotels, asking if they would be happy to stay there the night.

Vincent agreed, but he knew their journey was to be no holiday. Sufficiently rested from his earlier ordeal with the trains, his mind returned to the purpose of their journey.

"You reminded me today, why it is special."

Constantine waited for the wine to be served, and savoured its exotic flavours, before answering Vincent. "You are experiencing sensations no other human has before. We weren't sure you'd survive it!"

Vincent took a large sip of his wine on hearing this; his emotions were high, frightened by Constantine's words. He didn't realise his life has been at risk. Was his growing trust placed in a mad scientist? Even worse, a desperate scientist? But despite those concerns he had built an inner strength from the experience. He alone had faced a life threatening ordeal. A euphoric hunger lingered in him that provided him a growing taste for life and its challenges.

"These experiences are changing me. I'm gaining a strength that I haven't felt in a long time. But I fear it will not be enough to face this Entity."

"Perhaps, but these are early steps. You will have to face more. Then you will be ready." Constantine said, challenging him.

The thought horrified Vincent. He felt he had nearly died between the two trains. He had been tested to an extreme he was in no hurry to repeat. Any raising of the bar would be beyond his abilities, drug or no drug.

"You ask the impossible, no other human has faced what I endured."

Ella started to speak, but Constantine talked over her. "Look at the moon, so close to the skyline. Exquisite don't you think?" Stony silence greeted his attempt to change the subject, but he continued regardless.

"And there, five degrees above the moon, you can see the pale yellow star. That's Saturn. If we had a telescope you would see the rings and you would also see our home, Titan. How fitting," said Constantine, oblivious to Vincent's doubts, as he enjoyed the wine and the galactic view in the night sky.

"Galileo observed this night sky and changed everything. It was Galileo who first considered that light itself has limits to its speed.

He never accurately measured it but he motivated another to. Roemer used a Saturn moon's orbit to plot the first measurement of light, and not a bad estimate either, given his tools. But even at some hundred million kilometres per second short of the actual speed, Roemer learnt that light travelled very fast," he said, pausing and raising his glass to Vincent as a toast.

"That's how fast you must learn to travel."

Vincent drank more wine; a gulp more than his usual. The thought that he'd repeat the train experiment terrified him – but light speed? "I don't think I could face such a test."

Constantine thought to reply but decided against it, shooting a knowing glance Ella's way.

"Vincent, our time on this universe is short. We want to help you, but you'll have to make this choice yourself. This is your one chance to experience what you are destined to discover. You and Galileo are faced with similar challenges it seems," she said gazing at the Bell Tower.

"Is this why the Entity pursues me? Is it because of what I may discover?"

Constantine interjected. "It's possible, although the truth is we don't know why. We do know that both Entities sought only you and Jean. Despite our knowledge, it remains ambivalent toward us. I assume that we are invisible to it...or irrelevant. Sometimes I believe it does see Ella and I, yet it does not act or communicate. I'm hoping through you we may break that barrier. It will be dangerous for you, but I can think of no better alternative."

Vincent looked anything but convinced. "Vincent, I know this is difficult for you. All I ask is that you consider it carefully. Sleep on it. But then you will have to make your decision tomorrow. If you agree to do this, you will face terrifying challenges. But you must let me know in the morning."

Constantine stood ready to leave, but not before he shot a knowing glance to Ella. At that he left Vincent and Ella to explore the evening streets of Venice while he organised lodgings for the night. The crowds had, if anything swelled as more tourists filled the Piazza and Promenade. The night was still warm after a humid day, but an impending storm offered the promise of relief. Boats filled the harbour as they busily shunted passengers to and from the San Marco pier, giving life to the night-blue lagoon. The red moon's haze turned the horizon to a pink glow. The waters were now bathed with manmade lights that decorated the bustling ferries, giving a celebratory feel to Venice.

A pretty young Italian waitress, dressed in jeans, shirt and apron, wound open the restaurant canopy to provide shelter from the impending rains, before sitting in the covered courtyard alone, lighting a small self-rolled cigarette. The developing breezes caught her long fine dark hair as she sat talking on her mobile. The smoke from her cigarette drifted in all directions, carried by a combination of the wind and her expressive hands. A concoction of aromas filled the piazza - food, perfume, ocean salt, the wet oak of the boats and the distinctive smell of approaching rain.

"We should explore the streets before the rains arrive," said Ella, eager to see the beautiful city by night. Vincent agreed. *A perfect way to end his introduction to the lovers city*, he thought, hoping it might spark a hint of romance from her. Besides, he always felt comfortable with Ella, sharing conversation and laughter with ease, as if they were lovers. His emotions baffled him. He knew it impossible - Ella was not of this world - yet he held on to his fantasy.

"You've been quiet these last few days. I feel you wish to speak your mind, but Constantine stops you." He said, making Ella smile.

"Perceptive. I worry that he asks too much of you. But in another way he is right to do so. If we had more time..." she said, finishing in mid-sentence, unable to solve the dilemma that troubled her.

"Well at least you're worried about me. They are feelings of a sort," he said, detecting a reaction and for the briefest of moments receiving one. Her eyes welled with the hint of helplessness, a sadness, he hoped, for an unrequited love. Vincent wanted to understand her reaction, but the moment was broken by the sound of musicians in the Piazza drawing a crowd. Ella stood, eager to see the street entertainment.

"I love the sound of string instruments. Let's watch them play."

"You go. I want to wander the side streets for a while. I'll join you soon."

Ella walked briskly toward the appreciative crowd, leaving Vincent to explore the quiet lanes. He hadn't been alone much since leaving home and needed time to think, free from the noise of the crowds. Vincent enjoyed the peaceful surrounds after the bustle of the large throng of tourists. For the first time, he heard the sound of his own footsteps as he walked along the cobbled stone lanes.

He imagined how it would feel to live in the city of canals with its historic, rustic terrace homes of cream and peach. Would he become as expressive and passionate as the local people? Lights shone through apartment windows above him, some empty of noise, others filled with the chatter of family dinners. Lost in his thoughts, he strolled many lanes, some straight and long, others angled, and at times so sharp they almost turned back on themselves.

Before he knew it, he had strayed too far, losing his bearings. He could hear no sounds to help him and the street signs were sparse and at times confusing. He followed the larger signs that pointed to San Marco, only to find a dead end. The mix of roads and canals easily disoriented the unwary traveller in Venice, as Vincent now found out. He started out calmly walking up and down lanes, using logic to find his way, but soon his calm strides turned to nervous jogging as he doubled back over his mistakes more than once. He was about to seek a local for advice when a feeling of dread overtook him – and not because he was lost. The quiet was so absolute, like a void in space. Then he heard a sound he recognised.

The end of the small lane was shimmering as a transparent force covered the surrounding buildings and walkway in front of him. A familiar hissing rattle snake sound emanated from the force. Vincent's way out was blocked. A tart acid odour overpowered him, halting his movement. The transparent substance gathered mass, surrounding him. To his horror, sharp cactus like needles grew from it, threatening to envelope him in its painful lair. But its threatening advances stopped. A deadly silence ensued before Vincent heard the voice of Jean and then David as the Entity alternated their voices, mocking Vincent. Then they spoke in unison like a viper's choir. Vincent was trapped, only able to watch on as a human shape began to form before him.

"You think you can escape me using their little toys, but the truth is I can find you any time of my choosing," said the Entity, suddenly forming into the clear human shape of David.

David had aged years, yet it had only been days since their last meeting. He was a man in his thirties now, his powers fully developed and more threatening. He gazed at Vincent with piercing dark eyes, slowly moving closer, not speaking.

"I don't believe you can harm me, or you'd finish me now," said Vincent defiantly, trying to show no fear, but falling short. The Entity's powers terrified him.

"Hah, you try to imitate the false assurances of your so called friends. I could snap you in half in an instant should I desire it and yet I don't. Whereas your supposed friend and mentor killed the man closest to you, the man who helped you build your life again."

There was only one man David could have meant - his Uncle.

"Why do you speak about Jean?"

"I know you wondered about his sudden death. Don't deny it. A healthy man, in the prime of his life dies from unknown causes?"

"He died of natural causes, the Doctor's report..."

"The Doctor's report? Look around you. Your friends could do as they please. They could create any illusion for your eyes and you would never know any better," said the Entity, moving closer to Vincent.

"As you could," said Vincent.

"Yes I could, but I have no need to lie. I'm not trying to return home. Ask your so called friends and see what they have to say. For if they speak the truth, you'll know you have befriended murderers."

Vincent's anger grew; he loved Ella and did not believe the Entity's slanderous accusations.

"Kill me now or else leave me. I won't listen to your lies."

"You'll experience far worse than death if you befriend these murderers. Flee while you can. Never return and you will not see me again."

"How can I trust you? Your kind has haunted me for half my life!"

"I will more than haunt you, Earthling."

The Entity's eyes widened. It changed shape, gaining in height and mass, threatening Vincent as it moved closer.

"I shall not warn you again. Stop this game now or you will suffer."

The Entity laughed, mocking Vincent as it slowly faded to nothing before him. The force field also faded from view, leaving Vincent alone in the small lane lit only by the night sky. He was lost in Venice in more ways than one.

Vincent saw Ella still standing with the large crowd enjoying the music of local buskers as he crossed the Piazza. Her back was turned from him toward the music, so he called to her, immediately drawing her attention.

"I was beginning to worry," she said, before seeing Vincent's ashen expression. "What's happened?"

Vincent held back for the barest of moments, the Entity's words haunting his mind. *Who to trust?* He thought to himself. But if not Ella, who could he confide in? He felt truly alone, a pawn in a terrifying game between powerful creatures, before an idea formed in his mind.

"The Entity. It's returned. The same as in Brighton. It surrounded me in a narrow lane." His news genuinely surprised Ella.

"We must tell Constantine. This is too soon."

But Vincent cut her short. "Not yet," he said, more a plea.

"Vincent, you are in great danger. It got close to you. This means the immersant has not protected you."

"I'm aware of the danger, but promise me that you will leave it to me, when and how I tell him."

Vincent held her arm firmly, not letting go until she promised. Ella tried to persuade him otherwise but failed, reluctantly conceding to his demands.

"I will tell him soon, but for now dine with me, Ella. I need to know more."

As they walked back to Caffe Quadri, Vincent considered the soundness of his decision. He knew the danger he put himself in, but twice now, the Entity had accused his friends of deceit. In the first instance he refused to give it credence, but to raise the death of his uncle pinched a raw nerve in his mind. Jean's death was sudden, yet he had been in good health. Unanswered questions remained about his passing. Even worse, Vincent knew Jean had been greatly troubled just before his death. He owed it to Jean to learn the truth.

Vincent and Ella returned to Caffe Quadri, choosing a quiet outside table. Sheltered from light showers by a concreted arch structure spanning the dining precinct, the Piazzeta now filled with colourful umbrellas, as the tourists sought shelter. Vincent's mood was like the scurrying crowds, impatient and seeking resolution.

"The Entity taunts me about the true nature of our friendship. Even worse, he accused Constantine of being somehow responsible for the death of my uncle," Vincent's voice tapered off, in an attempt to control his emotions.

"Do you know anything of this? Please tell me if you do. I trust you, Ella."

"Constantine told me of your uncle's death. He has spoken to me about a lot of his experiences on Earth - that included. But he never spoke of how he died. You'd do better to speak to him directly about this. Constantine and your uncle were work associates for many years and good friends," said Ella, reaching out to console Vincent, her concern clearly growing.

"Be careful with this Entity. It will play on your emotions to unsettle and distract you. Did it make any physical contact? Think carefully, it's crucial to what we do next."

Vincent thought back over every minute detail of their encounter, but recalled no contact. Though it was impossible to be sure, the Entity had stood threateningly close and the mist and viscous liquid swirled around him from all directions. He could have easily been touched by the smallest of molecules and not known.

"I felt no contact. It stood close, but that's it."

Ella looked relieved. "Then the immersant has worked. We still have time."

"Time for what?" asked Vincent, still puzzled by her words.

"We still have time to show you what you need to know before we leave this universe. You have faced the Entity three times, now. You have ridden storms and sound waves. You have moved in time to see one of your greatest scientists. You must face another test and there is only one place in your world where you can do that without our help – Switzerland." A silence followed. Ella clearly wanted to say no more. But Vincent leaned forward in his seat, imploring Ella to confide in him.

"We can't leave while the Entity remains. If we don't destroy it, we will remain on this planet forever." Ella paused for a moment to look around her. *Could the Entity be listening or could it be Constantine?* Vincent thought. Either way he felt Ella was anxious about sharing the information.

"Constantine and I alone can't defeat the Entity, but the three of us can, because of the powers you possess. You hold the key. You have to develop them and I will help you."

"I hold no powers. It's the immersants," said Vincent, not believing.

"Vincent, you have felt the Entity's power. Our biggest weapon is the element of surprise. And your strength grows by the hour. If you learn to ride light you can face the Entity. Light is where its power lies. We do not fully understand. But if we can draw it to you and observe how it reacts to your changes, we could learn much."

"Where does it come from?"

"It's made of Dark Land Matter, so we believe it has evolved in the dark lands of our home – Titan. We have been aware of Dark Land Matter since Braccus Max discovered it. But we had never encountered a focused energy source such as the Entities."

"Why did it pursue my uncle and now me?"

"That remains a mystery. All we know is this force followed us when we crossed to your universe. It has never communicated with us. But it has with you. You hold the key, Vincent."

Vincent felt a chill in the air, as if the Entity lay close waiting for its opportunity to take him. "If my uncle couldn't defeat it, how can I?"

"I don't know. It may help if you tell me what Jean shared with you, during those last days?"

Vincent looked away, as he recollected the last time he saw his uncle alive. "He was my only ally as I grew up and that was all too brief. Jean was my father's younger brother. Dad used to tell me what an adventurer Jean was. Even at a young age, he spent little time at home. I met him only briefly as a young five-year-old. I was just beginning to see the hallucinations. Jean stayed with us for two days at most, so my memories are fleeting. I do remember that Jean and my father argued, which led to Jean's sudden departure. I didn't see or hear from him again for a decade. He didn't even return for my mother and father's funeral."

"You must have resented that?"

"Yes. I stopped thinking of him as an uncle."

"But he did ultimately help you?"

"Yes. To my surprise and some scepticism, I accepted Jean's assistance. I was grateful for his financial support, but didn't expect anything more. But again, to my surprise, Jean befriended me. He cut back on his travel commitments to support me for many years."

"So, when was your last conversation with him?"

"It was only days before he died. I had formed a close bond with Jean by then, meeting him every week. Jean was a dedicated science teacher and he had inspired me to follow in his footsteps. But unlike Jean, I balanced teaching with research. My passion was for research whereas his was teaching. We often joked about our differences. Jean described the beauty of inspiring others, whereas I preferred exploring the unknown through my research. But our common interest united us, becoming the best of friends."

"A good friend, but he kept secrets?"

Vincent looked at Ella inquisitively. She seemed to know what he was about to say. "On the last occasion we met, I thought he had an unusual seriousness about him, almost as if he knew something was about to happen. For the first time, Jean shared close personal thoughts with me, as if he'd had a premonition. He spoke as if he knew his time was running out. Yet Jean was not yet fifty, vibrant, healthy and full of life and hope. Then at the end of a long night of story-telling and wine, Jean shared a secret that shocked me to the core."

"What was that?"

"He said he never intended to share his secret with me. He thought I had faced enough problems in my life. But he had a sense of urgency that night."

"But he did share his secret with you?"

"Yes. He told me that the hauntings I had as a young boy were real. He knew that because he had the same visions for much of his life. I don't think I ever believed him, until these events with you this past week. So you see, Ella, if Jean could not deal with the Entity, how can I?"

"Alone, you have little chance. All the more reason we must go. Constantine has settled our lodgings and tomorrow we have an early start. Another long train journey awaits us. Our best chances lie in facing this intruder together."

Vincent wanted to ask more but he sensed Ella would offer no more that evening. As they walked back to the hotel, Vincent used his coat to offer some protection against the falling rain. He bridged his arm over Ella's slender shoulders, holding his coat - tent like - above them. His feelings were strong for her as their bodies rested close and for the first time he sensed Ella had similar feelings. They stopped briefly under a tree that offered a little more protection as the rains strengthened, giving Vincent another chance to share his feelings for her.

"Why won't you let me be closer to you? I know you have feelings for me. Does the sight of my human form repel you that much?"

Ella would normally have stepped back and resisted his advances, but that night, for the first time she stayed close, leaning her back into him, allowing the tender warmth of their bodies to be close.

"It's a strange sensation, but the warmth is pleasurable," she said.

Vincent held her close to him, shielding her from the chilly ocean breeze, enjoying their closeness and waiting for her to speak.

"One day soon you'll learn that my admiration for you is more than you could ever imagine," she said, resting her head back beside his. Vincent felt her warm desire building. He wanted to kiss her to show his true love. But as he moved to gently kiss her neck, Ella placed her outstretched hand between them.

"No, not now. Not like this. Another day soon. Then I'll show you my true feelings," she said, with a hunger in her tone he had not heard before.

EAGLES JOURNEY

"CI SARA TRA BREVE arrivera a Lucerna," announced an Italian porter over the train's loudspeaker. Vincent looked at the lush green landscape of Switzerland, feeling anxiousness rather than awe, as he knew that challenging trials, testing his courage and resolve lay ahead. The announcement woke him from his slumber. He slept fitfully for much of the journey, after a three a.m. early rise. He hadn't slept well in the hotel given his ordeal with the Entity and the intimate conversation with Ella. He trusted Ella, but his doubts ebbed and flowed about Constantine. He would not raise the Entity's accusations with Constantine until the right moment. To avoid the temptation, Vincent chose an unoccupied double seat in a quiet corner of the carriage and slept, missing the spectacular climb from Mediterranean Italy to the rocky snowcapped mountains of Switzerland.

They all felt the change in climate, disembarking from the warm comfort of the train. The long concrete platform of Lucerne Station was a spacious welcoming expanse, accentuated by its single framed 'curved' roof, situated in the heart of the city. Lucerne was a welcoming city, in its own stream-lined way, with an expansive crystal lagoon curved around its precinct and picture post-card mountains looming high in the background, expanding in all directions.

Vincent's skin tingled from the mint coolness of the winds that swept off snow-filled peaks, across the watery top. The locals seemingly ignored its beauty as they went about their daily chores - some on foot along uncrowded paths, others on modern, efficient trams that quietly whisked them through clean city streets. Swiss precision and efficiency were immediately evident.

The two bordering countries could not have been more different: Italy, a land of civic chaos but filled with human art and beauty; and Switzerland, the height of civic efficiency surrounded by nature's art. Here were two cultures with very different backgrounds, drawing their inspiration from the beauty of their unique landscape.

Bags secured in station lockers, all three were free to explore Lucerne until late in the evening when they would be boarding their second train for the day, an 'all nighter' to the north-west of Switzerland. The laid back nature of Lucerne offered them a chance to refresh after their long journey.

Lucerne was aptly named the 'lake city' as everything revolved around its crystal clear waters, fallen from some of the largest mountain ranges in the world. The water snaked from the main lagoon through the city proper, under man-made pedestrian bridges and past outdoor meeting places, filled with cafes and diners taking in the pleasant midday sun. The station was surrounded by the lake on two corners: at its front, ferries ready to take tourists on journeys deep into the mountains; to the western side, running the length of the station and beyond, smaller ferries for local commuters and private fishing and recreational boats.

"Go to pier two. We catch that ferry in twenty minutes. I'll meet you aboard shortly," Constantine said, heading back to the railway ticket office to arrange the night's train journey.

Vincent and Ella bought their ferry tickets and stepped on to the waiting ferry, a medium sized all white boat, holding upward of four hundred people. The main deck was in two main parts; the indoor section with catering and table dining for around three hundred and the outdoor section, also with tables and basic seating for the more adventurous. Although the sun shone bright that day, the breeze was chilly. The dining seats were filling quickly, so Ella chose a corner window seat toward the front of the boat, protected from the mountain breezes.

"The tour runs a half-day. We'll take a one hour cruise along Lake Lucerne to a small port at the base of Mount Rigi Kulm, then a cog train will take us to the top of the mountain where we can stay for a few hours, then back down the mountain for the return voyage."

Some forty minutes later the ferry had left the harbour. Its tree-lined promenades were in full view and on each side, with open grass parks and panoramic mountains as a backdrop. The ferry glided silently over the largest open expanse of the lake, with elongated views in every direction. The shoreline was dotted by elegant houses and at regular intervals, shops and a church, indicating another small township.

Vincent remained quiet over their meal, paying attention to the conversation, waiting for his moment. He was bursting to raise the issue of his Uncle, but like a wounded boxer, he held back his strike for the right moment. Ella sensing his building anxiety, made more conversation than she had the previous day, coaxing Constantine to explain Vincent's role on their journey.

"It's easy to get lost in the grandeur. A small ferry among these grand mountains makes us feel so very small," said Ella.

"We are small on a cosmic scale and yet as a species we loom large in that we have the ability to think about the universe," said Constantine, taking Ella's bait and turning to Vincent.

"As you know well, some of your greatest scientists pondered your place in the cosmos. Just four hundred years ago some risked their lives to change a world held view – that the Earth lay at the centre of the Universe, when in fact it was one of many planets that rotated the Sun." Receiving no reply from Vincent, Constantine continued.

"Kepler, there was a man rigidly guided by his religious beliefs. He spent the best part of his life trying to prove God's design of the world through elaborate theories. But when the evidence showed that no such design existed, that in fact Earth was a planet orbiting the Sun, he accepted the evidence, consigning a lifetime of beliefs to the scientific dustbin."

Talk of Kepler finally moved Vincent to enter the conversation. "It was the beginning of the new age of science. One of many remarkable turning points in human history. I wrote a thesis about it. It's why I teach. If I help just one bright up-and-coming student to work as hard as they can to make their own contribution, I'll be elated."

Constantine sat back and let Vincent talk about some of the different turning points in human history, as this subject more than any brought out Vincent's passion. He had a genuine desire to build a similar fervour in his students. He talked effortlessly about the contributions of Galileo, Kepler, Newton, through to Einstein, before Constantine interrupted him.

"Who knows, you might be the next?" he said, drawing only laughter from Vincent.

"You keep telling me this. Granted, I have seen many remarkable events on this journey which is changing my view of the world. But I am only seeing this because you are allowing it. I'm an ordinary man surrounded by extraordinary beings."

"Many of those great achievers were seemingly ordinary men in early life. Who's to say that you could not be one of them?" Constantine countered.

"For starters, I have written precious few papers compared to my peers. They are far more qualified for this task," Vincent said dismissively. But he did not shake Constantine from his line of thought.

"And what if you were wrong about that? What if you were the person that made such an astounding finding that the world would never again view itself in the same way?" he asked, holding his serious gaze on Vincent.

Vincent looked first at Constantine then to Ella, sure they were making fun of him, but Ella too held his gaze as if they both had shared an important secret, one he found too ludicrous to believe.

"It's true that I have an insatiable passion for scientific discovery, but I have so much more to learn from the many colleagues I admire."

"You readily believe us when we tell you we are from another universe - why would this be any less plausible?" Ella asked, joining the conversation, challenging Vincent to deny it.

"I believe what I see and your powers are beyond anything on this Earth. But I'm just beginning my research career. My capabilities don't extend much past holding my job down. Changing the world's view of itself is beyond me," he said firmly.

"Name another person on Earth who has experienced what you have these last few days? You have a unique ability. You may not yet understand it, but in time if you believed and persevered, your dormant abilities would surface."

"I'll be lucky to survive the week. In case you've forgotten, the Entity is determined to destroy me," said Vincent, drawing Constantine to respond.

"That alone should tell you something, Vincent. Why would this powerful Entity single you out? Think it through."

"Maybe I'm caught in the crossfire? Vincent said, drawing an angrier response from Constantine.

"I know you've faced many challenges and there will be more, but your lack of self-belief is your greatest enemy, not the Entity. One day you say you want to help, the next day you make veiled accusations," said Constantine, drawing his gaze away from the conversation toward the lake, in frustration. Vincent had his opening, but he looked to Ella first for her support and gained it with a knowing nod of her head.

"I said I'd help you no matter what, but I expect to trust my allies completely. Yet the Entity taunts me that our friendship is based on deceit," said Vincent, drawing Constantine back to the conversation.

"What do you mean?"

"For starters, were you there the day Jean died?"

Constantine looked to Ella, genuinely surprised by Vincent's question, before considering his reply. "Who told you this?"

"The Entity cornered me in a Venetian back lane. It could have easily killed me too, but chose only to taunt me. It made accusations that you and Ella are murderers."

"Did the Entity make physical contact?" said Constantine, looking to Vincent, then Ella.

"It made no contact," Ella said, revealing she knew of the incident. Constantine held his gaze on Ella, saying nothing, making clear his disappointment.

"You must tell me of any contact. It could mean a great deal as to whether we survive. The risk..." said Constantine, before Vincent cut him off.

"The risk is two way, I won't share confidences if it's not fully returned. So either you trust me or I leave here and now."

Constantine contained himself, saying little until after the approaching waitress had served their plated meals, seemingly deliberating over what he would say next.

"I'll tell you all I know about your Uncle, if you promise that you'll trust my judgement about future information I reveal. It's for your safety," said Constantine with an ultimatum of his own. Vincent begrudgingly agreed.

"Very well, but tell me everything you know about Jean," said Vincent, ignoring the dinner just served, waiting for a full reply.

Constantine pushed his hot meal to one side, showing his annoyance. He took a deep breath, seemingly to contain his anger and then he answered all of Vincent's questions.

"When I made the first fateful crossing of the multiverse, my intention was to study only Titan. My hope was that the Odorphin race had developed in another universe, not just ours. I intentionally scaled back my exploration of our own universe. I turned my back on the 'local voyages' as we called them, seeking to conquer new realms. Crossing from our universe to another became my new life-time quest. Would an alternate universe hold similar laws of physics? Would it be a replica of the universe, galaxy and solar system we knew? Was there a Titan that was inhabited by Odorphins? As it turned out, your universe did contain a replica of our solar system, but Titan was devoid of all life and in its early phase of development. A three month search delivered no results and I was left with a stark choice, abandon the project and return to my universe or continue to search. I chose the latter, searching Saturn and its moons and the planets closer to the Sun, looking for any sign of life."

"So you came to Earth?"

"Yes, there was an abundance of life there. Your race called humans were the most evolved, but without 'light web'. Yet you possessed the capability for astounding research, in part, beyond anything considered by Odorphins. That you had achieved this without full sight was a mystery, until I discovered your language of the imagination - 'mathmatica'. I studied its development for many Saturnine years. Its complexity was difficult to learn, but with diligence, I was rewarded. I learned new laws of the universe – principles supported by physical evidence. For the most part, the mathmatica dealt with a single universe, with scant attention paid to the multiverse, due in large part to the limitations of your senses. Your perception was confined to four dimensions, and given your research was more Socratic than speculative, advances in multiverse theory were considered controversial."

"Yet, you claim we have light webs?"

"Yes, your light webs exist, but they are less evolved. You possess auras, but I believe you use them subconsciously, in combination with your physical intelligence, the brain. What you can't physically see, you imagine, but the next leap in exploration – multiverse travel - would require an advance in the development of your auras. So I sought next to find those humans with strong auras and the potential to develop light web capability. Many 'spiritual' humans have developed their auras to a level that allows them some transcendental capability, but none had interacted with the Dark Land Matter – except one."

"Jean?" Vincent said.

"Yes. A Saturn year passed before I found him. I felt his presence at first, not in the sense of location, more so in my dreams which for Odorphins are very different from human dreams. Our dreams are indelibly linked to our light web, which allows us to retain and interpret dreams. Generally, they are considered as no more than a guide to our emotional state at the time, but on occasion dreams can be predictive.

"You saw Jean in your dreams?"

"Yes, almost a Saturn year before we met. I also saw the Entity, a powerful and mysterious force. The Entity appeared to have many of the characteristics of the Dark Land Matter, with one important difference. It had the capability to engage matter. In this case it was drawn only to Jean."

"What did it want of Jean?"

"I wasn't sure, but my dreams grew more vivid, providing me with images of Jean's life and his whereabouts. On the surface he appeared like any other human, except he was gifted with an aura that had similarities to our light web. As I had found no other human with a developed aura, I concluded the Entity was attracted to that."

"Excuse me, would you care to order any more drinks?" Asked a waiter.

"Just water, please," replied Ella.

"So you observed Jean...."

"Yes. In time I located Jean in the physical plain, observing him from a distance, unnoticed by either Jean or the Entity. But the Entity's powers steadily grew over time to a point where it recognised my holograph, too. I made contact, believing I had a breakthrough in my research into the Dark Land Matter. I welcomed our first meeting, convinced I had developed a bond."

"It spoke to you?"

"No. The Entity did not use human form to develop a bond – quite the opposite. On first contact, I experienced a slow crawling dark substance envelope my arm. In a short few minutes it covered my whole holographic body. Light holographs transferred sensory signals to my real self, allowing sensory experience, a kind of filtered feeling. Even that gave me extreme discomfort. The viscous dark substance was its true identity, a thinking molecular mass. Its sole purpose seemed to be predatory, seeking to destroy that which it sought. If it had struck me rather than my holograph, I fear my life would have ended swiftly."

"Why didn't you stop your research there?"

"I felt the encounter was worth the risk. I had gained vital information about the metabolic structure of the Entity. What I learnt was its structure was a moving target. It grew and adapted to its environment with frightening speed. As it grew, my dreams became more intense. Most revolved around the Entity's attraction to Jean. Its energy encircled, constantly observing Jean's unique aura, for what reason I was unsure. The only certainty was its aggression."

"So, it attacked Jean?"

"Not physically, but Jean suffered psychologically. He had constant dreams of a dark substance enveloping him as if insects crawled on his skin. He was losing the ability to distinguish his dreams from reality as his condition deteriorated. Jean had been placed on medication, an anti-hallucinatory drug that only added to his problems. Compelled to act, I contacted Jean, over time gaining his confidence and ultimately revealing the truth of his condition."

"So you cured him?"

"Never cured. I developed immersants using a combination of Jean's and the Entity's molecules and synthetic compounds I developed."

"This killed the Entity's invading molecules?"

"No. My immersants are somewhat like antiviral drugs. They act to inhibit the spread of the attacking virus rather than completely kill it. Every immersant repels the Entity's invading molecules for a time, but like a virulent virus, the Entity overcomes them, re-appearing stronger. The Entity's powers evolved. It developed a mist compound that could create holographic images, copying its surrounds, using simple forms at first but over time gaining more complexity. The first human like trait appeared from its mist, blurred but its shape was human and its intentions were aggressive. It had come to take Jean."

"The Entity claimed you murdered Jean?" Vincent asked, studying Constantine closely for his initial reactions, but Constantine gave off no clues as he answered Vincent's question fully and without emotion.

"I did all I could to help Jean, sidelining my aims to document the human race's achievements. My dreams became darker, haunting and threatening. One particular dream showed that I was the cause of Jean's condition. By crossing the universes, I had opened a trail that drew the Entity with it, drawing the aggressive force to Jean's universe. This disturbed me for if it were drawn here, why would it not follow me back to my homeland? Ultimately, Jean and I faced the Entity together to destroy it. I developed a new potent immersant that I hoped would contaminate the Entity as it engaged Jean and ultimately destroy it. We confronted the Entity where it first arrived on Earth, at the summit of Mount Rigi Kulm, on a water filled land – the metre deep frozen snow on the peak. The Entity could not penetrate water's molecular structure, no matter the temperature."

"That is where we are heading?"

"Yes. I had planned to tell you of this confrontation where it happened. I wanted you to see where Jean perished before you faced your biggest test," said Constantine, sighing with disappointment, before he continued. "We planned the confrontation together, over many weeks. The Entity was destroyed, but Jean's aura vanished with it, leaving him lifeless. I did all I could to revive him, but nothing worked. He died in my arms unable to speak, his life force spent."

Vincent sat quietly for some time, remembering his uncle's conversation, their last. What must he have felt facing the Entity's savage force? Vincent had a sense of it. He would have felt as though every atom of his body was being slowly torn out from inside his body, as the Entity devoured his life's essence.

"Were there any physical signs of the attack? Did Jean have bruising or cuts?"

"None. Jean died because the Entity shattered his will to live. The pain was too much for him to endure."

"You say the Entity was destroyed, yet we face it today?"

"This is another. Of that I'm sure. And this Entity didn't follow me into your universe, it followed another," said Constantine, looking to Ella.

"It followed Ella through the portal to your universe. But it pursues only you, Vincent," he said, prompting Ella to speak.

"My research focused on this very problem. Your scientists learned that dark matter forms a protective ring around galaxies to stop them from flying apart from the forces of dark energy. Similarly, it forms part of the protective ring circling each universe. Break it and there are consequences," said Ella.

"Ella brought new synthetic compounds from Titan. We hoped, together we would develop an immersant that would protect you and allow us to return home."

"So, I'm an experiment or a work in progress?" Vincent said, upsetting Ella with his accusations.

"There is another consequence of these confrontations," Ella interjected. "When the Entity vanished with Jean's death, so too did Constantine's portal between our universes, blocking his return. When this occurred, we set about to return Constantine to Titan safely. Would you not do the same for your greatest discoverer?" said Ella, still hurt from Vincent's words.

"From what I've experienced, you're no closer to controlling these Entities. What do we do next, Constantine?" Vincent asked.

"There is little difference between the two Entities. If anything, this Entity is more powerful, as if it learnt from the previous one. It could be that they have the ability to communicate across the multiverse. If that's the case, I fear we may not be able to defeat it."

"So why are we running? We may as well face it now." said Vincent.

"When it first approached you, I believed there was little hope for all of us. But there was one very large difference.

"Go on."

"My dreams have been different. It's as if this Entity is trying to communicate. The same threats are there, but something in the dreams give me hope."

"What possible hope is there? It seeks to take control of my body and destroy me."

"There are warnings in my dreams, the same as with Jean. Yet there are also hints, mysterious visions that I feel impelled to follow."

"What visions?"

"Visions of the places we have been visiting. It may be that the Entity is trying to influence where I take you, Vincent. But I can't be sure. It could also be a trap. My latest dream showed me that you and Ella would return to the place of your uncle's death, Mount Rigi Kulm. I know it is a risk, but I decided it was worth it. It may be that it is the best chance for us all to get home."

The ferry glided toward its destination, the port of Vitznau. Constantine remained on the ferry for the immediate return journey, leaving Ella and Vincent to join the connecting 'cog wheel' train journey to the top of Mount Rigi Kulm, an eighteen hundred metres high climb, the steepest rail journey in Europe.

"Why would he leave us, Ella?" Vincent asked, still fighting his lingering doubts about Constantine.

"In his dream, he saw only you and I on top of the mountain. He considered it a risk, but left the decision to me. I told him to let the prophecy unfold. Trust me in this, Vincent," she said. Vincent nodded his head and looked toward the mountain top. He pictures his uncle, this last train ride being his last Earthly action. He hoped that history did not repeat itself today.

The cog wheel train consisted of two carriages and had been in operation since the days of Mark Twain. The train, dubbed the Queen of the Mountains was just a hundred metres from where the ferry had docked and was being turned around on the circular turnstile for its trip back up the mountain. The carriages were vintage nineteenth century 'Belle Epoch' cars, simple in construction, reflecting the style of an earlier era.

The train soon began the slow climb up the steep slopes, taking thirty minutes to reach half way, the station of Rigi Kaltbad. The remaining thirty minute journey to the summit was marked by many spectacular scenic views over the mountain ranges in the east and Lake Lucerne in the west. Both Ella and Vincent walked up and down the near empty carriage, choosing various vantage points, offering the best views.

"This reminds me of my home, at the base of our tallest mountains. It's the same height as ours, perhaps a little higher," said Ella, breathing in the mountain air and the stunning views in the east. Vincent had not seen Ella so happy as when they caught sight of Lake Lucerne in the west. Ella was moved to tears as she spoke.

"When I see this, I want to return home. The shape is different but the height of the mountain and the size of the lake are as we see our own great lakes. I'd often fly to the summit of our highest mountain and enjoy the view of our lakes. The beauty and tranquillity invigorated me. Then I'd fly to the lakes, change form and swim in its soothing depths till the rings of Saturn disappeared. In my youth I'd do that every day. Even as an adult I'd find an excuse to return." For a while Ella appeared lost in her memories as the cog wheel train continued its crawl to the summit.

An hour after leaving, the small train pulled into the platform on top of the mountain. One of the most spectacular views in the world surrounded them, taking in the Eiger ranges and Black Forest. Both walked to the viewing platform jutting from the east face of Rigi Kulm. The view was clear except for an approaching cloud front in the north. The air chilled but in a refreshing way as its natural beauty lifted their spirits.

"This too reminds me of Titan, except the colours. We see the white, blue and greens on Saturn not Titan. Some of those snow covered rocky outcrops look like the orbs that make up Saturn's ring, don't you think?" she said. Vincent agreed, remembering their journey together through her light web.

"There is more at the top of the mountain." Playfully she took Vincent's hand, leading him back over the cog wheel track.

The station was just long enough to accommodate the two carriages of the train. Two trains operated on the line intermittently every hour. Earlier in the day the carriages were filled with tourists, but given the late hour, Vincent and Ella were two of just a handful.

"It's another five minute walk to the top," she said, pointing to the cream coloured concrete path that wound through the pure white snow covered hill top. Water puddles formed in parts where the snow had melted on the warmer concrete. The path was contoured, following the edges of the conical shaped mountain top. As they made their way up, Ella stopped momentarily. She stooped down to run her hand over the surface of the virgin snow, making shapes with her hands and fingers.

"The feel of water on Earth is one of my joys. On Titan our water is rock ice, whereas here it has so many textures. When I swim in Lucerne's crystal clear lakes, I feel as if every part of my body is free to dance, invigorating and soothing at the same time. I love how it reacts with the skin when it melts. These are the memories I'll hold dear."

They strolled hand in hand, to the western face of the mountain, where uninterrupted views of Lucerne and its surrounding lakes were in full view. Blue sky stretched clear to the horizon. It was fast becoming the remnants of a perfect day as a telltale breeze began to push at their backs signalling the coming change. With its chill came the slightest of snow flakes, followed by more, creating calm on the quiet mountain top. It was as if they floated on top of the world. Ella shivered with its enchantment.

"I never could have believed water to be so intoxicating," she said, breathing in the floating forms of ice. Vincent smiled, holding her close, warming her and sharing the moment.

"It's special for me too...for different reasons," he said, gazing lovingly at her, seeing the snow topped mountain reflected in her blue eyes, and touching the ice forming on her chilled cheeks. He wanted to kiss her. His desire was strong. Ella too felt his desire, at first wanting him closer, before she half turned, smiling warmly, inviting him to follow her to the top of the summit. Vincent followed, his gaze only for her beautiful slender form.

Both stood at the summit now, seeing unrestricted views in all directions. A series of lakes connected in the valley below like swimming pools in a park. Thick cumulus clouds gathered on the opposite side. Mountain top winds blew Ella's long, fine auburn hair over her woollen jumper. Snow had formed on the shoulders, so Vincent brushed it away, repeating the same action for the snow on her hair.

"You tell me you have no feelings for me, but when we're close like this, I feel you want more," he said, unable to hide his feelings.

Ella breathed in the freshness of the moment, gently taking his hand, studying its strong contours, softly caressing.

"I have feelings for you, but they're not the human feelings you experience." She took both his hands.

"Let me try to show you," she said. The snow fall gathered, all silent around them, except for the sound of an eagle's call high in the distance.

Ella revealed her light web to Vincent, a soft yellow hue against the pure white landscape. A force radiated from her body, connected to her two outstretched arms like blurred wings. Ella let go of one hand, waving her freed hand gently over Vincent's body as if she were a Spanish dancer fanning him with her desires. It felt softer than falling snow, soothing him, as if he floated in a calm mountain pond. His mind was totally immersed in the moment as if nothing else existed around him but the gentle fans of her touch. Then the sound of her soft voice broke the spell.

"Look now and you will see the world as I do."

His eyes had been open all the time and yet he felt as if he had opened them for the first time after a deep sleep. He was relaxed but disoriented. The snow-filled hills remained, but the falling snow took on an intensity, vibrating through the thick air as it fell to the earth. Sweet sounds emanated, like the strum of a fine harp. Vincent could have been in another world as he studied each and every snow drop playing in nature's chorus. He felt Ella's warmth all around him, as it radiated out in a stream of golden rays from her light web. Where her physical body remained hidden by the radiant force, her melodic voice floated in and through the intense light.

"I don't see you," he said, but he felt Ella gently touch his lips to hold back his words, reassuring him.

"Trust your senses and you will see me." The musicality of her voice stroked his emotions, with pure joy.

Vincent willed himself to see her true appearance, feeling her presence all around him, hovering close. Yet his gaze remained thwarted by the radiance.

"I feel you, but the light blinds me."

"Look within. Believe and you will see. Trust your senses and listen to the sound the light makes. Then follow its rhythm."

Vincent stepped closer into the glow, letting go his instinct to find Ella's melodies. It was then he heard her real voice, not human, indescribable. He could not understand but he felt fragments of her alien core. The falling snow's vibrations gathered strength, revealing rainbow colours of such clarity he wanted to stroke their soothing rhythms.

The patterns on each vibrating snow-drop linked, taking form. A presence slowly formed, circling him, building his desires, like an elusive drop of water in the desert. Vincent reached out to touch the mirage-like form and caressed the desert gold shadow before him. He felt an energy surge through his body, creating a subtle shift in his awareness, as if he were no longer in his body. The force drew him toward its centre. In that place, he felt Ella's warmth. His mind's eye floated, circling his body as if dancing around it. He felt an intense urge to look up. He was hungry to find Ella, to be with her.

And then his feelings willed him higher above the soft powdered landscape. He was bathed in a warm gold lit fountain of energy. There he saw an outline of Ella, like a rough sketch of her true self. She shimmered around him, gliding her light web softly across his face. Vincent felt her sweet force ripple across his skin. Its soothing sensation made him want more.

"I love you Ella. I always have," he said, desperate to show his true feelings for her. Ella laughed softly as she drew her force closer to him.

"I believe you do, my Earth friend. I think this is what Constantine dreamt of. Our developing bond here on the mountain top," she whispered in a musical tone so close to him he desired more.

"Is our love meant to be?" he said, hoping to hear her melodic tones concur. But instead Ella released Vincent from the gold lit fountain, returning him to the cool snow covered ground.

He looked to the sky. Clouds swirled above him, driven by soft winds. High above him was the eagle he heard earlier, now in clear sight, circling. At first he wondered if it might be Ella, but those soaring wings shimmered amongst the turbulence, a vibration he well recognised. For around it formed a grey mist, from which other shapes formed, until a flock of eagles gathered.

Vincent knew this was not Ella. It was her antithesis. The calm musical vibrations of the snow vanished. Vincent fell back too. Ella stood very still in front of him. She no longer danced. Instead her gaze was locked on to the flock of eagles gliding ever lower toward them as if they were their evenings prey.

"We must leave now," she said, aware of the gathering danger.

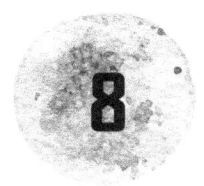

LIGHT SPEED

They left Lucerne in early morning darkness, three of just a handful of people boarding the train to Geneva. The cold of Lucerne matched their mood. They were weighted down by the sense of the Entity's presence, circling them like prey for the final kill. Geneva was less than an hour away and little was said as they continued their journey. Constantine was absorbed in his work as he carried out many calculations seeking a new chemical armoury to defend them against the Entity. His light web cast a spherical shaped light in front of him, like a holographic computer. Symbols, patterns and images flashed at a lightning-fast rate, operated it seemed by his mind. It was a blur to Vincent's eyes. Every now and then the screen slowed to one image that he studied at length – a kind of worm-like image that looked a cross between a serpent and a DNA helix. Vincent had never seen him so intent. Occasionally, he dared to interrupt Constantine from his calculations.

"Do you think the Entity will come only for me?"

"I'm not sure. It can see us all now, though," said Constantine, not raising his gaze from his work.

"How do you know?"

"It gazed down at you and Ella on the mountain top. If it can see Ella, it can see me also."

Vincent said no more. Constantine's demeanour had changed since the boat trip. There was an urgency about him, born from an experience he perhaps dared not share, or one of his dreams. Whatever the cause, it gave Vincent a greater feeling of foreboding, so he looked away from Constantine toward Ella.

Ella seemed unaffected as she sat cross legged, in a form of meditation. Vincent watched her in silence, as he remembered the events on the mountain. Could Ella's love for him be real? Or had the Entity's threats unnerved her? It was if she had seen the Entity for the first time. Maybe she had.

They arrived very early at Geneva station. Day light slowly crept into the pre-dawn skies, throwing a pinkish hue over the 'old town', an historic section of the sprawling city. This was not as Vincent had imagined it. For it was also an international city, housing the world's fledgling attempt at global governance, the United Nations. But they hadn't come to engage the world's political ideals. They had come for one purpose only - to prepare for the Entity. Constantine collected the hotel keys, handing one each to Ella and Vincent.

"We have a long and challenging day ahead. I suggest some rest from the journey, before we meet again here at the foyer," he said, providing the detail of when and where they would meet. Then he left the hotel. Ella headed toward the lift with her travel bag, turning to Vincent behind her.

"Shall we meet at eleven?"

"I don't need to rest. I want to talk about yesterday on the summit," said Vincent, determined to finish what they had started. Ella smiled, readily agreeing.

"There's a special place I'd like to show you."

Their luggage safely packed away, Ella led Vincent through the old town's narrow, winding streets, lined with centuries old buildings. Many were converted to restaurants and shops for the tourists. Cathedrale St. Pierre stood at the top of the historic town. Ella and Vincent enjoyed the sweeping view of Geneva, before ascending the steep staircase to the large oak doors of the church. Ella opened them for Vincent to enter.

"This is my favourite place in Geneva," she said, her eyes beaming with excitement.

Inside, they walked through an open, airy expanse. Its rectangular shape was surrounded by immense sandstone columns that framed the church from the stone and marble floor to the sixty metre high wooden ceiling. The spaciousness was created by its height, but also by expansive stained-glass windows that encircled the interior. Each window case consisted of half metre wide columns standing at least fifteen metres high bearing colourful depictions of Christ. Red and blue hues dominated with striking flashes of gold, adding a regal vibrancy to the interior. The sun was fully raised now and its rays seeped through, adding a purplish hue to the sandstone structure.

They continued through the main hall to the back of the cathedral to a second smaller chapel for worship. The miniature cathedral was equally impressive with intimate red velvet, marble and ivory used to great effect, creating a calming, more contemplative feel. Ella sat quietly for a time, seemingly taking in the introspective atmosphere, before finally speaking.

"I know your feelings for me are strong. But I wonder if it's for my human form only? How would you feel if you saw me, not my human holographic image? Until now, your limited sight has prevented that."

Vincent's spirits lifted, wishing nothing more than to show Ella his true feelings for her, his desire to be close outweighing any fear of confronting her alien form.

"You said until *now*. Is there a way?"

"There is, but you need Constantine's help. You have to trust him, Vincent. There is no other way." There was concern in her voice.

"I know you and Constantine have been friends and colleagues for a long time, but this last week I've felt some disconnect. Why?"

he asked, still unsure of their bond and probing to see if there was more than friendship.

"Constantine has worked and lived on your planet a hundred Earth years, gathering information and studying the mathmatica. To have all this destroyed by the Entity would be a tragic missed opportunity for the development of Odorphin culture and yours. On that, Constantine and I have always agreed. But sometimes we differ on how to bring that success about," said Ella, standing up to touch the small statues of marble and ivory.

"We value all the elements of the universe – from water to this marble - forged in the furnace of stars over billions of years. From its primordial fires came 'self-awareness', that rarest of commodities in the universe."

"You don't agree with Constantine on how we should confront the Entity?" he said, pressing Ella.

"No, I don't always agree, but I can't reveal those details. That would mean certain death for you," she said, frustrating Vincent.

"Riddles, always riddles!"

"When you confront the Entity, its force will be more powerful than you could imagine. It will know everything about you and use it to convince you the battle is unjust. This will feel like a confrontation of the flesh, but in fact it will be a battle of wills. When that moment comes, you must have resolve, and know that at the Entity's core lies only trickery."

"Ella, I'll never have powers to fight this force. It won't need trickery to defeat me."

"This is where your trust in Constantine is paramount, for only he can prepare you for what lies ahead."

"I will do that if you tell me more of your journey to Earth."

Ella shook her head playfully. "You are learning to drive a hard bargain. But it's quiet here. Sit down and ask me what you want to know."

"Constantine told me that you played a crucial part in deciphering the mathmatica?"

"He spent many years in your universe, unable to communicate with us. But after many of your Earth years he found a way. Then I worked on little else, deciphering the mathmatica, a language that made bold claims, many correct as proved by their own discoveries, many others sounding the ramblings of a fertile imagination. Yet time and again, the Earth scientists' proposed theories were backed by exhaustive research that tested its validity. In time, I admired the work of the Earth scientists, proving gravity, light speed, electro-magnetism – and all achieved with no physical capability to see the world as it really was. Through pure imagination and a unique skill to manipulate the mathmatica your kind identified much of their physical universe."

"So you came here to research Earth?"

"Yes. I have spent the last year collating and refining my knowledge of the mathmatica and to voyage your world."

"Tell me about your voyages here."

"I will, but not now. We should return to the hotel and refresh before we meet with Constantine."

The three met as arranged at the hotel foyer before walking to the small square, a popular meeting place for locals. A restaurant in its centre and outdoor seating positioned under a hundred year old oak and adjoining church, gave the cobblestoned expanse an air of history. A little further down, children rode on an 'original' Swiss merry-go-round that piped playful music to the exuberant youngsters who rapturously engaged its swings and rounds. It was an infectiously happy scene, the antithesis of their mood as they planned their defence against the Entity.

"Vincent, I know you have faced many challenges in too short a time," said Constantine, with one eye to Ella, seemingly saying it to appease her. At times I have not said enough to deserve your trust, but I did this to protect, not deceive you. So today I want to be very clear. Ella and I are asking you to face a challenge that your scientists would call impossible."

Vincent looked to both for some encouragement, but they sat quietly, waiting for his reply. Vincent was too fearful to make a decision, so he turned to Ella.

"What would you do if you were me?"

"I'd consider the possibility that I may be the Earthling who made a telling discovery that accelerated the human race's understanding of their place in the cosmos."

"You really believe I'm that man?"

"I do," Ella replied with conviction." "But what matters is that you do."

Vincent turned to Constantine. "How dangerous is the experiment?"

"We can come to your aid if you're in danger. But unlike the previous experiment, we cannot predict every potential outcome of the journey you will take, hence our reaction time will be slower."

"Meaning?"

"There is a small element of risk that could prove fatal."

Vincent knew he had come to a crossroad. Should he step into the unknown?

"Given the unpredictability, what would you choose, Ella?"

"I would say to myself that an experiment that could lead to a major turning point in how humanity saw itself, by its very implication, would entail a leap into unchartered territory. That is the very nature of discovery. You have to choose if that is your purpose in life."

"What is the experiment, Constantine?"

"We must lift your speed and awareness levels. You experienced the speed of sound at a sub-atomic level. Now you must see more."

"Go on," said Vincent, concerned about where Constantine was leading.

"Light speed – that's what we want you to experience, so that you can reach your destiny and that's where you need to be, if you're to see and defend against the Entity's attack."

Vincent remembered the previous experiment. He nearly died between two trains. The physical requirement to concentrate at such speeds had left him exhausted. What would light speed do to him?

"I'm not sure I can do this," he said, again turning to Ella for support and not receiving it.

"You can do this. It's your destiny," said Constantine, drawing out the familiar orb.

"Your body has developed a tolerance for the immersants now. This new immersant is based on the same atomic structure, but its power will lift your reaction speed to the levels required, just as it did previously," said Constantine confidently.

"So what vehicle am I riding on this time? Is it a light ray?"

"Close, but photons can't be smashed. That's why we came to Geneva. There's a machine here that smashes atoms at near the speed of light, the Large Hadron Collider. You may have heard of it?"

Vincent nodded but said no more. He knew any more questions were pointless. He had to choose. He felt fear mostly. Unable to say yes, he nodded acceptance for his next challenge - a training run around the Hadron Collider, the world's fastest machine, where particles were fired at near light speed, with the sole purpose to destroy them in a cataclysmic collision at the end of a twenty-seven kilometre tunnel. On one of those particles would be a passenger – Vincent. And Vincent knew after the last experiment, that there was a strong chance that every atom in his body would be destroyed too.

The Hadron Collider looked every bit the international collaborative effort it was. Security was akin to a prison lock down as they assembled with other visitors to inspect the world's most expensive scientific experiment. Its contentious budget was around ten billion Euros. The park-like entry of lawn and lined trees counter balanced the 'bunker style' main building of concrete, steel and glass. Well protected behind two check points were more sombre darkened rooms belying the benevolence of the Hadron Collider's lofty aims.

"Passports please," said the security officer, the third and final guard to inspect Vincent's credentials. Satisfied with his documentation, the officer returned his passport.

"Just sit here, sir, in front of the camera," he said. Vincent dutifully followed his orders, not knowing whether to smile or show his true mood. He expected security, for he wasn't inspecting the 'Iconic Globe' that most tourists inspected. This was a 'higher level' area reserved only for the most important dignitaries, such as Constantine, who was a highly regarded theoretical physicist. But an hour separated their first check point to this final entry, leaving Vincent on the verge of leaving in frustration.

"Thank you sir, if you could wait while I finish your badge," said the guard. True to his word, he left Vincent to wait a further fifteen minutes for his 'visitors tag', before finally allowing him through to the main hall to join the assembled party.

Their official guide, Adrien Egger gathered the group together, quickly commencing the guided tour with an apologetic tone in his voice and resignation toward the security that pervaded the complex. But now quickly moving, Adrien was awash with scientific facts and figures. His smooth Swiss accent provided a relaxed tone.

"The Large Hadron Collidor is the world's largest and highest energy particle accelerator, contained in a circular tunnel. Its circumference is twenty-seven kilometres, buried a hundred metres under the ground. The four metre wide concrete-lined tunnel is so large it crosses the border between Switzerland and France. To give you a sense of the speed required to smash protons: a normal 27 kilometre train journey on your underground in England would take maybe an hour – on a good day! The protons in this machine would do that same journey eleven thousand times – not in an hour but in one second!"

The tour area of the complex was well laid out with instructional demonstrations and videos strategically placed in rooms that slowly descended the hundred metres below ground level, to where the concrete tunnels had been constructed.

"The collider tunnel within the concrete pipe contains two adjacent parallel beam pipes that intersect at four points; each contains a proton beam that travels in opposite directions around the ring. The beams are powered by over twelve hundred dipole magnets that maintain their path, while an additional four hundred quadrupole magnets are used to keep the beams focused on their path. This of course maximises the chance of a collision between the beams," said the guide, before asking for final questions.

The official tour ended one hour after they commenced, leaving one final 'optional' movie that provided more background history of its development. Constantine, Ella and Vincent were the only visitors of the tour that remained to see the movie. All three sat in the semi-darkness of the amphitheatre. The sound track provided enough cover for them to discuss their plans without being overheard. Vincent's anxiety grew. Having heard the full details of what happened beneath the thick concrete encasing, Vincent thought only about withdrawing from the experiment, but Constantine's attempts at persuasion were relentless.

"This immersant will give you reactive abilities to cope with this extreme environment, plus some," he said reassuringly.

Vincent could only think about the previous experiment, a part exhilarating, part terrifying experience that felt the longest day of his life. But here he was, about to experience a journey that would make his train ride feel like a stroll in the park. He could still walk away and would have, except for Ella. She sat beside him, re-assuring and motivating him in equal proportions. *Do this and I will see the real Ella for the first time*, he thought. In truth, this was the main reason he considered going through with it. The movie played on in the background, reinforcing the challenge he was about to face.

"Both protons will travel toward each other at close to the speed of light, where they will smash each other's proton into smaller particles."

Vincent pointed to the movie screen, its grim details unsettling him.

"You're sending me to a deliberate collision. What purpose could this achieve, except kill me?" he said, looking for some comfort where little was on supply.

"The immersant will allow you to visualise down to the level of fundamental particles – quarks. At that level, you'll feel you're surrounded in a vast space, the proton. The collision will free those particles, which will scatter in an outward direction at faster than the speed of light. You will experience what your current science considers impossible. You will be protected within the quark field as long as you hold the visualisation that you are a quark, not a human. Remain in that visualisation and you'll be unaffected," said Constantine.

"But I felt the trains."

"You believed the images true, so you made them true, but it never happened. The immersant flowing through your veins allowed your mind to vividly absorb the world around, but your body was not there. Your ability to see the world was raised to another dimension. Let go your normal perception, for if you don't, it will trick your brain into believing your body is actually there and the shock will kill you. You nearly got through the last experiment. Just at the end, your human perception took over, but even then your strong mind helped you remain steady when you faced what you believed to be certain death. Because of your experience, you'll know not to lose your focus. You have that capability. Trust me," said Constantine.

"Can't we do this on another day? I'm not ready."

"That is impossible. The machine will not run for another month. This is your one and only chance."

Vincent had exhausted every rational reason to abort the experiment, so he turned to Ella for emotional support. His gaze was an open book as he showed Ella his fear and vulnerability.

"At the other end of this, we'll meet," said Ella, her hand lightly rested on Vincent's shoulder. He gazed at her, reassured by her supportive gestures. He trusted her.

"I'm ready," he agreed, feeling anything but.

Chemicals reacted. The immersant ran through Vincent's veins for a second time, oozing a cold chill that shook every atom in his body and more, until his alertness frightened him. In this place he sensed every movement. A hive of activity exploded around him. He interpreted his immediate surroundings in an instant and he craved more information to feed his insatiable appetite for the world around him. Every breath, movement, electric charge, sound - all were indelibly recorded in his drug enhanced mind. He craved more information like an infant with a new world to decode. Restless, his attention span expanded to the only activity that could satiate his appetite. Voices, hundreds of voices focused for the most part on the Large Hadron Collidor with a synchronicity of common purpose, trained on one momentary, momentous event.

Then he heard the call, *ten-nine-eight*. Countdown had started. There was an expectation in their tone and a confidence in their multi-billion dollar software. They commenced the experiment that would last no longer than the blink of an eye. Magnetic fields sent waves of pulses that would hold his 'quark vessel' on its steady, exact passage. Vincent's mind tracked the countdown whilst he vigilantly maintained a review of his surrounds. Every pulse, sound wave and vibration instantaneously accounted for, *four-three*, he was ready.

His mind stepping inside the collider, he took a final look back at his body, frozen in the moment, fear written large on his face. But he instantly forgot his physical shell, for he saw his destination - his vessel - a single quark pulsing within a massive expanse – the proton. Vincent's body was a dim memory as his mind flew to join the universe's smallest particle.

He had no heartbeat now, becoming one with a single pulsating mass about to be flung on a journey powered by super magnets toward the impossible, light speed. He would be the first human to travel at a speed considered impossible before colliding into another proton travelling toward him at equal speed, smashing him out at close to light speed.

He stood firm in a world within a world. The rotations began, slowly at first, like a bob sledder testing a runway for the first time. Forces enveloped the proton encasement, gripping it with an impenetrable power that nothing could break but an equivalent opposite force. The acceleration lit up the proton like a sun. Magnetic waves pulsed their steady rhythms, balancing and counterbalancing potential movement in any direction. Perfect unwavering momentum held, while violent speed lashed all round in ever increasing intensity. One hundred...two hundred... one thousand...two thousand rounds were rapidly reached as the rotation count itself accelerated exponentially.

Closer to impact, Vincent recalled; *eleven thousand rotations of twenty seven kilometres must be reached before impact.* But he quickly wiped the thought from his mind. *Must not think like a human,* he thought, burying his emotions deep and heeding Constantine's warning, *seven thousand...eight thousand rounds.* Vincent focused his line of sight to the front. The colliders cylindrical pipe looked more like a wormhole between two nebulas, a swirling, seething mass, lit by electric charges creating a perfect storm, *nine thousand...ten thousand rounds*. Still as a rock now, he was ready to witness a collision not seen by human eyes – an event privy only to the universe itself, in its early birth.

Eleven thousand.

Vincent's world ceased. The translucent expanse of the proton shook with violent waves felt far out in the misty distance. Tsunamis from every direction bore down on Vincent's quark vessel, as if a hundred cyclones encircled him, trapped in a vast violent ocean. Large planet like masses flew past, as charges exploded white lightning on a blood red ocean.

Vincent's gaze held steadfast, until a photon struck his shell like a supernova smashing the earth's sun, a terrifying collision. The quark spun, blurring Vincent's line of sight. His resolve shrunk in that violent place. His mind was lost in the storm. He sank into an ocean of tidal waves, with no sign of calm on its savage currents. Vincent submitted to his human emotions - sheer terror. His protective shell began to crack in its deadly waters, threatening a torturous end.

He was drowning in its turbulence. Then another large orb passed him, carrying a voice that trailed behind its trajectory, like a scream from a bullet train.

"Here Vincent...." It was Ella. He saw only the orb, but he knew Ella rode on it, willing him to join her.

The thought she was near calmed him, but his position was becoming unstable, firstly free falling, then violent rotating that pushed him perilously further from Ella's voice. The fierce storm exploded around him. Its force applied enormous pressure on the spherical structure, its protection about to give way at any moment, exposing him to the full force of the storm's deadly tide.

"Stay with me," said Ella, her voice more distant.

Vincent centred his focus into the calm eye of the tornado, forgetting the viper winds that raged around him. Quarks exploded as they freed from the gluon force, destroyed by fragments of protons that had been smashed in the collision.

As the final pulse of his quark sounded, Vincent saw the proton sphere turn in on itself, as if it was a dying Red Dwarf Sun, about to become a Black Hole. The quark was about to return back to its inevitable compacted world, taking Vincent to its oblivion. Then he saw Ella's light force. Her web fanned out, powerful enough to resist the inner gravitational force of the dying proton.

"Now Vincent, you see me, come to the light."

He leapt against the gathering gravity toward Ella's light web, tremendous forces pulling him back toward the developing black hole, where the quarks of smashed protons were being drawn to their finality. Vincent tried to ignore his human reactions but failed. His body fell toward the vortex. Yet Ella's orb remained a sole surviving sphere undisturbed by the deadly whirlpool.

His fear grew, not for his death but rather that he'd die never knowing the true identity of the woman he loved. He had to be there - with her. He first imagined traversing the violent winds to the safety of her orb. There beside her, the raging storm no longer surrounded him, but was below him. The dying quark orbs and the smashed protons exploded like nebulas before evaporating in the vortex, a last gasp of matter, then life extinguished.

"Now," said Ella, and Vincent looked toward the fan of light outstretched, willing himself to immerse his hand into the light of her web. Vincent made his fateful jump and touched Ella's light web, setting off a star light reaction, dazzling then blinding him with its intensity. Its force struck him like a thunderbolt, jolting him back to his human form. The power of the surge convinced him he'd die, but just before passing out he felt only happiness. He was blind now but he sensed the warmth of Ella close by.

9

Revelation

VINCENT WAS STILL ON the mountain top of Rigi Kulm, yet Constantine and Ella were with him. Was he dreaming? The Entity swept high above them, still in the form of an eagle. The snow was thick, blurring Vincent's vision of its grand wing span as it drifted closer to the earth.

"Another Entity flew here, before taking Jean," said Constantine. Fear was in his eyes.

"Order must be maintained, chaos avoided," came words from the voice of Jean, but seemingly from the eagle.

"How can you restore balance to that which you do not try to understand?" Constantine said.

The eagles form shimmered as it replied. "You sentient beings roam recklessly through the multiverse like destructive fires in a forest, unleashing indiscriminate forces you neither recognise nor understand. You claim to believe in causes, but in truth you are little more than vandals, leaving scorched markers, like graffiti carvings on the most beautiful tree. When the signs are clear, I will act. Your insignificant world of Baryon matter is ruled only by cause and effect in a diminishing cosmos bound only by entropy."

The eagle came to ground ten metres from them. The grand bird was unaware of its environment. Its earthly state had been long extinguished. It was now a mere carrier of a force from another dimension. Its wings were folded in and its head lay on the cold snow as if it listened for echoes from another place. Then it stood upright and transformed into the human form of Jean.

"A storm rages through the multiverse. Balance must be restored."

"We wish the same. Tell us how," said Constantine. The Entity ignored Constantine, gazing only at Vincent.

"What do you want of me?" Vincent asked.

"I want much more than you, Earthling," it said, moving closer to Vincent.

Constantine and Ella reacted, moving closer to Vincent to protect him, but the Entity opened his palms, unleashing a mist-like force of energy that bound them in the finest of webs. The Entity then directed its palms in his direction, unleashing a similar force. He braced, expecting capture, but instead saw the web like mist in intricate detail. Each was filled with a universe of atoms that contained information. His mind was drawn to one of the webs and a blinding light flashed momentarily before his sight returned. He was no longer on the mountain. He felt as if he were floating in space witnessing a cosmological event.

A universe sized mass collided with the edge of the empty space in which he floated, like a grand liner swiping an iceberg on a vast ocean. The force of the collision sent out a shockwave that made an instant universe. Waves rose up like a whirlpool, mixing and expanding matter and anti-matter - action and reaction. All the elements were in place in that compact area of infinite possibility - the singularity - a place of high energy density, soaring temperatures and extreme pressures. Rapid expansion followed as the baby cosmos cooled. Cosmic inflation ensued.

The seismic event flung Vincent at inflationary speed across the universe until he reached an evolutionary turning point – the birth of light.

The Universe grew exponentially, like a colossal supernova spilling out its secrets to form new stars and planets in time and space. In the early universe only energy existed, but soon Baryon Matter and Dark Matter followed. Then the universe expanded, allowing the basic codes to create the world Vincent was familiar with. The Universe cooled sufficiently, energy converted into subatomic particles, combining to form the first atomic nuclei only a few minutes after the collision. A thousand years passed every second, as electrons merged with the nuclei to create the first atoms, the building blocks of matter.

All the while, Vincent floated in a cosmic front row seat with an uninterrupted viewing of the ultimate science lesson.

The first element produced was hydrogen, along with traces of helium and lithium. Giant clouds of primordial elements coalesced through gravity to form stars and galaxies, and the heavier elements were synthesized within stars. Then planets emerged to coalesce with the cosmos of matter – all orchestrated by a hidden realm that held the galaxies of Baryon and Dark Matter in place. This force was hidden from human eyes until now. Vincent watched the building of a universe as if it were a favourite painting on canvas that had suddenly been turned into the most intricate of holographs.

"I could never have imagined this," he said, awe struck by the wonder of what he was witnessing.

The two fundamental building blocks of the universe emerged like Siamese twins at birth. They were merged at conception but ultimately separated to ensure both survived. Everything that was, and is, streamed through to the baby universe, filling it with the elixir of life so that it may grow to self-awareness. The ability to conceive was planted. This was the law of the multiverse, which was the essence or DNA code of every baby universe.

"Your life was created by stars. Your people of carbon are little more than stardust with limited self-awareness and an inability to comprehend your place in the universe. Those insights are locked away in the DNA implanted in Dark Matter, the fundamental elements of our existence. We alone are born to know what you were not."

"Teach us."

"How can we teach those who cannot see? Would you teach a single celled organism your mathmatica? Here is your future," said the Entity, opening its palms and revealing a force that swept his friends away, as if they were no more than sand in a desert. Then he turned to Vincent, unleashing the same force. Vincent felt an excruciating pain as his skin slowly began to peel away from the force.

"No, no, please stop," cried Vincent, as he woke from his ordeal, unsure of his whereabouts. He lay on a large bed, but saw little else. His eyes ached and his sight was blurred. He was disoriented until he heard the comforting sound of Ella and Constantine. The familiarity of their voices reassured him, although all was not right as they sounded to be arguing.

"...every time you join him...brings it closer..."

"...I won't sit idly...another way..."

He heard fragments of their heated conversation, muffled as they were in an adjoining room. Vincent attempted to get up from the bed, wanting to see Ella but pain jabbed his skin as if his dream had been real, making him cry out and forcing him to lay back. Vincent wanted to call to them but he dared not risk the pain again. Then he heard them approach the room, Ella first, who sat beside him and Constantine, not far behind, who remained standing. He was the first to speak.

"How are you feeling, Vincent?"

"My skin...pain all over," he whispered, looking to his arms and body, convinced his flesh had been peeled away.

"It's the effects of the drug," said Constantine, gliding his light web over Vincent's body.

"The pain will ease soon. There'll be no residual effects."

"Do you remember anything from the Hadron Collidor?" said Ella, applying a cold towel to his forehead.

"Falling...I was falling...then...you...I saw you," he said, his memory of the events slowly returning.

"Yes, good, you'll remember everything in time, but rest now."

Vincent was tired, but his fear of the Entity's force would not allow him to relax.

"We are in great danger. We can't rest. We have to leave this place, before it destroys all of us," said Vincent, desperately trying again to get out of the bed, before the pain forced him back. His fear prompted Constantine to speak.

"What is it, Vincent? What happened in the Hadron Collidor?"

"It came to me and told me things...showed me things."

"What did it tell you?'

"It told me that we should stop what we are doing. It came from another place...dark matter. It lived across all universes...saw all things. It showed me wondrous things...then terrible things."

"What did you see, Vincent?" Constantine asked, as he fanned his light web over Vincent.

"What no human has seen before. Then pain...terrible pain," he repeated until he fell back to sleep.

Vincent awoke alone in the hotel suite. The last sun light was pouring into his room, the day nearly spent. He listened for sounds nearby but all was quiet, bar the hum of the small refrigerator next door. The sky was a violet blue and the neighbouring oak tree was motionless as only stillness pervaded the air.

He felt no pain and his strength had returned as he stretched arms and legs to wake. The memory of the Hadron Collidor and meeting the Entity continuously re-played in his mind. The acuteness of his drug-induced mind had diminished, except his hearing. He found if he focused his mind to listen, his ability to hear took on a super human quality. The sound of the fridge motor grew clear as if it was in the same room. He heard other sounds from afar. The desk clerk was welcoming a new arrival, two storeys below. Had the immersant's effects remained?

Thoughts of Ella suddenly filled his memory, of how she saved him. The feel of her light web still tingled at the ends of his fingers. He listened for her, hoping she was close. Then something strange occurred. As he focused his mind toward her, all around him turned silent.

He could hear Ella as clearly as if she were beside him. There was no other sound near her bar her own deep breathing. He could tell she was meditating as her breath was rhythmical. Vincent imagined Ella sat beside him in her meditative posture, so that he could imitate her action. He sat upright and crossed his legs and relaxed his mind, remembering the comfort he felt when shielded by Ella's light web.

He was reaching a calm state when a familiar mist disturbed his focus by seeping into Vincent's meditative haven. A dark viscous substance formed from the mist's wake, lining his mind's eye with its toxic, crawling mass. The Entity slowly formed into the shape of David, older now, in his late thirties, more threatening and more certain.

"All your little games are for nothing," it mocked. "Isn't this perfect? I have found Vincent and his lover together in their own private refuge. But it isn't private anymore, is it? Now, I see both of you."

The power of Vincent's meditation was more vivid than any dream he'd had. He looked to Ella. She remained in her meditative state, eyes closed, seemingly unmoved by the invader. He wanted to remain impervious to the Entity's threats like her. Perhaps it was no different to his experiences with sound and light waves. He was safe if he focused and did not allow his human emotions to take over. This is not real, he repeated to himself, trying to imagine he was in the protective bubble of a proton orb, but the Entity broke his determined attempts.

"I am much more than a light wave. You can't escape me with their mind tricks. The Entity's mist thickened to a suffocating level. Vincent was unable to hold his meditation as he choked on the hazardous concoction. Only then, Ella opened her eyes and reached out for Vincent. He reached out also, just before closing his eyes, to protect them from the mist's sting.

"Vincent...Vincent," said Ella.

"Vincent...Vincent."

Vincent opened his eyes. To his surprise, he was back in his room and the mist had disappeared. Ella was holding his shoulder.

"We have left the meditative state. Are you all right, Vincent?"

Vincent wanted to say he was fine, but the vivid meditation burnt into his mind. For the first time, the Entity invaded his thoughts. Was there no escape from its threatening shadows? The thought of this made him stand up, wanting only to leave the room. He walked to the lounge area, grabbed a juice from the fridge and sat at the small table beside the window.

"I don't like this hotel. I want to leave. There's death everywhere."

Ella studied him for a time, before speaking. "Let's go back to the church. It's a calming place. You'll feel better there. Safer," she said. Vincent quickly agreed. He needed fresh air, time with Ella and a chance to speak his mind. Something terrible was unfolding and he felt more vulnerable by the day. His only hope was to learn all he could about his situation. They walked out into the fading light of the day, hand-in-hand, as they strolled to the beautiful old church high on the hill, overlooking the old town.

"Something has changed. My senses are more acute."

"The immersant was powerful. It'll change you in many ways. Some forever," she said, hope in her eyes.

"I have changed. I know what I want," he said, strength and purpose in his tone, surprising Ella. "I want to see you. Not just your light web. All of you. Then I will tell you how I've changed and what I know."

Cathedrale St. Pierre's expansive main hall was filled with colourful textures from the setting western sun as its rays bathed through twelfth century stained glass windows. The cathedral was empty, as if by design. Warm coloured rays shone across the northern main altar. Its impressive gothic sculptures were awash with the colour and the fragrance of a dozen bouquets of fresh flowers. Ella stood in front of Vincent, breathing the natural and manmade fragrances of the cedar and flowers that decorated the altar.

"Our home is not unlike your cathedrals, except ours are natural wonders, vast church-like caves. That's where we choose to live and work when not exploring our world's wonders. One particular cave is lit up with plants that shine continuously, turning the night to day. I sometimes explore deeper into the large underground mazes, where no light penetrates. Even in those cold recesses of our planet, I shine my light web and find life everywhere. If not for my light web…" Ella broke off momentarily, holding a flower close to her to take in its fragrance of rose.

"I can't imagine living without 'true sight', yet it hasn't hindered the imagination of your great scientists." Ella smiled and gently touched Vincent's cheek, slowly gliding the back of her fingers around Vincent's face. Her light web glowed a cardinal hue. It felt as if a hundred rose petals softly caressed his skin.

"Would you like to see what I see?" she said.

"More than anything."

"Close your eyes and imagine my true image, standing next to you," she said, still gently stroking his cheek. Suddenly she floated above him. Vincent's mind felt disconnected as if he too floated upward in union with Ella. Then he saw Ella's light web gliding, its euphoric vibrations pulsing above. He reached out, immersing his hand into her sun gold force, toward her inner body deep within. She laughed with the happiness of a lover, guiding him to feel the texture of her skin, lovingly encouraging him to explore.

Vincent felt a charge surround his body. He could see fine electrical currents interact with his own aura. Gold light cascaded through his opaque thin aura. He felt as if another immersant had filled his veins. This immersant allowed him to touch her light web as if it were skin. Vincent parted Ella's web to slowly reveal her inner body.

"I feel a power in my hands. What's happening to me?"

Ella guided his hand as he explored her. "Your powers are growing. If you believe in your changes you will see me."

Vincent softly stroked Ella's alien body. It was a texture not unlike skin. Her warmth drew Vincent's aura to her. He gazed in fascination as his aura danced across her pale smoothness, revealing more of her slim alien lines. She had unmistakable human characteristics, but her body was elongated, smooth and shining as her light web ebbed and flowed across her skin. Vincent wanted to explore further. His hunger grew.

"I know what I seek is impossible. But you must have some feelings for me. Our bond feels so strong - so right."

Ella did not try to stop Vincent, her desires growing, too. "There is something special that can never be broken. I feel that, too," she said, as she bathed Vincent in the glow of her web.

But then Vincent was transported to another place. A cascade of images flashed before Vincent's eyes of people and places, some he knew, many not. Ella stood on Brighton Pier, her auburn hair windswept. She spoke softly, but it wasn't Ella's voice. Yet Vincent felt he had heard the voice before. He searched his memory but could not remember. He was about to ask Ella but she vanished.

Another image of a young girl, no more than six-years-old took her place. She danced playfully on the beach below him. She stopped to gaze out to the ocean, before turning to look up at Vincent on the pier. Warm love filled her gaze before she pointed out to the horizon. A dark cloud formed. Was it the Entity? Vincent could not tell. It circled rapidly across the ocean's surface, like a tornado on its side. Vincent sensed danger. But he did not run. The ocean image changed to a forest, then a desert. The little girl remained in the foreground oblivious to the changing scenery and the approaching storm. He wanted to warn her. But the black ridge of storm swallowed them both, casting them to an uncertain future. Vincent lost the little girl in the violent darkness, losing all bearings in the storm's fury. It felt too powerful for him to hold his ground as he was nearly swept away, but then he felt Ella's hand. On touching her, they returned to a familiar place – Brighton Pier.

"What were those images? I don't understand." Vincent said.

"Don't try to understand. Those were images from your past, present and future, blended in with your imagination. They were no more than a montage of what defines your essence. It is something that you should observe, but interpret at your peril."

"How do you know all this? Make me understand?"

Ella took Vincent's hand and walked with him along Brighton Pier. It was the new pier, but it was strangely empty for such a perfect day. The sun warmed the skin, just as the gentle breeze cooled it, filling the day with a gentle harmony.

"What is it that you want to understand, Vincent?"

"There is so much I need to understand and I now see that I need to learn quickly. Start with your voyage to Earth. Why did you follow Constantine on such a perilous journey?"

"I was very much like my great-grandfather, driven to explore the unknown. And fate was on my side as the research field of Dark Land matter had advanced in exciting new directions. The work, commenced by Braccus Max and furthered by Constantine became my grand obsession. Constantine became my mentor. Together, we unlocked the secrets of Dark Land matter. It was inevitable that I would follow in Constantine's footsteps and attempt a voyage to another universe."

"It amazed me when Constantine told me that you supported his research over the long period he was missing. He could have been dead, for all you knew," said Vincent.

"Yes, passion can make you do the most amazing things. I worked tirelessly on the study of our light web and its interaction with Dark Land matter for all of the hundred Earth years Constantine left our universe. Odorphins in our small team had given up on the research. Many demanded Constantine's body be released from the cocooned shell of Dark Land matter where it lay in an induced sleep. But I stood alone in defending Constantine's wishes, allowing his holographic avatar to continue to function in another universe. In time, our work was forgotten, leaving us to continue the study of the 'other universe' free from interference. Ultimately, I became the second Odorphin to cross the unknown into your universe."

"What was it like?" Vincent asked.

"What was what like?"

"Crossing a universe?"

"It felt more like a dream. My avatar body was lighter than light, so I floated like a whisper in the cosmic noise, riding on a photon encircled by Dark Land matter. My avatar was drawn to your universe through a funnel like cortex where two universes intersected. It took only a microsecond, yet it felt a lifetime - like an elongated shimmer. At the critical juncture, I felt a cramp tear me from the inside, building as if a battle raged atom by atom. I fell to your world sensing only pain. Any sense of achievement was lost to its agonising claws."

"Could you have died?"

"Possibly. But the destructive reverberations on my body dimmed. I searched my surroundings, feeling as if I had not left my home. I remained in the same inner most recess of my home cavern. Instinctively, I knew it was different. I soon realised the cave was devoid of all life, as was our moon. My world had disappeared, leaving not a single trace of my culture's footprint. Days and nights of fruitless search confirmed my fears. This land was barren."

Vincent and Ella reached the end of Brighton pier. Ella let go Vincent's hand, placing both on the railing as she leant forward and gazed out to the vast ocean. Vincent breathed in the cooling breeze before turning to her.

"What did you do next?"

"I turned to where life existed in your universe. It was sad to leave my home, but I knew Constantine was on Earth. We re-united on a world vastly different from ours. I'll never forget the first time I saw your ocean. It was filled with an astonishing array of life forms – a complex world filled with natural and man-made wonders - your world Vincent."

"Where did you travel?"

"Constantine took me to the 'water world 'of Earth. Your oceans most reminded me of home. There beneath its waters, I could change to my true form and explore your oceans, unhindered by human eyes. We voyaged the Earth's great oceans – the Pacific, Atlantic, Indian, Antarctic and Arctic Oceans. I observed the wonder and diversity of your sea creatures, all the while learning from Constantine about the animals that dominated the land surface – humans."

"How could you possibly learn the complexities of our Earth in such a short time?"

"I had already learnt much about your kind through Constantine's holographic transmissions. I had deciphered much of the mathmatica and human science but little about your culture. For your civilisation is a complex maze of tribes, vast in number. I understood basic information, facts and figures mainly, but social norms and customs had to be experienced, not studied, so I had to focus on western culture - your culture, Vincent.

"You also had to face the Entity?"

"It was my main purpose." Ella paused to look around her, as if someone had interrupted her.

"What is it?"

"We must return," Ella replied, maintaining a watchful eye on the Brighton ocean, then the church as they returned. She held her gaze toward the back of the church, not speaking.

"Is it the Entity?"

Ella did not reply, instead signalling Vincent to move to the main pulpit facing the wide expanse of pews. Then the silence was broken by the familiar voice of Jean, which reverberated around the cathedrals high walls.

"Now I see you," said the Entity.

Suddenly Ella's body was rocked violently by an invisible blow. The force momentarily deformed her right side, as if a car had struck head on sweeping her from Vincent. Her body rolled uncontrollably, smashing rows of pews, as if an invisible wave from the oceans depths held her in its powerful grasp.

Vincent thought her dead, such was the savagery of the blow. Her body distorted and bloodied, lay motionless against broken wooden pews. But miraculously, her eyes opened, and her steely gaze swept the large cathedral, momentarily resting on Vincent, before continuing her search for the invisible enemy. Vincent stood frozen to the wooden pulpit floor, helpless, vulnerable to the invisible force.

"Don't move. Stay very still," Ella said, before suddenly vanishing.

An eerie silence hung over the gothic expanse, belying what had just happened. For there in front of Vincent was a mangled explosion of wood where once were pews. His instincts told him to run, but where? Suddenly Ella reappeared in a flash, with no sign of her earlier injuries. Her light web now open, she ran down the church's centre aisle, away from Vincent, veering left before vanishing again. A force exploded with a wave of sound that nearly felled him.

Another human came into vision, as it was hurtled back uncontrollably into the pews, creating a second mound of broken, splintered, mangled wood. It was Jean. It was stunned, shaken by the force it had encountered, its gaze now directed toward Vincent, violent intent written on its contorted face. In a flash it vanished, throwing the cathedral again into an eerie silence.

Vincent braced, wanting to run, but holding on to Ella's words. Don't move...don't move, he whispered to himself, helpless before the invisible enemy, his only defence, to focus his mind and remain still as he had when the trains had hurtled toward him. He had no drug induced help this time, but his perception was still heightened, allowing him to see the Entity with greater clarity, as a massive mist like force threatened to sweep him away to an unknown abyss. Vincent heeded Ella's warning, remaining deadly still as the force approached. But a second force stopped its charge - Ella's light web. The sound of impact was deafening as her fiery field flashed like a thousand solar flares exploding.

"You hold back the inevitable," said the Entity, its voice roaring as charged flares continued to flash like fireworks.

"This human is your sacrifice. Give him to me now, or you both will die." Violent fields charged between them, building to a corona like intensity.

Ella held the force for a time, her focus strong, but her powers waned, overwhelmed by the Entity's relentless power. Ella's web weakened, until it was almost transparent, leaving her vulnerable to the Entity's savage force. Then another invisible wave of energy entered the fray, smashing the Entity with an intensity that shook the stone church to its foundations. Any pews still standing were now rubble. The gothic sculptures were fallen and all stained glass windows had shattered.

EMISSARY

Constantine appeared before Ella and Vincent, his light web spread wide, readying himself for a second charge at the Entity.

"At last we meet," it said, its form blurring but its voice crystal clear. Constantine remained calm, not showing any fear.

"Why are you here, why are you pursuing us?"

The Entity's form hovered now, its misty mass pulsating like a heart.

"You already know the answer. Or don't you believe in your dreams?" it said, mocking Constantine.

Constantine held firm his defence of Ella and Vincent. The Entity was aware of them all now, yet it backed away, choosing not to attack.

"You are different from the other. You talk to me through my dreams. Work with me? Together we can bring change for good," he said, before being cut off by the Entity.

"Like how you helped the other, Earthling? We tried to show you the folly of your actions, but you would not listen."

"Then why do you guide me through my dreams? It can only be you."

The Entity floated closer to Constantine, all the while its mist slowly took the human form of Jean. It studied Constantine's hands, as if it were looking for a way to invade his body, but Constantine stood his ground, before fearlessly reaching out to the Entity, grasping Jean's arm.

"Kill me now if you can, but I don't believe that is what you seek."

The Entity reacted to his touch, showing Constantine that his immersant was still potent.

"Perhaps it is not. You will never know what we truly seek. You are blind to the truth. But you will learn what you have done – what you have all done," it said. The Entity waved its arm across all three, plunging them into the cold depths of Lake Lucerne. Constantine did not resist as they plunged ever deeper in an inter-universe dance. They soared over the sandy sea bed, coming to rest at its deepest point.

"This is where your so called friend's lives faced our wrath."

"What do you mean by lives?" Vincent asked, seemingly unhindered by the ocean depths.

"We take more than one life, in one universe, human."

Constantine opened his light web to peruse the murky depths, seemingly hoping he'd find out how and why he disappeared.

"What did you do to him? We fought on land, not here. Jean vanished on Mt. Rigi Kulm."

"You will learn soon enough, Odorphin."

"Is he alive?"

"Your questions show your ignorance. He is not on this Earth, or any other Earths. He is with us, so that order remains."

"I want to help you. Why can't you see that? Or is it that you don't want to?"

"I won't play any of your games. What is will be. Run wherever you will, but know this. Nothing you do, none of your concoctions will alter what is. There are no more hiding places left and when your little immersants dry, there is just you and I. Then you will feel my force and never forget its pain."

In an instant, the Entity vanished, leaving them alone, instantly transported back to the church. Constantine appeared to be considering the Entity's words. Perhaps for the first time, he feared for his life, for all their lives. What was certain, all were visible to the Entity now, as its powers continued to grow and adapt. The question was – had the Entity come for Vincent or would all three of them die at the hands of this force?

The church fell silent again. Constantine held vigil for any sign of its return, but the silence held. There would be no more confrontations that day. Seemingly sensing it was now safe, he closed his light web, walking in human form back to Ella who was drained from the encounter as Vincent held her near.

"Come, we must go now. It will return," said Constantine, extending a hand to Vincent as they left the war zone that just an hour earlier had been a gothic jewel. Constantine carried Ella in his arms back toward the hotel, showing no sign of strain and demonstrating his unearthly strength. The violence that had unfolded reinforced the deadly powers Vincent faced both from friend and foe. He wasn't a religious man, but as he left the church, he whispered a small prayer to himself before taking a last look at the carnage unleashed. What he saw shocked him.

The church looked as it did an hour earlier. There was no sign of any damage. Vincent knew then that he lived in two worlds: the Earth that he knew; and another world, seemingly created by his friends and the Entity.

The early morning fog had not yet cleared over Lake Geneva. Its expansive waters were hidden from their view, as they sat at a small park table considering their next move. Vincent was pensive, more out of concern for Ella, still weakened from her church encounter. Doubts too lingered in his mind over the Entities words, the human is your sacrifice. Was that to be his ultimate fate, to die like his uncle, carried from this world into the Entity's hellish pit, so that the others might live? True, Constantine had saved them both last night, but was his intention to save only Ella?

The fog unsettled everyone that morning. Its thick blanket reminded them of what they faced. Ella sat meditating, rebuilding her strength, whilst Constantine poured over equations and images that constantly flashed across his light web. Vincent's strength was returning and with it, his frustration of knowing little.

"So what next," he said, breaking Constantine's concentration.

"We weakened it last night, but not for long. It'll return stronger," Constantine said, alarming Vincent. Could it possibly be any stronger than what he experienced that night? Its violence had been a terrifying demonstration of its power.

"Can you stop it?"

"Possibly, but for now we must put some distance between us and its threats. We can't face it here."

Vincent sighed at the prospect of more train travel. "What country this time?"

Constantine smiled, "We can't fight it on Earth!"

"You're leaving me here alone, to face this monster?" said Vincent, alarmed at the prospect, for he feared the Entity's warning of his sacrifice was true.

"That choice is in your hands, but either way, we face it for the last time on our homeland."

On Titan, thought Vincent. A day earlier and he would have thought the idea implausible. But everything that had happened to him seemed to be occurring on another plane. The destruction of the church felt so real and yet in the real world, Vincent's physical world, it had all been an illusion.

"So how do I survive this plan of yours?"

"You'll have to take a third immersant, a drug far more powerful than your last two. So powerful it will change you - forever."

"In what way?'

"You will lose some of your humanness and take on some of our characteristics. Some of those changes will be permanent. Your body has had to gradually adjust to the ever increasing doses we've been administering. If I'd have used this more powerful immersant the first time, you most surely would've died. There's still a chance it could kill you. That's why it's your choice."

Vincent lay back against the wooden park bench, watching the fog slowly lift, revealing Geneva Lake. The Jet d'Eau, one of the city's most famous landmarks, streamed five hundred litres of water a second, one hundred and forty metres into the air. He enjoyed its power and imagined riding the water as it sprung high above the lake. Compared to what he had done in the last few days, it would be an easy feat. How would this next drug make him feel? Would he experience boundless power and capabilities? The thought terrified him before a single idea reassured him. He'd see where Ella lived.

"And if I don't take it?"

"We leave you here, Vincent. We cannot fight the Entity here, not now. By facing him last night, you both unwittingly revealed more about us," said Constantine, glancing to Ella.

"The Entity is like a virus. When it fails to penetrate our bodies, it analyses the reasons. When it has immunity to that defence it will return to attack. We have to face it under new circumstances, if we're to have any chance of destroying it."

Vincent looked Ella's way. Her face was drawn, weakened from the previous day's battle. The truth of Constantine's words was etched in her tired, drawn face and listless body. She could not offer him advice, though he desperately searched for it in her eyes. But she kept her gaze from his, leaving the final, fatal choice with Vincent. The fog had completely lifted now, showing a perfect blue sky day on planet Earth. Vincent took in the calm waters of Lake Geneva for a time, perhaps for the last time, before turning to Constantine.

"I'm ready. I don't want to run anymore."

HOMECOMING

CONSTANTINE WAS TRUE TO his word. The immersant ran through every atom of Vincent's body, chilling him and charging his senses. His human frailties were purged, as he felt a power surge through his body giving super human strength to his limbs. The Jet d'Eau emitted water as if an aircraft engine lay below, cannoning an eclectic storm of electrically charged atoms and ionised light high, before sprouting wings at its peak and drifting back to the continuing flow.

"Ride one just before it starts to fall. Focus on its charge and follow us," said Constantine. Vincent could see harmonic shaped air molecules vibrate from Constantine's lips. "Focus on one atom," was his last advice, before all vanished from the physical world.

Vincent merged with a single atom, centred between neutrons and protons, dazzled by photon charged electrons that lit the vast spherical case. Lightning rods from high, cast solar flares around Vincent's protective atomic sphere. His world view was at the quantum level and the turbulent skies he looked up to flashed from day to night by the orbiting electrons.

Constantine led them to the bottom of the lake and to the edge of a crater formed deep in the lifeless sandy floor, plunging further to the darkness with no base.

"Lie flat and very still!" he said, as an intense light similar to the colours of Ella's light web, radiated from the bottom of the crater but on a larger scale. The force gripped his sphere with the power of a thousand tornadoes, spinning the encasement of his atom until the electron flashes blurred to an intense red light. Then a force slung shot him upward with the power of a supernova, directly into the middle of a giant whirlpool. A blinding flash of red then white light stretched out before him. The light of a dozen suns blinded him temporarily before everything stopped.

He was on solid ground. Slowly, Vincent's vision adapted. He lay high on a mountain bathed by a red sky and bound by lakes of black. Constantine and Ella stood some metres away on a ridge, their gaze on him filled with welcoming smiles, for they stood on their home land, Titan.

Minutes passed before Vincent's full vision returned and he joined Ella and Constantine on the high rock ice ledge, gazing over chocolate and tangerine lakes. The landscape was awash with evening twilight tinges, giving it a desert-like atmosphere, except it was the coldest of deserts - minus one hundred and eighty degrees centigrade.

Vincent felt as light as a proton, in the thick nitrogen atmosphere, unaffected by the extreme cold. His senses had returned to normal, no longer seeing matter in the 'hyper' detail of earlier.

"The immersant. It's left my body already?"

"This immersant is different. It's formulated to respond when required, akin to adrenalin. It fills your body when the right signals to the brain are sent," said Constantine.

In fact, Vincent felt normal standing on Titan, as if this was his world. His body was fully adapted to its atmosphere and gravity, whereas the thought of standing on Earth would be unthinkable, its extreme hot conditions hostile to him now.

"The sky is clearing, Vincent," said Ella, holding his arm and pointing in the direction of the clouds as they rolled toward the horizon. Titan's sky was a blood orange haze, lit by what appeared to be a sun covered by thick fog. But the clearing haze revealed Titan's neighbouring planet. Saturn's rings emerged, creating a rainbow arch of cinnamon and cream that reflected across the mirror-like lakes, blending shades of sparkling colour across the vast methane expanse.

Soon Saturn came in to full view, brighter than the Earth's moon, ten times larger, jacinthe and smooth. The majesty of Titan's mother planet reigned like a goddess come to watch over her disciples. It was little wonder the Odorphins held celestial travel as their core life purpose. Countless tales of their world were passed down as folk lore, forming their own unique culture. Most of these stories centred on the ringed planet and its sixty moons - and why not? A veritable feast of activity on a solar scale orbited their land. A unique cosmic clock of a grand scale surrounded Titan.

"Such a sight only occurs in the long dry season, when the cloud dissipates. Past ancestors celebrated this event in meditation, paying respects to the mother. Folk lore has it that the mother's rings provided us with our light web, so that we might shine like her," said Ella, hypnotised by Saturn's beauty. "Is it not beautiful?"

"It's like you have a solar system on your doorstep," said Vincent.

"It's why we live to voyage. Each moon's our fellow traveller on the journey. Constantine and I share that love for the voyage. From our worlds to the limits of our reach - the multiverse," said Ella, smiling with Constantine as they stood to honour Saturn as it revealed its full beauty.

The majesty of Saturn's rise would stay with Vincent forever. He stood in wonder at the sight of the gas giant illuminating the vast lake-filled valley of Titan. The dark lakes took on a colourful hue of Saturn's vibrant indigos and gold, shining like Egyptian jewellery.

"We have no religion as you know it. Our lives are inspired by the pulse of our mother planet. We serve as a reminder to it of the life it forges in the great cosmos. We want you to share our passion for the voyage with the mother and with us," said Ella, turning away from Vincent now, her head bowed, eyes closed, in meditation.

Vincent stood for a time on the high ledge, thinking over the trials of his earlier troubled life – the unfairness of it all, its pain. Yet it all made sense now. The struggle had been worth it. He was the first of all human kind to witness firsthand the celestial wonders of their solar system. He no longer questioned why he should be the first. For it no longer mattered. He felt as if the colossus that was Saturn had chosen him. He could not explain the feeling. He didn't need to. And as Ella and Constantine openly worshipped the giant planet, he felt for the first time that they genuinely accepted him as their friend, someone they trusted.

"Do not question your abilities anymore, Vincent. You stand alone amongst humans. No other could have joined us this day," said Constantine, in a determined tone. He held his arm as a friend, before continuing.

"You'll face great danger. Expect the unexpected. But remember in the darkest hour, we share the love for the voyage. Your life was destined to cross ours. Your new life has just begun. Breathe every last molecule from it. For you know in your heart that this is what you seek."

Saturn had fully emerged from its slumber filling the sky like a royal crown. Then the ice white moon Encelidus joined her mother, shining like a diamond among the sapphires. Two jewels merrily danced in Titan's precious sky.

Constantine then turned to Ella. "Take him to the caverns, where the Entity cannot penetrate. I'll go to the great lakes, for the last immersant. Then with the mother's will we'll face the final hour and emerge free to again voyage." There was a calm resignation in his voice as if he knew the confrontation was close.

Constantine smiled warmly and a satisfaction crept around his lips, as he revealed his light web. He leapt high in to the thick air, before soaring from the mountain top down toward the great lakes below. His web illuminated the methane lake with gold as he flew over it toward the horizon.

"Come with me now," said Ella. She too flew down the mountain side to its base. Without a thought, Vincent leapt from the mountain side and flew also. His immersant responded as if flying were his natural state. His aura was like a light web, allowing him to glide effortlessly.

The mountain side was smooth, compared to Earth's rockier formations, and a lighter colour. Its rocks were a mix of ice rock and earth-like boulders. As they descended to the mountain's base, Ella turned from the vast lake and walked back toward a naturally formed cavern, etched out over a millennium of seasons shaped by the ebb and flow of the lakes changing tides.

The cavern was as Ella had described it to him on Earth. It did remind him of the giant columns of a gothic church, but this natural wonder ran five hundred metres high up to its cavernous ceiling of 'helocites' made of ice and methane. Its space was grander than three of Earth's largest cathedrals combined.

"Odorphins' live simply, requiring few possessions. We travel often and explore our solar system, but we always return to the sacred caves, to share our voyage and learn of new wonders. I'll share the mathmatica with my fellow Odorphins in a cave such as this," said Ella, walking deeper into the recesses of the giant cave, the outside light fading from view.

As the darkness took hold, Ella re-opened her light web, revealing a long narrow tunnel to a second chamber. The second smaller cave lit up with flying insects, their wings finer than a bee. Thousands of them flew away from Ella's light web deeper into the cave where its ceiling height fell dramatically. Ella described them.

"They're called muskins because of the faint violet colour of their aura. I have sat with them for many hours." She spread her web further and the remaining muskins disappeared, leaving just the bare rock ice cave walls.

"There's life here?"

"Sadly no, I created them for you. I wish you could see all the creatures on our home. Their collective energies sing with life, like the animals on your Earth."

"You have such wonderful powers," said Vincent, awe struck by her light web capabilities.

"It's a complex recreation but it can never replace reality," said Ella, fanning Vincent's face with her web.

"Can I see the real you, rather than a holograph?" Vincent's desires for her were stronger than ever.

"You carry a strong immersant in your body. This gives you the capability to see Constantine and I, as we really are. That's why I've brought you here, to become used to our true form, for we will face the Entity in our Odorphin bodies. Creating human form requires effort, energy we'll need when we confront the Entity."

Ella explained the looming battle, all the while slowly circling him, as she had done in the church in Geneva. Soft violet light flowed from her hands as she lightly stroked his face with her finger tips.

Vincent reacted to the soothing violet force. His immersant allowed him to draw his gaze closer. He longed to immerse himself in her light web. As he did, he felt his mind float free above his body. Ella's light web grew brighter, taking form, not unlike wings that beat so quickly they blurred. He floated closer to her so he could see her inner body, a long narrow frame with slender arms, but small stump-like legs. She was some three metres tall with a light skin that appeared to vibrate, blurring its form. Her face was the clearest feature, elongated, smooth and featureless, like a sculptor's mould waiting to be worked. Her eyes were as dark as a swirling ocean on a moonlit night. She turned to face Vincent and he could see no reflection in her eyes, as if they absorbed all light.

"You are with me now," said Ella, her appearance powerful.

At first he feared her alien form. Her shape had some human qualities. But if there was an evolutionary link, it was many millennium removed. However Ella possessed a powerful beauty. He wanted to hold her close, but held back, unsure she wanted him. Ella sensed it and guided his hand to touch her alien body. The texture of her skin pleased him as he delighted in the feel of her smooth, soft form. Energy enfolded around his fingers as he slowly glided his palm over her.

"Your skin is so soft. It feels familiar, like we have always been close. I wish we could be together like this for a lifetime."

"Trust your feelings Vincent, they will never mislead you. We can always remain close – in our thoughts. You'll learn one day that there is little difference."

Vincent wanted to explain his feelings, but he sensed a tension in Ella, born from nearby events.

"How long do we have before the Entity finds us?"

"It's close and its power will be great. We'll need our full powers now," said Ella.

"We'll do all in our power to protect you," she said. Her emotions showed in her voice, where her alien features could not.

"Why does the Entity seek me, I have none of your powers. What possible threat could I pose?"

"You have more power than you could ever imagine. You're born of a race with limited sight and yet an imagination that stretches beyond your universe. It's that rare capability, one perhaps we do not possess that has drawn us to you. You have something it wants, perhaps even fears. We hope to find out what that is. But if we can't, we must find a way to protect you. And because I drew the Entity to you, I must do all I can to protect you. I'd lay my life down for you," she said, her web brushing his face, seeking his trust.

"As I would for you Ella, but how can I fight such powers?"

"Use your imagination, that's your gift. The immersant will react to it. If you listen to your foe, as if you were he, in that place it is foretold you'll prevail."

"Foretold? What do you mean?" He reached out to her web, wanting to understand, but Ella stopped him, as her gaze turned to the cave entry.

"I can say no more. Trust your deepest instincts for you will need them. Constantine returns. The time has come."

Ella changed back to human form as she walked to the lake-side shore where Constantine stood, looking out across the smooth lakes, holding orbs containing a newly created immersant. He turned and greeted Ella and Vincent as they neared him.

"It prepares an approach. I sense its power building. It will have speed beyond our reach."

Ella looked at him, unable to hide her concern. "Do we have time?"

"There are three of us against just one. We must use this to our advantage," he said, thinking for a time, before turning to Vincent.

"But it will make contact with you first. We can't stop it. You must prepare for that moment."

The thought of the deadly mist attacking his body, devouring him atom by atom, terrified Vincent. The real sensation was worse than any of the nightmares that haunted him for much of his young life.

"Is there nothing I can do to fight it?'

"You can't outrun it, nor fight. Its power is too great. You must outsmart it." Constantine briefly returned to his light web, reviewing his strategies before revealing his plan to them.

"We'll wait for its attack in the open expanse," he said. He turned and pointed to the centre of the great lake. His light web lit up like a transparent computer screen, showing his plan.

"I'll hover in the lakes centre, like your Earth's Sun. Ella, you'll be below the lake's surface orbiting me as Saturn. Vincent, you'll rotate Ella as Titan. We must maintain pinpoint accuracy, relative to our scale and timed to our nearest pulsar star. When the Entity disturbs our model field of gravity, we'll be ready to react to its attack within a quark rotation. It's our only chance to defend you."

"I'm the bait," said Vincent, resigned to his fate and getting no contrary argument.

"Take this immersant now," said Constantine, laying the orbs in front of them.

"A smaller dose for you Vincent, your body would reject any more. But this dose should be sufficient."

"So it's similar to the last?" he said, gripping the orb tightly.

"Every immersant must be different. You'll face much, but you must stay true to your feelings. Remember this when events are at their darkest." He positioned his light web over the orb, as did Ella. The orb evaporated as the immersant filled Vincent's veins.

At that, both Constantine and Ella transformed into their Odorphin bodies, two giants hovering a metre above the ground beside him, spreading their light webs like wings. Their grandeur lit the lake's edge as if a bonfire burned bright, as they flew towards their destination.

Vincent's immersant allowed him to react immediately, as all three flew low over methane liquid toward their fateful encounter. The shores soon disappeared from view. Titan looked more like a 'water planet' to Vincent. The thick viscous methane liquid was the colour of clay. Above them, the majesty of Saturn shone its regal reflection from the mirror-like lake creating an eerie effect, as if they were to do battle on Saturn itself.

All moved to their positions. Constantine hovered above the surface, dead centre of the miniature solar system they had re-created. Ella positioned her movement to recreate that of Saturn to the Sun. She rotated at the correct elliptical speed as did Vincent to her, locking his rotation to hers as Titan to Saturn. The precise laws of physics were now their first form of defence against an approaching interstellar storm.

Vincent felt alone and vulnerable as he waited in the deadly quiet for the Entity's attack. Constantine and Ella could abandon him to face the Entity alone, for all he knew. But he trusted Ella. Focus on the physics, he thought, maintaining precise movement. Newton's Law ($F=G(m1m2/r2)$) was his only focus as his sphere maintained a perfect elliptical path around Constantine and Ella's conflicting forces.

"When you feel the Entity's energy disturb the laws, flee as fast as you can from him, for every micro-second could mean the difference between success and failure," Constantine had warned him. Time would be his only friend.

Vincent's senses were on a knife edge, knowing the attack could come from any direction without warning. He orbited between the real Saturn and its mirror image, floating in a foreign world, as if lost on Titan's mother planet. He retreated further within himself, calculating the number of atoms he breathed as he maintained pulsar-like precision. He wondered whether his survival would be determined by his reaction time, given he'd have no more than a microsecond warning of the Entity's strike. He retreated into his mind further until he thought nothing except that he was Titan. Vincent no longer existed.

But then the predictability of gravity was rocked by a force akin to a supernova. Vincent felt the first of the atoms smash into their orbits, changing Newton's projected trajectory. His instinct reacted instantly as his orbit changed. It was an almost undetectable shift, but his adrenalin charged immersant detected it. He headed for Ella, aware of her precise location and approaching close to light speed in a fraction of a second. But he could not out-run the Entity. Its mist poured around him. Time stopped in that place. He felt trapped in a large sphere from which he had no escape. The mist gained form. The familiar, threatening human shape of David stood before him. His flight toward Ella extended to what now felt like a lifetime.

"They won't save you. They never intended to," it said, eyes wide, wild and victorious, before it extended powerful hands to firmly grasp Vincent's wrist. A pain roared through the tips of his fingers. He felt his hand burn from the inside out as a dark mass containing poisonous microscopic spines tore at him atom by atom. He was paralysed with the pain, unable to stop the crawling mass as it relentlessly crept from his fingers to his wrist.

"All your running and hiding. And to think your true enemy was with you all the time, waiting to betray you."

Vincent's arm throbbed with the pain, before an odour of rotting flesh permeated his sense of smell. He felt his body die, though his mind had not. He wouldn't allow the Entity victory without a fight. His mind was the only resistance he had left.

"I'll never believe your lies," were his last words, before he looked away from the viscous mass as it oozed closer to his life force. Time slowed. Death held him in its claws, as his body fell to the shadows.

But a second force, he knew to be Constantine, swept his assailant away from him. With the force of a second supernova, every atom of the Entity was wrenched from him in an explosion of light that cleansed him of the poison. A third force, Ella, carried him to the safety of the mountain top, from where they had come. She lay him down on the smooth rock ice, before she stood sentinel on the mountain edge maintaining her vigil.

Vincent wanted to speak, but the memory of his pain lingered so powerfully it filled every crevice of his thoughts. Then shock set in. He felt as if his right arm had been torn from him.

"What has happened? Has it been destroyed?"

Ella either didn't hear him, or chose not to as she held a steely gaze toward the great lake where an energy of light advanced. Vincent saw it in the distance, convinced it was the Entity, until to his relief Constantine greeted them victoriously. Both hovered together on the mountain edge, before reverting to human form.

"It's done," said Constantine.

"Will it work?" asked Ella, desperation in her voice and face.

"We will know..." his reply was interrupted by a violent eruption that thundered along the mountain top surface, as if a hundred quakes shook the ground and threatened to swallow the mountain in its fury. Vincent looked to Constantine and Ella for explanation, but their faces were filled with a fear that scared him more than the earthquake. Before he could react, a force gripped him from behind and in a microsecond pulled him through Titan's rock ice as if water. Vincent's physical form was taken, but his mind held tenuously to Ella and Constantine. He saw his friends alone on the mountain and could hear them. Ella looked to Constantine, shock in her eyes.

"We have little time," she said.

"There's time. We must rest now and build our strength, for there is only one more chance. It will soon return to take us all," said Constantine.

He walked over to where Vincent had just been taken, gliding his hand over the rock ice. Vincent called to him, but Constantine did not hear his cries for help. There was no sign of any disturbance. It was as if he fell through another dimension. Constantine shook his head. Fear was etched on his face.

"For now we return to the cavern. It cannot penetrate the dark. There we'll rest and rebuild our strength."

"Shall we fight it on the lake again?" Ella asked.

"No, we'll fight it where it was born - in the Dark Lands."

Both looked south before they flew back to the safety of the cavern, leaving Vincent alone. He repeatedly cried out to them in the hope that they may hear him, but they did not respond.

"How readily they leave you, human. I have you now," said the Entity with power in its voice and the confidence of a victor.

Vincent didn't turn to face his captor, until Ella and Constantine faded from his view. He finally turned to face it. It was no longer in human form, reverting to its shadowy, menacing mist. He would have fallen into a state of complete submission but for something that surprised him. He could still hear his friends, as if they stood beside him, even though they had disappeared over Titan's horizon.

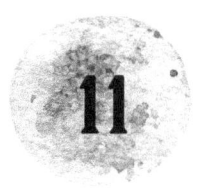

11

THE ABYSS

VINCENT FELL DEEPER INTO the abyss, nightmares realised, memories of a life disturbed by dark dreams. He was overtaken by the sombreness. The daylight had left him. Atom by parting atom, his past physical form stripped away. But with finality came renewal, a new form shaped from the earth's underbelly and time. Was he human flesh anymore? Or consciousness lost in the falling darkness, his soul vacant. His descent was broken by a cold rocky surface. Was this his death? Scattered memories raced through his mind, unconnected. Dark dreams, crowded lecture halls, hospitals, injections...endless injections, people he thought he once knew but could no longer place. All floating slowly from his mind in the dark pit in to which he had fallen.

But he still possessed memory, faded as it was. He knew to look up through the darkness, follow his instinct. He searched through the rock ice until the dark of the Earth's cold crust was replaced by Saturn's glow of the sky. Then he remembered light and life. His senses were reborn. He could again observe the world of matter - the changing universe, atoms moving forward, entropy in action, formless, a chaotic symphony of matter ever moving, creating time itself.

He observed his surrounds with new born eyes, sensing a terrible wrong had been done. He then turned his gaze back to Saturn, Ella's mother planet. He searched for her in the ever moving ice rocks that circled the planet. He remembered as he fell deeply into the abyss that he could still hear his friends. Vincent focused his mind on sound waves and imagined he rode one as he did on the train. He thought of his friends' voices as he searched for a similar frequency. To his surprise, he found a wave that exactly matched Constantine's voice. He immediately reacted and rode the wave that deflected from solid ground back to where his voice came from. Soon, the sound wave mixed with the surrounding light waves and he saw his friends again.

Constantine gazed upon the empty cavern walls. He looked sad, as if he was imagining life back on his home Titan, not the barren moon of this universe. His light web and Ella's threw a light hue on the cavern rock ice wall as they studied a montage of information, some of it seemingly about him. Were they transferring information to each other? Vincent wondered. The light provided a camp fire effect in the normally pitch black cave. Both were in Odorphin form, no doubt, conserving their energy for the looming confrontation half a world away. Ella asked many questions of Constantine in the quiet of the cave.

"So, if the new immersant fails?"

"Then the transference is all the more important. We have acquired a hundred Earth years of discoveries from another universe – irreplaceable," said Constantine. Ella maintained her inquisitive gaze, seemingly wanting more information.

"If Vincent meets the same fate as Jean, the transference would all be for nought. If the immersant has taken, we have a chance." Constantine said.

"But Vincent's future?" Ella asked, in a determined tone.

"We can never be sure. What is, cannot be changed. Our responsibility is to our race. If there is any opportunity left, we must take it and fight with every part of our being to return to our homeland."

Constantine closed his web and turned his body toward the cavern's rock ice walls, sitting in a meditative position, seemingly shutting down their conversation. But Ella held her gaze toward him, agitation in her eyes. "I would do anything to protect our people. You know that?"

"Yes, Ella. I would never think otherwise of you." He turned to face her, at first showing annoyance, but then his expression warmed. "What is troubling you?"

"I'm also responsible for what has happened to Vincent. I will not turn my back on him."

"We haven't. He carries the other immersant. If he loves you as much as he claims, he will reject the Entity's grip on him."

"It's a huge risk."

"What else could we have done?"

"Resisted it and protected Vincent," she said, spanning her web and revealing an opal blue hue.

Constantine cast a violet light with his web as he spoke. "The Entity is more powerful than you know. It would have defeated us."

"You can't be sure of that."

"That's true, but I have faced two Entities. Experience has taught me to not underestimate its powers. It is like a malignant cancer. At best, we can hold it at bay, but we can't destroy it."

"Then we can never escape it?" Ella asked, as she cast her opal blue light deep into Constantine's web, as if she were confronting him. Constantine reflected before answering.

We can't defeat it by ourselves. But the three of us can. We have to rely on the new immersant in Vincent."

"Are you sure it worked? I was with him for some time after the battle on the lake. I could not detect it."

"I'm sure, Ellatine."

"Show me, now."

Constantine did not act on her request, but Ella maintained a determined gaze and her light continued to pierce Constantine's light web. Finally he cast a light on to the rock wall and images started to flow at a rapid rate.

"We are risking our advantage. I cannot be sure that the Entity does not see what we see."

Vincent floated close to both but neither were aware of his presence. He feared Constantine was right. If he could see them, so too could the Entity. He called to them but his words fell away to his world of darkness. He had to find a way to talk to his friends in the world of light. In that instant, his force moved to the light waves on the wall, shaping and moulding the photons to patterns he wanted to convey. He had mastered his power over the light waves by the time an image of him shone on to the ice rock. He had found a way to communicate with them.

I see you. Help me!

Constantine reacted immediately, closing down his web light. Ella reacted.

"It's Vincent. We should speak to him."

"It could also be the Entity," replied Constantine.

"But..."

Constantine silenced Ella with a single wave of his light web. Both searched the cave, looking for signs of their invisible intruder. Vincent called out continuously, in the hope they may eventually hear him, but to no avail. Ella's alien face made it difficult to read her emotions, but he sensed sadness in her that he believed were feelings for him. He buried the images he had seen deep inside him, fearing the Entity would see what he had seen, before he returned to his dark abyss. It was a place of no light, but now he could fill its insidious cold with the tiny embers of hope. He held an immersant that he believed the Entity was not aware of.

Back in the dark, he sat in a meditative position, as Ella often did, waiting for the Entity's inevitable return, all the while listening to the voices from his friends of the light.

"I will not show you again," said Constantine, sternly.

Ella did not respond for some time.

"You kept information from me, didn't you?"

"It feeds on our communication as if it were our very atoms. So there are some things I will not reveal. You have to trust me, Ellatine."

"I have trusted and supported you for most of my life. But I will not fight this Entity, blind to the facts," she said, in an angry tone.

"Even if sharing those facts may put at jeopardy everything we have worked for?"

"You're asking me to play with another's life. I don't think I can do that."

"That decision may put the survival of our race in jeopardy."

"We are responsible for two races, not one."

"Are you sure it is two races?"

"What are you saying?"

"I have studied other universes, Ellatine. You know that. All of them harboured intelligent Earthlings, but not Odorphins. In every case, Titan was lifeless. Why would that be?"

"In each of those universes, you have travelled to a different time period."

"Exactly. The time of the Earthlings is in a period before or after the Odorphin civilisation. That we know. But on the evidence, there are too many similarities to separate us as different species. They are less developed physically, lacking light webs, but they share many more similarities."

"We are the same race?"

"I believe so. We evolved from them at some point in time."

"Then all the more reason to do all we can to save Vincent. Not acting could put our very being at stake!"

"He is one human. His death would be significant, given the Entity's interest in him. But it's unlikely that one death would bring about the extinction of the entire human race or ours."

"But you do agree that he is significant?"

"I have no doubt about that. But the puzzle is impossible to decipher. The Entity will not reveal its intentions. It seems that it believes we could never comprehend its reasoning anyway. Given that, we must firstly act to ensure the safety for our people."

Vincent held his meditation, focusing on hearing his friends. There was a long pause, before Constantine broke the silence.

"Ellatine, don't despair. I believe there is hope. Together with Vincent, we can prevail. Look at me....closer. Let me wipe your tears away."

"I am responsible for Vincent. I brought this Entity to his Earth."

"I think you are feeling more than responsibility toward this Earthling. Tell me I'm wrong."

Vincent desperately wanted to hear Ella's response, but he was disturbed by another voice, much closer than his friends.

"Where have you been, Earthling?" came a powerful voice. It was not Jean's or David's voice, but he knew it was the Entity.

"I have been alone with my thoughts, held hostage by you," he replied, trying to maintain a calm manner.

The Entity was a formless mist that ebbed and flowed, floating close to the ground. From it, emanated the smallest of lights, giving Vincent his first look at where he had been taken. He appeared to be floating in a dark void, offering him no sense of direction.

"What do you want from me?" Vincent asked.

"I'm not sure. I am waiting."

"For what?"

"I'm waiting until you are ready."

"Ready to die?" Vincent asked, preparing himself for the end.

"Your essence will never die, human."

"You have tortured me most of my life. So much so, I have often wanted to die."

"You could end your life, but your essence is much more than that. It spreads for an eternity, through infinite life forms."

"How do you know this? Or are you justifying your threatening nature?"

"We are life forms, like you, but we are made from a very different stream to your kind."

"If you are so wise, tell me of your race, instead of threatening me. I cannot harm you," said Vincent.

"Again, you know not what you say."

"How could I threaten your kind? I have no powers to cross universes."

"In your world, they say that the movement of a butterfly's wings can influence climate on the other side of your planet." The Entity drifted toward Vincent, before enclosing its mist around Vincent's arm. "This discussion alone could change everything."

Vincent tried to move his arm from the mist, but was unable. "Again, you offer me no more than physical threats."

"I'm not threatening you. I'm reading your essence. But if it is information you seek, ask me questions."

"Why the sudden change? You and your kind have shared nothing with me, only pain."

"You have changed, human. Your so called allies have lifted your powers."

Vincent feared the Entity knew he was able to hear his friends' voices. "What powers do you mean?"

"You can travel on light. You have also seen the multiverse. Have you not?"

"Perhaps. But they may only be visions created by my friends. Why not leave me to learn off Constantine and Ella?"

"Your essence seeks far more than that."

Vincent shook his head in frustration. "If what you say is true, I need your guidance. Explain your life and perhaps I will begin to understand."

The Entity shrouded Vincent in its mist before replying. "You are ready to learn."

Before Vincent could speak, the void in which he was trapped transformed into a twilight land, lit by the far off stars of the universe. They floated on a plateau, high above a lifeless plain, swept by unrelenting winds.

"Where are we?" Vincent asked.

"You know."

"The Dark Lands of Titan?"

"Yes. My home."

"We are in the Odorphin's universe?"

"No. We remain in your universe, but you are seeing my home, as it appears in my universe. We will not cross the multiverse until the right time," the Entity said, before transforming into the human form of Jean. "This is your world of Baryon matter," he said, pointing to himself. "But in our universe, we see two fundamental building blocks."

The Entity transformed from human form into the shape of an Odorphin. "And this is what half a billion years of evolution can do. Unlike your race, the advanced sentient beings consist of two types of matter. Odorphins developed powerful light webs forged from Dark Matter and an inner body made of your Baryon Matter. The interaction of the two forces led to the creation of a new strain of self-awareness. The Odorphins' intricate light web allowed them to see their complex universe in greater detail by harnessing the powers of 'radiant light'. You have been made aware of its power, haven't you?"

"Yes, they have showed me how to use its power, with the help of immersants."

"Dark Matter evolved in two races in our universe. In the light web of Odorphins and in us. And there it remained until the 'great fusion' could take place."

"Did you bring about that fusion?"

"We have no need to create change to time frames. That is only important in the world of Baryon Matter. We are made up entirely of dark matter. We have no form, just instinct for the multiverse. We hold memories that were born in the time before there was time. This was the place of no beginnings, a continuation of what will always be. There is no beginning or end."

The Entity reverted back to a mist, before spreading and diluting its form until it evaporated out of sight into the Titan atmosphere.

"This is our natural state. I believe we are called Hollow people."

"Then you are brothers of Titan?"

"We couldn't be more different. That is why we will face them, together."

"Face them? When? Where?"

"Soon, they will be coming for us, here on the plains of the Dark Lands."

"I will happily face them, I am their friend."

"Do you think so, Earthling?" The Entity unleashed a powerful mist that surrounded Vincent's body, like a second skin. Vincent felt pain at first, but then his body relaxed, accepting the foreign substance. He fell blind for an instant, but on recovering his vision, he could see the Dark Lands as if it were a city of lights. Energy streamed and swirled with the great gusts of the plain, like a modern highway filled with cars that sped past at high speed on a freeway that extended out beyond anywhere he'd seen or imagined. Was it the multiverse?

"Do you see it?"

"Yes. I feel like I'm an electrical charge inside a giant brain."

"This is my home."

Vincent searched his memory, but had few. There was the land of light, but the solution could not to be found there. Did the answers lie in the Entity's homeland?

"Now do you fear death?" said the Entity, its invisible form now visible to him, like a vast, thick fog.

"There is no death, only an infinite number of lives," said Vincent, understanding now. "Just purpose."

"And what is your purpose?"

Vincent scanned the last of his memories – of the life he had just lived. But he found no purpose. He felt a calm building around him in the vastness of the Dark Lands. His initial fear had been replaced by a warm glow. It was as if the poisonous barbs that had previously stripped his body from his soul had awakened a new consciousness.

"I don't remember my purpose," he said, the growing warmth overpowering any other feeling or memory he ever had.

The mist no longer felt threatening. The Entity cloaked him in its soothing energy before repeating his question. "Look and you will understand your purpose."

Glowing light radiated out in all directions, infinite in length. Vincent felt the contents interact with every particle of his being. Then his particles streamed out along the waves of light into infinity. Vincent focused on the swirling energy and to his surprise, he could see at the quantum level.

"Did you create this?" Vincent asked.

"Yes. Now do you see?"

"I do. The particles are steaming toward an intense field. Is it a black hole?"

"Do not think as a human. It will trick you."

Vincent was encased in a transparent capsule as he sped toward a large field. Particles poured into the large expanse, creating flashes of light as they crashed into the unknown substance. It made Vincent think of how people described their near-death experiences. Was he experiencing death? Fear and fascination overtook him in equal measure, as he tried to make sense of what was happening.

"This is not to dissimilar to how people have described near-death."

"In a way, you're right. But you continue to think human thoughts. What have I told you?"

"There is no death."

"Yes. All that exists are the cycles of the cosmos."

Vincent approached the substance, something akin to a thick fog. "Am I looking at a Higgs Field? Are these particles gaining mass?"

"That event occurs in your world, human."

"They are losing their mass?"

"They are returning to the source."

Somewhere in the dense fog lay Vincent's purpose. His capsule followed the disappearing particles into the dense soup. He expected his view to clear as he became one with the field, but instead all vision disappeared in a snowfield-like whiteout.

He called to the Entity, but he was no longer with him on the plateau. Vincent was alone. Strangely, he felt to be in a place of perfect harmony, but for one thing. He kept hearing faded voices in the recesses of his mind. They were the voices of his friends.

Vincent followed the sounds of their voices until he saw the two Odorphins as they journeyed across the remote twilight deserts. Then he remembered the Odorphins' tales and legends told by their forefathers. Ella, he knew had turned down offers to explore the Dark Land. Many Odorphins believed the death of her famous grandfather left its mark, a fear she often denied. Either way, her resolve would be tested this day as she faced the Entity on the plains of the twilight desert, the door between the Braccus Plain and the Dark Land.

Vincent flew alongside Ella and Constantine. They were unaware of his presence as they headed west across the great lakes to Braccus Plain. Its landscape was identical to their own Titan, an earlier version of their home, before life took hold. Constantine talked of his experiences in that turbulent hostile land as they flew toward their final destination, where faded light turned the Saturn light to grey.

The coldness of the colourless desert was immediate. Icy winds swept from the pitch black unknown of the Dark Land across a contoured plain of frozen methane and rock ice. Its hostility was on full show as cyclonic winds whipped the two voyagers. Ella said little. Perhaps her mind turned to her grandfather as she flew into the storm?

Her great-grandfather, Braccus Max had spent a good deal of his life exploring its mysteries. Today's voyagers had unlocked the science behind night vision, whereas Braccus Max journeyed the difficult terrain without it, guided more by the stars. Ella had told him of how she admired Braccus's courage. It was likely her admiration grew, as she felt firsthand the hostility of the terrain. The nitrogen storms were violent as they buffered them from the Dark Lands into the warmer winds of the Braccus Plain, creating intermittent lightning and thunder that filled the land with its charges. The millennium old wind storms were savage as they twisted and ripped contours across the Braccus Plain.

"The Entity entered this universe here and this is where it must leave it," said Constantine, studying his light web, and pinpointing the exact location.

"Where should we wait for it?" said Ella, gazing across the expanse.

"It doesn't matter where. He will seek us. He has Vincent, but I sense he wants another."

"Shall we use the same plan as on the Great Lakes?" she asked.

"We cannot. The Entity grows stronger and wiser every time we engage it. Every immersant I have administered has worked, but only for a short period of time. The only predictability about this creature is it quickly develops immunity."

They came to rest on the smooth methane and rock ice plain, both with light webs fully powered, protecting and compensating for the extreme conditions.

"It's coming for me?" Ella asked.

"It came to this universe because you made the crossover. Its instinct has been to find you, but it recognised Vincent's importance and took him first as his forebear took Jean. I survived the first Entity, but in losing Jean, I lost the way back to our Universe. If it fails to take you, it will want to maroon you here too."

"And still we know little of why. We only know that Vincent is somehow important to it."

Constantine appeared not to hear Ella. Perhaps he recalled the loss of his friend Jean who had placed trust in him. Uncertainty crept into his expression, as if he feared failing again.

"Maybe it's the natural order of things. The Entity knows only to correct what has been broken. It's instinctively drawn to us, of that I'm sure. Why it ignored us up until now is a mystery. I don't believe it's fear. There's a higher purpose at play here."

Ella held her gaze on Constantine for a time, as if seeking answers she did not have. "What is it you want me to do?"

"It will come for us soon. When that time comes, you strike it with a blow to weaken it only. At that moment I must read its reaction. When it is at its most vulnerable, I hope to be able to find its reasoning for this confrontation."

"Then shall I destroy it?"

"No, if I'm right about it, you must allow it to strike you at your most vulnerable," his gaze fixed on Ella now.

Ella looked away, toward the wind-swept plains, seemingly searching for her reply. Finally she turned toward Constantine.

"I've followed you without question because I believe in you, but now, you ask the impossible. I'd risk all to defeat it, but I'll not meekly allow it to take me without a fight. That is no plan," said Ella, refusing him for the first time, seemingly surprising Constantine.

"Then I'm afraid we have already lost." He opened his web and floated green light toward her. "Come. Follow me."

He led Ella toward a small rise of rock ice, offering shelter from the raging storm. "We can reserve our energy here. The battle is close and we will need all our strength." He gazed upon Ella as a proud father would, before pointing toward the frozen plain.

"The Braccus Plain was named in honour of your grandfather, for being the first to journey to the Dark Lands. His feat changed everything for our people. Braccus Max was the first to confront the old superstitions of our forefathers. Because of his efforts, a new age of voyaging followed, first to the Dark Lands and then the Solar System," he said, gazing toward the eternal darkness on the horizon. Constantine moved closer to the shelter, extinguishing his light web. He breathed the nitrogen air in with deep slow breaths, before feeling the smoothness of the rock ice.

"Your grandfather inspired me more than any Odorphin. Every time I have faced the dark abyss, I wondered if I had the courage to journey through it again and face my fears. If we get through this, I'll make the trek of the Braccus Plain again, but without the full protection of my light web."

Ella had heard the tale of her grandfather many times, but sitting on the vast plane, recalling his famous journey, seemingly touched her in a way she had not expected.

"He is one of the most courageous Odorphins I know. I have been blessed to know two," she said, brushing Constantine with rainbow light from her web. "He had the courage to be the first, to face the end of the world, as the Odorphins' culture believed it to be back then, just as you have faced the multiverse."

"Your Grandfather had a great vision of the future. The Entity too envisages a future. A future it protects. For some reason it will not share it with us. We have to find its vision, so that we understand and make the right choice."

"You don't believe it will kill me?"

"It has had many chances to kill you and Vincent already. Yet it holds back, as if it is uncertain."

"It would have taken us both if you hadn't intervened in the church."

"You think so? I struck it with a powerful force, true. But I don't believe I harmed it at all. It chose to retreat, but not from fear. I felt it made a calculated decision."

"Then it doesn't seek to destroy any of us?"

"I didn't say that. I made that mistake last time and it cost Jean his life. I misread the other Entity's intentions. Not this time. I know it intends to stop us. If I can find out why, I believe I can make the right choice."

Ella shook her head. "So many uncertainties."

"I would not ask this of you if I didn't believe it was our only course of action," said Constantine. A silence ensued.

Ella stood quietly, thoughtfully. "Your deeds and the spirit of Braccus Max loom large here. Three Odorphin generations have been shaped by its rugged beauty. I feel Braccus Max's energy close," she said, as she gazed at her mentor, Constantine.

"You and he have shaped my life and inspired me to walk in your footsteps."

Ella extinguished her light web, to feel the rock ice. She breathed in the exhilarating air and then sat closer to Constantine.

"Strange, but I feel Vincent's presence here, too."

Vincent stood near the two Odorphins, willing them to hear his pleas, but they were unable to feel his presence. Ella looked around her, seemingly willing Vincent to reveal his presence, before she spoke.

"I'll do as you ask." Ella said.

Vincent wanted to speak to them. But his feelings about the Entity were changing, too. Were they in a battle with a friend or foe? He was not so sure now. What he did know, was he carried secrets. He held a hidden ability that neither Hollow People nor Odorphin could penetrate. There remained one certainty. A battle was about to be fought that carried consequences for two worlds.

WHIRLPOOL

THE BLASTING WINDS DROPPED, as if even Titan trembled briefly at a disturbance high in the western sky. A shimmering force split the deep nitrogen filled clouds with a force that dislodged heavy rains. Droplets a metre in length fell from the thick grey cumulus and froze instantly as they crashed to the rock ice and methane plain, forming concentric circles on the frozen ground, from which steam vapour rose a metre high. Vincent flew not with the Entity, but above it, now. Inexplicably, it had released him, not to Vincent's universe, but to another place between universes, perhaps another dimension. He wanted to speak to his friends and tell them of his experiences, but they appeared unable to see or hear him. His twilight view of the plains was blurred by the droplets. The icy plains and the thick cumulus created two mirror images, connected by the fountain-like flow.

Vincent felt the 'topsy-turvy' world. Its misty haze resembled a sunbeam in the shadowy world as he descended to the ice plain. Constantine and Ella came to view. They stood together, tall and proud. They were in Odorphin form, their light webs fully exposed, seemingly ready for confrontation. The Entity drew form, building into the human shape of Jean. With a single raising of his arms, Jean drew a lightning charge from the storm, crashing it to the ground nearby, revealing his new powers.

Constantine retaliated, striking the Entity with the power of a solar flare. His force smashed the Entity deep into the plain, near the border of the Dark Land. He followed, sucked along by the whirlpool force he had created, ready to strike again and again across the twilight of the plain into the pitch black Dark Land.

Ella sat alone, gazing to the night sky as it intermittently flashed fireballs from Constantine's relentless strikes, unaware that Vincent stood beside her.

A final strike lit up the Dark Land for the first time in a millennium, as if a rogue comet had crashed through its weak gravity, spreading heat across the land. Then the flashes ceased, signalling a potential outcome. Ella held her gaze toward the night sky, hope of victory in her eyes, but a hint of fear, too. Her hopes were quickly dashed as the Entity returned, not Constantine.

"How many more concoctions have you left?" it said, sensing Ella was protected by a new immersant.

"Where is Constantine?" Ella demanded. The Entity did not reply.

Ella drew her light web and struck the Entity across the face. Jean's face burned from the blow as if a laser flame cut a fine line across his cheek. The Entity was forced to retreat. Anger burned in its eyes as it summoned all its strength to control the pain. Then it made the wound disappear, seemingly returning to full strength.

"Any more tricks?" it said, gloating at its rapid conquest over Ella's immersant.

Ella desperately struck the Entity repeatedly with all the force she could summon. But her blows had little effect. The Entity effortlessly brushed her strikes away, before pushing its hand through Ella's web force as if through butter. He grasped her slender neck and began to choke the life from her.

The Entity turned to Alan, showing it alone had the power to see him.

"Where am I? Why can't I help my friends?" Alan cried.

"You could if you chose to," it replied, taunting Alan to respond.

Ella could not see Vincent, but she called out to him. "Leave this place if you can, Vincent. You can't help me."

The Entity held Ella high above him as he slowly choked her to death.

"Don't your kind say that you will sacrifice all for the one you love?"

Vincent could not find the words to reply.

"It seems not. So now watch your pitiful lover die, human," it said, mocking Vincent.

Vincent watched helplessly before his fear was replaced by anger. His body reacted to a surge of power that filled his aura. He stood tall and approached the Entity with a fixed gaze that transmitted his rage. He wanted to attack, but how? He desperately searched for a point of weakness as Ella neared death. Her light web was all but extinguished, except for the remaining power surrounding her neck. If that was extinguished she would surely die.

Then Vincent saw something. The light that surrounded her throat streamed from the skies in all directions. An infinite array of laser light beams lit Titan, at first confusing Vincent. But then the rays merged, forming infinite scenes of the two combatants. Some ended in Ella's death, some her victory. The universe filled with infinite scenarios, like his dream when he was held captive by the Entity.

Then he saw Constantine in the distance. He instantly knew Constantine saw the same images. Could Constantine see him? Vincent shrugged his shoulders at Constantine, not sure what the complex montage of scenes meant, but then he remembered Constantine's words – trust your instincts. The immersants extended his field of vision to many dimensions and he instinctively chose the one he needed. In that universe, he had one hand stretched skyward, summoning a power emanating from Saturn. Vincent suddenly found himself in that scene, standing with one arm raised, summoning the strength he needed to face his enemy. A super nova of light streamed around his aura powering his entire body. He effortlessly broke the Entity's grasp on Ella as he struck it with all his power. The Entity slumped to the ground, its attention fully on Vincent now.

"So, you've found your purpose," it said, as it approached Vincent in a threatening manner. Vincent instantly reacted, grasping the Entity by the throat and applying a vice-like pressure.

"I know you now. I no longer fear you. But you will fear me," said Vincent, his aura lit by radiant light.

For a brief second the Entity smiled, as if it wished to die. But its expression changed as did its shape, turning to mist before flying comet-like from Titan's surface. Constantine prepared to follow it, before Vincent called out to him.

"Don't follow. Leave it. We need to talk," he said.

"I know I can defeat this creature," said Constantine, anger in his voice, ready to seek vengeance for Ella.

"No. The battle is not what it seeks? Please!" Vincent pleaded.

"This monster nearly killed Ella, as it killed your uncle!"

"I don't think that's true. And I don't think you believe that's true, either. Do you?"

Constantine made no response, instead turning to his human form, revealing unbridled anger. "I have given this monster the benefit of the doubt too many times, but for you, I will make one last attempt. Let's talk. But if you can't convince me, I'll track this beast and confront it. You realise it will soon have immunity to our new immersant?"

"That's the one certainty. Its power is beyond ours."

"You don't know that. You nearly defeated it just now. What have you learned that has changed your view about it?"

Vincent wanted to ease Constantine's doubts, but the truth was he couldn't be certain, himself. All he knew was the Entity made threats, even carried out violent acts, but he did not follow through with any of them. His violent act against Ella concerned him, but even then it appeared it was challenging Vincent to act.

"It showed me its home."

"On Titan?"

"Yes. In the Dark Lands."

"Does that mean you should suddenly trust its motives?"

"No. But it needn't have shown me its home. It could have killed me at any moment. But it chose not to."

"What did you see on its homeland?"

"More than the Dark Lands. It allowed me to see with its eyes."

"And..."

"It showed me the forces of the multiverse surround us everywhere. Just as we both saw our alternate lives stretch out to perhaps infinity. That's how I chose the right way to defend Ella. You saw that too, didn't you?"

"Yes. I did. What I and you don't know is if it was real or of the Entity's making. It could have been a ruse."

"We can never be sure. As I can't be sure that what you show me is real or not. But I accept you show me in good faith, so that you may teach me. What other reason could you have? Your power is beyond mine."

"So, you believe the Entity is acting in good faith? It has threatened us all. Look at Ella! Look at you. You're locked in another dimension."

"I didn't even realise what had happened until I tried to talk to Ella."

"It removed you from your universe to what is known as a subtle dimension, less than an atom removed from the universe you perceive, but a place where light cannot reach."

"Why did the Entity do this to me?"

"That is truly a mystery, for it seems it put itself at risk, by doing that."

"I was able to attack it?"

"Yes. But it would appear separating you from Ella, more important than its safety. It's logic, I'm afraid, is unpredictable and unfathomable."

Constantine walked over to Ella and waved violet light over her resting body.

"Is she okay?"

"She'll be fine with rest. I only hope that the Entity give us that time? This is the risk we take by not acting now."

"It could have killed us all, long before now. Instead it has drawn out powers in me that I did not believe I had. It wants something from the three of us. That's our challenge. To find it."

Constantine continued to brush Ella's weak body with his light web. For the first time, Vincent saw tears form around Constantine's eyes.

"Ella is like a daughter to me. We have worked together for many Saturnine years, achieving so much. My work would mean nothing if I lost her."

Vincent walked over to Constantine and held his shoulder in an assuring manner, before speaking.

"I love Ella, too. Trust me Constantine, I wouldn't propose we wait, unless I believed it offered a better chance to survive. I learnt much in my short time with the Entity and I admit that I'm not certain about what I believe, but I am certain that if we treat this as a contest, we will lose."

Constantine shook his head in resignation. "Very well, we will rest here and recuperate, before talking more of our next move. Go rest for a while, so that I can heal Ella. She is responding well. Another hour should see her return to full health. I just hope we are allowed that time."

All three lay in the quiet of the Dark Land. One light web shone, illuminating the sheltered space where they rested. The other web, Ella's remained in darkness. Constantine sat quietly, gently fanning Ella with his light web, like a doting father, all the while looking Vincent's way as he rested.

"You look so much like Jean at times."

Vincent nodded and smiled briefly, before gazing beyond Constantine, out to the darkness. "Perhaps Jean will return one day, if we could..."

"The only thing that will return is the Entity and soon," interrupted Constantine.

Vincent nodded. "I will do all I can to protect Ella, but I still don't understand why the Entity let me see the multiverse. Why would it show me such wonders, only to attack Ella shortly after?"

"It thinks of many lives, not just one," replied Constantine.

"I know you from my many lives, don't I?"

Constantine smiled, knowingly." Your instincts serve you well. Your race doesn't yet realise the depth of your imprint on the universes, a depth I discovered in my journeys. When I arrived in your universe, everything happened as I told you. I explored Titan, then the Solar System, before coming to Earth and discovering your uncle and then you. What I didn't tell you was that your universe was not the first I visited. I have met you in another universe."

Vincent had changed in so many ways, this last week. He would have considered Constantine's words as fanciful before he headed overseas. But, he had seen other universes himself.

"You travelled to my future?"

"In a way yes. But not your future here. I travelled to your future on another Earth, in another Universe. As you are beginning to see, your life is so much more than what you experience here and now. You're part of a greater cosmos, linked by forces we don't and may never fully understand. But when I crossed the universe, I was drawn to you. For like Braccus Max was the first of our kind to voyage the Dark Lands, you were the first human to successfully cross the universes."

"So why here with me now? Why not with the other?"

"I have seen two of your lives, but it's possible you have an infinite number of lives. Each life is equally important to the whole. But it was you the Entity sought and you alone. That is why I have acted against the Entity in your universe. For a reason I don't yet understand, you are important to it. So I believed it important you experience more than any other, to experience our race, to experience our history and yours, to face the Entity, to face yourself."

"To face myself? What do you mean?"

"My holographic image, my voice, is a copy of you on that other universe. I wanted you to be the first to experience part of your true nature. I believe you have many lives across an infinite number of universes, all different, yet bound by a common purpose."

Vincent pondered Constantine's words. "To travel the multiverse?"

"I believe that is your unique destiny. All of these lives are what makes you your true self. It also seems to be a part of what the Entities fear."

Vincent wondered whether he would fulfil such a destiny. His own life was perhaps in the balance, for all he knew.

"So if the Entity kills me, do my other lives die, too?"

"I don't know for certain. I believe it will send a ripple through the multiverse. How large we can never know. The only evidence I have is that Jean's death affected one other of his lives – erased, it seems."

"So there's a price for crossing the multiverse," said Vincent.

"For every action, there's a reaction. We can never know who or what we will affect. We may unwittingly destroy whole civilisations. We may build new ones. But that's part of life. It is filled with random events and random consequences. But does that mean we should not investigate our world, so that we may learn?"

Vincent deliberated Constantine's words as he looked out to the horizon for inspiration. "Perhaps, that is our mistake?"

"What do you mean?"

"Instead of searching for the solution in our universe, we have to look in the Entity's."

"I have tried to communicate with both Entities and on every occasion, I met with hostility," said Constantine, frustration in his tone.

"Precisely. Its hostility toward you is clear, as it has been to us all. But it hasn't harmed any of us. We don't even know if Jean was harmed."

"Go on."

"It claims we cannot die. Perhaps it seeks something from us that cannot be explained in words."

"It seems a strange way to communicate, given it has mastered language. What can't be described in words?"

"We say on Earth that actions speak louder than words. Perhaps our words are limited to one universe and can't adequately explain perceptions beyond that. The Entity has already claimed time is irrelevant to it. So would not the concept of life or death be irrelevant also? Perhaps it senses something deeper in our actions, a kind of highly developed instinct."

"Vincent, this creature probably killed your uncle. It tortured you for much of your young life. How do you intend to change that?"

"That's just it. We can't change it. We have to somehow understand it. Let's think about its actions this past week. It has made veiled threats to me, all the while warning me about you and Ella. It cornered me in Venice."

"I released you, remember?"

"Perhaps. It cornered Ella and I in the church in Geneva. Ella defended me."

"At great risk to herself. She could have died, but again, I released her."

"Yes, twice you defended us and both times it retreated rather than attack you."

"I held new immersants, both times. It had to retreat so that it could develop an immunity."

"Didn't Ella and I carry the same immersants in our bodies?"

"True. But your powers were only beginning to develop. You didn't know how to control or use the immersants effectively."

"And Ella?"

Constantine stood up abruptly, seemingly agitated, before he walked over to Ella.

"Well?"

He continued to ignore Vincent, choosing to fan Ella with his light web. Violet hues wafted over her sleeping body, seemingly soothing her as she reacted to the rays.

"She is gaining strength. Another half hour and I will wake her," said Constantine, extinguishing his web light and returning to Vincent.

"Are you keeping something from me?" Vincent probed.

Constantine did not immediately reply, instead choosing to breathe in the Titan atmosphere.

"This atmosphere is younger than our atmosphere back home. Ella particularly misses our home. She may not show it, but it has been very hard on her."

"I hoped I made a difference, but I was naive to think that she could love me," said Vincent.

"She does love you, in a way, but not how you would ever understand. But you are special to her. Why do you think I have been leaving you both on this journey?"

"You want our love to develop?"

"Of course. Your developing bond has been a surprise to both Ella and I. Our race values love in the universe, just as yours does. It should never be stifled."

"I know well enough to sense that there is something wrong. Tell me," said Vincent, almost demanding. Constantine appeared torn as he pondered his reply.

"Vincent, think this through. You are not even in our universe. You reside in another dimension, put there by our foe. I could be talking directly to the Entity, for all I know. Can you be sure that I am not?"

"No, I can't. But I think our time of developing strategies as if we are at war with this Entity are long gone. Don't you?" Constantine threw his hands in the air, as a sign of resignation.

"Very well. I hope you're right, Vincent. Our last chance has perhaps passed us anyway."

"So tell me what is wrong with Ella?"

"Wrong is not exactly the best way to describe her situation. Look, like humans, Odorphins' have different body types, capabilities and weaknesses. For one, I can see you in another dimension, whereas Ella cannot."

"Why not?"

"Why do some Earthlings understand science, whereas many don't? I think you have misinterpreted the capabilities of our light webs. They do not immediately give us superhuman capabilities. They provide us a more seamless way to interpret information, but if we do not study, as you do to understand science, we develop less capabilities. Ella is my student, remember. She has learned much in her young life, but she has many Saturn years of study to reach her full capability."

"Then why are you concerned about Ella?"

"The journey to cross a multiverse is dangerous and comes at a cost. I lost some capabilities in my journey to your universe, as did Ella."

"Life threatening?"

"In a way, yes."

"What do you mean?"

"I have had to carefully manage the dosages of every immersant she and you have taken. If I had given you the same dose as either Ella or I, you most certainly would have died."

"You told me that we took the same immersant."

"Well, technically, we did, but the dosages varied."

Vincent shook his head, showing his displeasure.

"Yes alright, I lied to you, but for good reason. The point is, that Ella was given far less potent doses than I."

"Did she know?"

"No. For if Ella knew, she would have to be made aware of her situation."

"It could kill her?"

"No. But she could face a life sentence. She may not be able to return to her home."

"Why wouldn't you tell her the truth?"

"If Ella knew that, she would willingly sacrifice herself, so that I could return home. Her loyalty to me and the Odorphin cause knows no bounds. I love Ella as daughter. I won't allow that to happen. I didn't want the Entity to know that either, hence you see the terrible risk we are taking, by talking about this."

Their conversation was interrupted by the sound of Ella, calling out as she slept. Constantine immediately went to her side. "She's dreaming. She's okay. I will wake her soon."

Vincent was about to ask more before the pitch black sky filled with a streak of light, streaming across the sky like a comet. It struck the surface not far from where they lay. A mist like substance began to take form. Then the shadowy swirling mass of gases revealed the Entity. It had grown bigger and was now spherical in shape. The Entity no longer had a human form. It looked more a miniature Jupiter, its grey mass swirling and rotating. Snake like currents flashed across its surface giving off light from the friction of its rapid movement.

The Entity was some hundred metres away and closing as it hovered toward them, massive in size, some ten metres in diameter. Mist emanated from its sphere, surrounding the three and filling the area with fog. Then it stopped some fifty metres from them as it appeared to be examining its situation. Constantine woke Ella.

"Stay behind me," he demanded his light web outstretched.

He had reverted to Odorphin form, standing between Ella and the Entity. Their deadly battle was about to commence. Vincent wanted to join him, but Vincent signalled him not to.

"Try to understand it," said Vincent.

"I will only defend myself, unless I believe it means us harm. You have played your part. It is my turn. On this night you will see the passion of the Odorphin spirit. I will fight to my last breath if it attacks," he said, a warrior ready for battle. His smooth inner body looked less blurred as if he had created carbon armour with his light web. Constantine stood three metres tall and then taller as he levitated higher from the rock ice. He cautiously circled the Entity like a moon orbiting a planet.

The Entity made no sounds, as if they sparred in another dimension. It had moved to within twenty metres of Ella, seemingly signalling its intent. Constantine responded, circling closer to the Entity, halving the distance between them, making the Entity stand its ground.

"We mean you no harm," said Constantine.

"Help us understand what you seek," added Vincent.

A deadly still ensued like two gun-slingers daring each other to draw, before the Entity broke the deadlock.

Waves of energy rippled from its shadowy sphere, like horizontal lightning, striking Constantine's light web. He absorbed its strike then deflected the force back into the giant sphere. Shock waves emanated from the point of entry, before it fell back into the mist, fully absorbed.

"You don't have to attack. Constantine means you no harm," Vincent implored.

The Entity ignored Vincent's plea and struck at Constantine a second time. The showdown had begun.

Constantine built his energy as he moved from an upright to horizontal position, hovering a metre from the ground. His web cloak glistened like finely cut diamond, glowing like an aerodynamic missile ready for launch. A power emanated from his web that sent waves of light cascading across the Dark Land, making it look more like Mercury than the dark side of a moon.

Vincent shielded his ears from the roar, but dared not move his gaze from the battle. He expected a charge of super nova proportions, but instead Constantine appeared to move at lightning speed through the Entity and back again, repeating the action again. The only tell-tale sign that he had attacked it were the ripples of coloured energy that charged like a lightning storm. Its concentric circles rotated in the centre of the Entity's gaseous mass, like a gaping wound.

The giant sphere hovered lower to the ground. Its only movement was a slow rotation that matched its adversary's as he continued to circle like a wrestler ready to strike. The silence extended. Constantine held attack position, waiting for a small opening in the Entity's formidable defence.

The Entity suddenly feigned an attack, sending waves toward him, less powerful, more a ruse as it seemingly vanished from its precarious position. A micro second later, Constantine vanished before Vincent's eyes too, he believed in pursuit. The arena of battle lost its intense light, leaving Vincent in an eerie silence, wondering if the Entity had developed immunity to his newly formed powers. Feelings of vulnerability overwhelmed him as he tried to use his immersant powers, to communicate with Ella, but she was still too weak to move, let alone sense him. He could only observe Ella's fate from his twilight world.

A noise suddenly echoed from above that heightened his fear. The Entity's misty force flashed with sparks, lighting the dark hollow, turning night to day. To Vincent's surprise, Ella responded to its presence with confidence in her commands.

"This is where your life ends its reign of torture," she said. With one powerful surge of force from her web, Ella made good her threat, holding the Entity like a limp rag doll, seemingly powerless to stop her.

"Release Vincent or die with me," Ella threatened. The Entity made no counter threat, instead yielding to Ella's demand. Vincent detected no change, but Ella turned her gaze in his direction, showing she could now see him.

Then, with one motion, she struck the Entity with a laser like wave of energy, forcing it back across the cold plains of Titan, until it appeared just a small fading light on the horizon. Ella held her gaze until a second power source – Constantine – struck the Entity again with violent force, cannoning it at near light speed from Titan's atmosphere.

"Have you destroyed it?" Vincent asked.

Ella held her gaze in the direction of the sphere's path along an infrared view not afforded Vincent, not responding for a time before she felt it safe to do so.

"The final immersant has worked. We developed it from your blood after you were taken by the Entity. It was our last chance before it gained total immunity. We have control of it for a short period of time," she said, waving her light web across Vincent's face, almost as if a final gesture.

"How will you kill it?"

"We must strike it at light speed and destroy every one of its atoms, so that it can't form mass again. Constantine is drawing it toward Jupiter before using its gravity to sling shot it back toward Titan. I must strike it at equal velocity. Then it will be left vulnerable."

"For a final force to shatter its atoms?"

"We don't possess such a force," she said, reverting to human form, her web now a human hand, stroking him gently.

"Then what?"

"Soon, with luck, we will be free of it, Vincent."

"Tell me, Ella. How will you destroy it?"

"I'll tell you soon, but for now you must wait," she said.

Vincent laid his head back against the rock ice, his eyes firmly fixed on Ella's beauty. But it was a beauty he knew to be manufactured by an alien force.

"We shared the last year as friends and one eventful week that may change the course of history for both our worlds." Ella said. Both smiled.

Ella looked skywards to the darkness, but Vincent knew she saw beyond the thick clouds that blocked the star filled sky.

"How long?"

"Soon."

"I thought we could reason with it, but I was wrong. It is filled with deceit. I want to face our foe with you, not cowering in the shadows."

"I can't allow that."

"You must, if you want me to be everything you claim I will be," said Vincent, determined.

Ella thought to reply but embraced him instead. "The risk..."

Vincent pressed his fingers on Ella's lips, silencing her reply, before he stood closer. "I will only become what you say is my destiny if we face the Entity together. Only then will we seal our bond across two universes."

Ella studied Vincent for a time, seemingly looking for any reluctance on his part, before resigning herself to accept Vincent's wishes. She drew a final immersant from her pocket and placed it in Vincent's open palm, before closing her hand around Vincent's and activating the orb. A crimson light cascaded from the orb, surrounding them in the radiant light.

"Two universes," she agreed.

Their lips met as two lovers who had shared a lifetime together. In a way they had. They both willingly embraced the fleeting, loving warmth, until all too soon, their lips parted.

"I love you, Ella," Vincent said, kissing her soft cheeks, knowing he may never caress her again.

Ella smiled warmly. "Then let's show our adversary what love means," she replied, before softly kissing his lips.

Affection gave way to the task as they flew toward the Entity. Ella transformed to her Odorphin form. Vincent flew beside her, his radiant light aura shining in the darkness. They hovered low to the ground, their force building, soon to disappear in a motion so quick no human eye could see. Their speed built to an intensity sufficient to destroy their adversary, or die trying.

Ella had calculated their position to the precision of a pulsar star. She looked to Vincent, who nodded, confirming he could see her calculations.

"You hear us, now?" Ella communicated telepathically.

"Yes. I have been able to hear you and Constantine since the Entity captured me," he replied, telepathically, also.

"We hoped that would happen, but we did not know. Your abilities are growing with every immersant. The three of us can finally communicate as Odorphins."

"I understand the plans on your light web, too. Images. Many images."

"You are tapping into our light webs."

"Will these abilities only stay with me while the immersants remain in my system?"

"There will be some permanent changes. What that will be, we can't be sure," said Ella, before raising her hand to signal Vincent to remain quiet.

Vincent saw the myriad of images that Ella and Constantine now shared. He saw that Constantine was orchestrating the coming collision. It almost felt as if he were masterminding the attack, not Constantine. Constantine held the position of the three fast moving objects clear in his mind, precision crucial. The Entity was held in place by both his and Ella's force, travelling at two hundred thousand kilometres per second as it rounded the gravitational pull of Jupiter. By the time it reached Constantine it would have accelerated to nearly the speed of light. At that point two forces would meet in a final fateful collision.

Their plan was in place. Constantine's trajectory accelerated towards the largest of the Galilean moons Ganymede, velocity near light speed. By his calculation, the Entity had no time to develop immunity to the immersant that held it captive, locked in a journey to oblivion. But his calculations were based on its past adaption speeds. Was it more powerful than before? There was every likelihood its power had grown and with it, its capability to adapt ever faster. He had to draw a second path, one it would not consider.

Ellatine Braccus Max and Vincent had reached near light speed, perfect control as they locked on to the speeding missile that approached them at the exact same speed. Two points of matter were about to collide with such force they'd achieve singularity. Billions of atoms that made them both would be crushed to such a density that every atom would be squeezed out of their normal existence, never to return. The Entity's entrapment was maintained. It came down to its ability to break free of the immersant code that controlled it. If it did, all would be lost. Calculations maintained pinpoint positioning of the coming collision.

"Twenty Earth minutes," said Ella, as she turned to Vincent. "Remember, focus your mind on the photon that you are riding. Do not think human thoughts."

Vincent rode the light wave with ease, the opposite of his first fateful trials. His experience riding sound waves seemed an eternity removed. He knew that his life was just one cog in a wheel that perhaps stretched out to an infinite number of lives that made him who he was. He faced this confrontation for Ella and their multiverse of existences. The future would be handed to his many lives to forge change to the multiverse – his destiny.

Fifteen minutes. "Remain on the trajectory set; no matter the circumstance, do not waver," said Constantine, telepathically.

All three focused solely on enacting their plan, to finish what had been started, their belief in their voyages filled with conviction.

Ten minutes. There was an eerie silence before the inevitable fire storm, before they all sited the approaching missile through Ella's light web images. They were exactly on course for their fateful meeting.

"I opened the multiverse, through which the Entity and I entered. I am responsible for closing it." Ella said.

"We are responsible," added Vincent.

Five minutes. Constantine's trajectory varied from the set plan. "I have to alter my course. The Entity's immunity to the immersant may be achieved, outcome unpredictable. Hold your course, Ella." Constantine said, as doubt swept into their carefully laid plan.

The only certainty left was that atoms would be merged beyond repair, forming singularity, melded with such a force that electrons would simply disappear, allowing the protons and neutrons to be crushed into another physics, no longer matter as the 'mathmatica' had described it. But the Entity was not born of the mathmatica world. The disappearance of the atoms would occur, but to where and what was the unknown.

A minute remained. "I'm making a slight speed shift. We both may need to engage it," said Constantine, building to a light speed approach.

Vincent looked to Ella for perhaps the last time. Images transferred at the speed of light in that final minute. Calculations of their impending collision were interspersed with Ella's memories of her year on Earth. She had formed a friendship in another universe with a human – a friendship destined. For if not, how had the human language crossed the largest of divides? Odorphins lived their life on Titan, never knowing humans, yet everywhere were signs of humanity, from the Great Lakes to the Great Escarpment Mountains, human names, made by the discoverers of the mathmatica. Names forged by her forefathers, replicated in an unknown parallel universe. How could this be, in a world of randomness? There had to be a connection between these two races that spanned a millennia - the bond of evolution - a bond Vincent believed worth dying for.

Final seconds seemed to stretch out into a lifetime of memories floating among the collage of images from Constantine and Ella's light webs. They approached light speed now, holding speed and course to a pulsar accuracy. Do not veer...hold...hold...

Then as they approached their fateful collision, time suddenly slowed to nearly a standstill. Vincent could clearly see the Entity as they were no more than twenty metres from it. What he saw shocked him. The Entity was in human form, but his identity was hidden by a long flowing robe and hood, not dissimilar to that of a religious monk. He, Ella and Constantine were all locked in a slow motion momentum toward the same target, the Entity. Within ten metres, the Entity removed its hood, revealing the face of an elderly man, who Vincent did not immediately recognise. Where its identity surprised Vincent, its next action shocked him to his core. The monk seemed unconcerned about the forthcoming collision, as he spread his arms wide smiling as he uttered a single word.

"Welcome"

Then instantaneously, Vincent and his two friends' momentum returned to near light speed. Contact was made between four forces, lighting up the solar system like a super nova.

And darkness swept Vincent's world.

13

A New World

VINCENT WOKE DISORIENTED AND unsure of what had unfolded. He remembered the approaching firestorm and then the mysterious monk, before he blacked out. He looked around him, then realised he was back on Titan. Had Ella returned him before the collision? Had he died? Why had the Entity said welcome? He was alone and needed answers! But all he could do was wait. It felt an eternity as he held his gaze toward the emptiness of Titan's dark sky, but then a single comet-like flash appeared, signalling someone's return. Had they failed? Had they survived? His mind filled with dread as to the outcome. Then a glimmer of hope rose as the light approached, close to where he lay. It was slower than a comet – much slower. A light descended through the thick Titan atmosphere, clear to Vincent's view, distinctly human in shape. He considered hiding, but where? His life would be over anyway if they failed. He waited, resigned to his fate, eyes locked on the glow as it descended further toward the rock ice where he lay.

Long minutes passed. At times, Vincent was convinced the light was the Entity as mist enshrouded the glowing object. But it was the thick atmosphere of Titan, playing tricks on his willing mind. A shape formed, reassuringly Odorphin, the smaller of the two -

Ella. Fear built in Vincent's mind as he believed she harboured bad news.

"Where is Constantine?" Asked Vincent, finding the silence unbearable.

The sombre Odorphin sat for a time, gazing up to the sky, before finally speaking. "I don't know," said Ella, emotion in her tone.

Vincent hid his feelings of joy for Ella's return. "Thank heavens you're safe!" Before fear again returned. Were they all doomed? Was the Entity simply too powerful?

"Did Constantine survive?"

Ella transformed from Odorphin shape to human before responding. Vincent could see the hurt in her eyes, now. She maintained her vigilance overhead. But hope slowly faded for Constantine, as the sky remained dark. Reluctantly she sat with Vincent, her head laid back against the rock ice, resigned to an outcome she didn't want to believe true, as she recounted what she thought happened.

"We were on course, less than a minute to collision. I could see its approach. I could taste its death. Our plan was perfect. Constantine was to be behind Jupiter at the point of collision, protected from the blast. But he changed his trajectory and accelerated toward the Entity. Also..." She held her words, too choked with emotion to say more, before Vincent comforted her, drawing out her full account.

"He returned you to Titan, Vincent."

"We were all close to impact. But then our light speed was suddenly slowed to a snail's pace," Vincent recalled.

"Yes, the Entity found an antidote to our immersant and regained control at the last micro-second."

"It chose human shape. A hooded man who looked like a monk."

"Was the human familiar to you?" Ella asked.

"Yes. It was David, but he was much older." Ella nodded her head in agreement before she continued her recollection of events.

"We were as close as that boulder. Then suddenly it vanished. I stayed on the course though, in case it was a trick, holding my line until I fell into Jupiter's gravity. Only then did I dare to contact Constantine. There was no reply. I swept all areas of space where they could be but there was no sign of either. They have both vanished from this universe."

"So he could still be alive?"

"I don't know. Even at light speed they couldn't have passed the detection range of my light web, so they're no longer in this universe. The only good news is that the crossing remains open. They crossed universes through another portal, but where I'll never know. It occurred after my failed collision but before reaching Jupiter. During that time, every atom of Constantine and the Entity vanished from this universe."

"What do you think happened?"

"There's the possibility Constantine planned it all along, so that we both might live," said Ella, her sadness deep.

"There's also the possibility that we still remain in danger. The monk said 'welcome', as if it had always been in control."

Vincent's sadness gave way to guilt, for having doubted Constantine. At times, he had believed there was some truth in the Entity's accusations, when it was possible Constantine had sacrificed his life for him.

"What now?"

Ella sat beside him and leaned back against the rock ice, eyes closed, not answering, as if she was not sure herself, still shocked at the loss. She stood finally, walking from Vincent, eyes gazing upward, re-checking for any sign of life, before letting go all hope.

"We return...to Earth."

Vincent grieved for Constantine and his selfless sacrifice, if that had occurred. He wanted to tell Ella of the discussions and plans they made while she was recovering from the Entity's attack on her, but he dared not while their situation remained tenuous. Had he misread the Entity, thus exposing Constantine to the danger and possibly his death? The latter appeared more likely, given Ella's disturbing news.

"Are you sure there is no sign of them? No trace?"

Ella nodded, to sad to respond. Unanswered questions haunted Vincent's mind. Why would the Entity share insights with him? Was it a mere ploy, to catch his friends off-guard? It seemed senseless that a superior being such as the Entity would entertain such thoughts. At least for now, Vincent no longer needed to be vigilant against its attack. Finally, exhaustion gave way to slumber. His body slid from the rock ice wall to the flat ground. His last memory was the cold flat surface of Titan, its darkness lit by the soft glow of Ella's light web.

Vincent woke. His head was hard against the earth. But rather than rock ice, he felt soft grass parklands and the gentle slope of rolling hills. The air was filled with the sounds of life. Pigeons cooed above as a young squirrel scampered down a tree trunk that sheltered Vincent from the sunny spring day. The squirrel observed Vincent for a time. Its small front paws rubbed together as if feeding on food. Its brown fur glistened with flecks of silver and its tail was filled with fine silver hairs, shining in the sun's rays. The little creature tired of Vincent as he offered it no food. So it scampered back up the tree, only to be chased by another larger squirrel, protecting its patch of the parkland.

Two pigeons perched together above him, lightly pecking each other's beaks and necks of grey, purple and green hue feathers, in lovers embrace, preening each other with complete devotion. Vincent soaked up the energy of the peaceful park land, so full of life and sound. The park's gentle rolling hills stretched to a water line he recognised. Surrounded by snow peaked mountains in the distance, the crystal clear still waters of Lake Lucerne lapped gently on the grassy shores.

White clouds drifted high in the blue sky. Everything was peaceful until a small moving object approached from on high. The familiar shape of Ella, light web extended, flew toward him, descending from the cloud and hovering just above the lake's rippleless waters, to finally rest at his side. She too looked relaxed. It appeared that the pain of her loss was less intense. She sat beside him, gently stroking his hair with her hand before speaking.

"How are you feeling?"

"Rested, as if I slept a hundred hours. But we're in Lucerne. I don't remember any of the journey," said Vincent confused.

"You'll need more rest to fully recover. Your ordeal with the Entity and the many immersants, took much of your energy."

"No sign of them?"

"They're gone from this world."

"I dreamt of Constantine," said Vincent, hoping to provide some hope for Ella.

"A good dream, I hope," said Ella, light heartedly.

"It was so vivid, unlike any dream I have had before."

"Was the Entity in your dream, too?"

"At first, no. The dream reminded me of the visions I had when the Entity held me captive."

"Were you on Earth or Titan?"

"Titan, I think. Not in your lands, but in a vast, twilight expanse."

"The Dark Land?"

"Based on your descriptions, I'd say it was. Yes. I was walking alongside Constantine. It was bitterly cold and the twilight was rapidly fading. We were using the stars to guide us to our destination. But then I told Constantine that I knew where we were, because the Entity had taken me there. We walked for what felt like hours, deeper into the darkening desert, until we arrived at a large mountain. That was where the Entity lived, or so I believed. We walked together into a large cavern at the base of the mountain. It was pitch black, so Constantine lit the cavern with his light web.

The cavern was empty, so I told him we should leave it and climb to the top of the mountain. But he shook his head and told me that it was not empty. He cried out into the empty cave, his words echoing into the distance."

"Did you see anything, then?"

"No, and I told Constantine so. But he shook his head again and told me that the Entity's presence was all around us and only his immersant saved us from being swept up in their barbs."

"He said their barbs?" Ella asked.

"Yes, I remember that clearly. It was as if he saw an army of its kind, but he felt protected. Then he disappeared from the cave, but I heard his voice."

You have the power to see me now, no matter where I travel," he said and I could see him. I felt so close, I could touch him. I felt what he felt, as if I were him," said Vincent.

"What did Constantine feel?" Ella asked, hope in her tone.

"Constantine felt that he struck the force exactly as he planned, accelerating at greater than light speed into the Entity. In fact, the Entity had not manoeuvred in any way, even though it had overcome Constantine's last immersant. Their collision had obliterated all matter, leaving dark matter, only."

"Where is he?"

"He floats in a large sphere, somewhere in deep space. Ribbon-shaped streams of laser beams surround it. He touched the borders of the sphere with his light web, causing ripples to spread over the sphere, before slowly fading."

"A force field?" Ella asked.

"I don't know. But I suppose it was, for he felt trapped. At first, he thought he was alone. But then the Entity's mist appeared. It moved toward him, so he struck it with his light web."

"So, he remains in danger?"

"I'm not sure." Vincent shook his head, as if he were trying to remember the events that unfolded."

"Try to recall, Vincent. It could be important," said Ella. Vincent continued to shake his head, but then he started to laugh to himself.

"That's the funny thing. I can remember every word spoken between them. Is it the immersant?"

"Yes. Constantine has given you a very powerful immersant. Your aura is as strong as my light web, now. Perhaps even stronger, given I cannot reach him, whereas you can." Vincent continued to shake his head, almost disbelieving he could have such powers.

"Describe what happened, as if you were Constantine. He was trapped and the Entity appeared...." Ella recalled, encouraging Vincent to describe Constantine's situation. "Yes, I remember the Entity's first words," said Vincent, as he recollected the events.

"You cannot harm me now, Odorphin."

They circled in the sphere, sparring as if in a deadly standoff, feigning attack and defence, waiting for an opening.

"If I can't harm you, why do you defend yourself?" Constantine asked.

"I'm not defending myself. I defend this sphere."

"Where are we?"

"At the beginning of everything."

"The multiverse?"

"A portal? Strike the sphere too hard and you could unwittingly plunge us into another universe."

Constantine cautiously streamed light from his web toward the sphere, observing the ripple of light that weaved in a seemingly infinite thread.

"Strike it there," said the Entity, as it ran a fine mist toward a particular cord of laser-light. Constantine obliged, holding a cautious eye on his adversary. A portal opened to an event he was familiar with.

It was a scene of their most famous - Braccus Max.

"He is venturing deep into the Dark Lands, opening the bridge between Baryon matter and Dark matter," said the Entity, as he transformed into the form of Braccus Max.

"Ironically, his discovery occurred at his most vulnerable moment. He lay near exhaustion, his light web near extinguished. His cry for help was the faintest of signals, like a single leaf on a vast ocean. But even that faint signal was sufficient to draw us to him – our first contact with your kind. We created a cloak around his weakened body, protecting him from the extreme cold of the Dark Lands, and sustaining him until he recovered his strength."

"Did Braccus Max communicate with you?" Constantine asked.

"In a way. In that desperate moment, a new life form emerged from the symbiosis between our force and his light web. Braccus Max sensed a presence, but his mind was vague and confused by his ordeal. His light web had changed in a subtle way, but he didn't immediately recognise it. Dark matter had fused into every fundamental particle of his light web. Ultimately, he did sense Dark matter. Then, he recreated it with his light web."

"It was our greatest discovery. I followed his work."

"Yet, it was as if the discovery of light had been made by a blind man," said the Entity, as it streamed mist to another multiverse cord, opening another scene.

"The fusion changed the Dark matter too. Braccus Max's light web spilled into the field of Dark matter that protected him. Both Baryon and Dark matter had been altered, accelerating the evolutionary process."

"It created a new species?"

"Yes, the Hollow People. But where Odorphins evolved in the world of matter in half a billion years, the Hollow People evolved in a fraction of that time."

"Why didn't you communicate with us?"

"We did, but our perception of the cosmos was very different to yours. You sensed a five dimensional world – height, length, width, time and transension, whereas we perceived the complexity of the multiverse. We live in a multiverse of equilibrium and oneness – a higher plane that branches out to infinity. We aren't driven by time and motion. Rather, we live in a perpetual moment of perfection, as if it were an exquisite pitch of music held for an eternity."

"So, why would you be affected by us?"

"Braccus Max's symbiosis and that of the other Odorphins who followed him to the Dark Lands, changed us. We could now detect the world of Baryon matter. At first, we thought we could make you aware of the multiverse, but you were blind to the reality. How could beings that relied on photons to see, comprehend its vastness?"

"Then, ignore us," challenged Constantine.

"We couldn't. We were drawn to the light web of any Odorphin that ventured into the Dark Lands. Connections were irreversible and forged at the fundamental level, forever linked to a chain that could never be broken. Like hot water had been poured on an ice block, both Hollow people and Odorphin had been forever changed. Those Odorphins that travelled the Dark Lands further deepened the symbiosis between us. We followed your voyages, so that we could better understand our developing connection. It was only natural that we followed the most daring voyager of them all." The Entity pointed at Constantine.

"You were the first to fully understand the connection that had occurred between us. You successfully recreated the Dark Matter on your light web, freeing yourself to voyage to all corners of the Dark Lands, not for days like your predecessors, but for as long as you wished. You alone, connected at the deepest level with our world."

"I discovered that our cosmos was more than just one universe. It stretched further to a multiverse."

"Yes. You crossed a crucial bridge. For the first time, a being made of Baryon matter sensed the deeper truths of the universe.

You did not have the ability to sense the infinite universes, just as you could not detect us. But you learned to cross universes. We sensed an important divide had been bridged. The linking of both matters had the potential to transform the multiverse, bringing a new perspective of itself. Another layer of self-awareness was being created."

"I crossed to another and discovered similar conditions to my own, but Titan was at an earlier stage of development. We had yet to evolve. It was the time of the humans, a race evolved from African apes," said Constantine.

"Your race evolved from them. They forged the mathmatica that allowed them to better understand the cosmos. Without their discoveries, you would not have a light web."

"I voyaged to another universe. Again, humans were the most advanced race in their solar system. I learnt from them, too. Some of their discoveries are new to us, even now."

"We learnt too, Odorphin. One of our own followed you across the multiverse, drawn by your light web. We have learned to see worlds of Baryon matter as you do, changing our perception of the multiverse. As you have seen, we can now walk on the world of Baryon matter."

"You abused your new powers," said Constantine, trying to draw a response. But the Entity continued its story, ignoring Constantine's barbs.

"We made small gains to begin with, attaching to the living cells of plant life so that we could roam the Earth, following your interactions from a distance. Then we attached to inanimate manmade objects, still remaining undetected. In time, we began to understand humans better. But then you did something unexpected. Inexplicably, you turned against us."

"It was never my intention."

"Goodwill was lost. Our hopes for a new self-awareness for the multiverse was about to be compromised. You had affected the multiverse in a dangerous way. You confided with the very people that meant it harm."

"I have never intentionally acted in a way to harm you or the multiverse!" Constantine exclaimed, frustrated that the Entity was ignoring him.

"We did consider that you were blind to the threat. It's true that you do not possess full sight. You can sense multiple universes, but you lack the ability to see the infinite beauty of the multiverse."

"All of that is true!"

"At that point we resolved to reveal our powers to you, well before we intended. You held the power to bring great change. Yet you protected those who posed danger to the multiverse. We could not communicate directly to the human, Jean. We had yet to develop the ability to take human form. Instead, we demonstrated that supporting the Earthling was dangerous and would have consequences. Ultimately we learnt to take on human form. Then we attacked you, as a way of testing your allegiances."

Constantine shook his head in disbelief, before a realisation came. "You act like a human does to an ant. You look upon them and never seek to understand. Communication between sentient beings is how we learn about our world. We are not born with your abilities. We have no insights into a deeper reality you so easily see." Constantine's pleas to be understood seemed to be ignored, as the Entity continued.

"We attacked on two fronts, threatening the human and enveloping your dreams. But our warnings were ignored, as you took it upon yourself to protect the Earthling and treat us as your enemy. We were left with two choices. Take you back to our universe and close the opening that you had created, permanently."

"That was not your choice. Why?"

"Removing you from the multiverse meant a grand opportunity for the multiverse's self-awareness to blossom would be lost - perhaps forever."

"So you took Jean."

"It too, had risks. But yes, we took the human. We left you stranded on Earth with no way of escape."

"What risk were you taking?"

"We left you alone with another equally dangerous Earthling – Vincent."

"But what of the other? Is Jean alive?"

"We took him to the Source."

"Jean is on Titan?"

"We closed the gateway permanently. The multiverse re-stabilised. Harmony returned. The only threat left would be if another bridge opened."

"Once knowledge is gained, it can't be closed off, as if it's a dam holding back water."

"That is true, but two forces will always flow through cosmic openings made in the multiverse. When an Odorphin crosses that bridge, we will follow. I followed your Odorphin friend to face an Earthling that poses great peril for our multiverse. He has the potential to be the most dangerous of all. And you in your wisdom chose to help him."

"I have acted on my instincts. This human is not bad. He didn't deserve your torment. Would you kill him, too? Like Jean?"

The Entity laughed at Constantine. "As always, you show your ignorance in matters of importance. There is no such thing as death."

"My dream ended with the Entity's haunting words. He said it with such conviction. His eyes were piercing as if he was speaking beyond Constantine, directly to me. Is that possible? Or was it just a dream?" Vincent asked.

Ella smiled, nodding her head, seemingly understanding Vincent's dream.

"What does it mean?" Vincent asked. Ella did not answer. Instead she lay back on the grass, seemingly digesting the significance of what Vincent had just told her.

They sat for a time on the green hill top. One tree provided soothing shade from the bright rays. They were comfortable in its cover, soaking up the natural beauty of their surrounds. A boat full of tourists slowly cruised past them, heading for the snowcapped mountains, reminding them of their own earlier journey.

"I was so happy that day, with you on the mountain top. I felt your love for the first time that day," said Vincent.

Ella giggled with delight as if she were truly human. She smelled the air and earth, before speaking.

"You'll feel that special love again."

Vincent hoped more than anything for a return to a normal existence, free of the shadows that had haunted him for much of his life, a life changed forever. He had been visited by another universe of creatures, good and evil, who claimed he was something more. One day, he wanted to find that, but for now Vincent just wanted to enjoy the idyllic beauty of their surrounds. He wished he could find a way to stay with Ella.

"So what next? Will you return?"

"Soon. But not before we share one last voyage."

Ella drew her light web around him, soothing his mind with soft caresses of white light. The gentle petal-like caress relaxed him until he fell into a calm trance. Ella's embrace was the antithesis of the Entity's dark force.

Vincent found himself not on the lakes of Lucerne, but by the oceans of Brighton amidst the sounds of seagulls, gliding high above in the breezes and hovering in still flight. He then looked down hearing waves pass under him. His view was blanketed by a thick fog. Further east was the familiar Brighton pier and 'The Booster' where he'd first experienced inter-planetary flight. It was clear of low lying cloud there, as the sun struck the white pier and small white capped waves surged across the structure toward the pebbled shore.

He then realised they stood on the old pier, no longer the rusted relic decayed by the universe's entropy, but a new pier, shining white with angled promenade boards. Vincent either stood on West Pier from the past or the future, but he had no way of telling, for the shoreline too was blanketed by thick fog, making him feel it had been built in the clouds.

"Is this real, or am I dreaming?"

Ella did not respond, instead taking his hand, walking together out along the pier, toward the deck's end, where a large concert hall filled the pier head. Every now and then she let go of his hand, to dance in the cooling sea breeze, circling him in a playful mood, as if all the horrors of the past week had never occurred.

"I guess you could say, it's your future," she said, finally answering Vincent's question.

"This place is so beautiful, why leave it at all?"

Ella smiled, continuing her flirtatious mood, holding Vincent's hand again and walking to the very end of the pier. Out in the distance the fog had cleared. A blue horizon filled with emerald shades across the ocean surface, the breezes in their face, cool and calming. Ella let go of Vincent's hand to lean on the rail and study the vast horizon.

"That's where I belong, I am Odorphin, born to travel and explore the universe. Our people live for the voyage."

Vincent knew that all too well, now. He studied the distant horizon, wishing he could join her, but knowing he had none of her capabilities. They were indeed alien to each other and yet his instincts still told him otherwise.

"When will you leave?"

"Soon. We may never meet again, but our spirits are tied for eternity. This is our bond," she said, her gaze drifting across the vast blue horizon.

"I'll never forget you or your people. I owe Constantine my life and you my undying love."

"Your love is true, but it's misplaced. Do you accept that Constantine was of your image, but from another time and universe?"

"I do. There is little other explanation."

"Then what of my identity?"

Vincent hadn't considered it until now. His feelings had run so deep for Ella that his heart had overruled any rational thought.

"You've visited another universe too?" he said.

"Yes, I too saw another of your lives on another world where your deeds had shone across the vast ocean of space. It has shone brightly throughout my voyage. It's what drew us to you. It's what drew her to me."

"Ella lives on Earth?" he said, excitement rising.

"Each life is different, yet the core never changes. I crossed the verse to one other Earth solar system, as did Constantine. He spoke of your other life where you were famous for your discoveries, like Galileo and those scientists that followed. You brought the first proof of the multiverse to your people, turning the tide, making them understand and believe. It's likely, your energy spreads across the multiverse, attracting many followers, but also detractors."

"The Entity?"

"Yes, you alone faced it, where the others did not. This event is important to your life, or should I say your multiverse lives."

"Why just me?"

"We don't know. We saw two Earths in what may be an infinite number. What we do know is your civilisation existed in both, whereas ours did not."

"Why would a power as superior as the Entity seek our destruction? Why did it share information with me, then attack and capture Constantine. There are still too many questions left, to believe this is the end of the matter."

"In our own minds, we mean it no harm, but did your civilisation mean harm to the many million species you made extinct through global warming? Imagine if those species had the capability to fight back."

"If that's true, we should stop the voyage until we know more?"

"Constantine started the multiverse voyages a hundred Earth years ago. We discovered humans and the mathmatica, but we drew an apparent enemy – the Entity. So we face new problems, but we must develop new capabilities to find solutions. We cannot undo what we have already begun. The multiverse has been crossed and powerful adversaries appear to resist it. Reasoning has failed, as if the Entity's survival is at stake. Up until your dream, it has chosen not to communicate, preferring aggression to reconciliation."

"So, you believe my dream was something more?"

"Perhaps. We will never be sure. But it is the only information we can go on."

"So it sees me as part of the threat?"

"Or the solution," said Ella.

"And what now for you, Ella?"

"Constantine's crossing was closed by the first Entity, but the second crossing was not. I can return home, which means I can try to right wrongs using the research we shared. So my voyage continues. I now know why Constantine was adamant it not be reviewed until our return to Titan - to save you and I."

"What can I do? It will take me decades to convince the sceptics of what I witnessed, if ever!"

"Convince them with new insights and discoveries. Live your life as it was intended to be. But know this. You are the first human to face the Entity and live. Your other lives have sensed its force, in dreams, but you are the first to encounter it directly."

"The university will call my observations fanciful. They'll fear I've lost my mind."

"All radical new ideas face derision. Some of those brave new thinkers paid with their lives. You nearly did. It's the way of the universe that new thinking is feared in the beginning. Humans crave certainty in an uncertain, random universe. You will challenge that comfort."

Vincent looked away from Ella, out to the ocean. He had faced much this last week: atomic travel at speeds of sound and light and deadly entrapment by a force that attacked like an insidious cancer and devoured the fundamental atoms that made up his life force. But a potentially worse fate crossed his mind. Had every one of his infinite lives been assaulted by the creeping darkness, as if in a deadly fight toward extinction - annihilation of 'his' species?

"We have no choice. The consequences of failing are too dire to contemplate. I hope I never cross such a force again, but if what you say is true, the gateway between our universes makes it inevitable."

"We have opened a bridge that has disturbed a universal force that we are only beginning to understand. We must continue our investigations before we again 'voyage' the multiverse. That's our challenge, but voyaging is inevitable. It's our way."

"I find it hard enough to convince my students of the fundamental laws of our own universe. But this...I'm alone."

Ella lightly touched Vincent's arm, reassuring and encouraging him with her warmth.

"You're not alone. The truth is on your side. People will believe, if you believe. And you have acquired new power," said Ella. She held an immersant in her open palm, as if offering a gift. It surprised Vincent.

"Do you want me to make another journey?"

Ella smiled and drew his hands to hers to hold the orb tightly. They both gazed at the warm glow that streamed from it through their loving clasp.

"No journey. This will protect you and bring you the strength you require when you most need it."

"You developed a stronger immersant?"

"The three of us did. Remember when I told you that only the three of us could defeat the Entity.

"I did nothing."

"You fell into the Entity's clutches and survived. We learnt a great deal from your interaction with it. It released you, but some of its makeup remained in you. That allowed us to develop an immersant that would be harder for it to defeat. Constantine carried that immersant in his final encounter."

"You don't think he died?"

"That's difficult to say."

"Riddles, always riddles," said Vincent in frustration, making Ella laugh.

"It's not a riddle. I'm telling you what I know." Vincent looked put out, as if Ella had slighted him. "Look, I think he no longer lives as we know it, otherwise I would have detected his presence. I believe your dream is true and he is among them, but not defeated."

"The immersant?"

"Yes."

"The Entity bypassed all other immersants, why not this one?"

"We emulated the most difficult process to control that we know. It is a process that exists only on Earth – cancer. Constantine knew this process would be virtually impregnable, even to the Entity, but we had to understand the capability that allowed the Entity to break through our immersant's immune systems so easily. To do that, we needed a sample of the Entity's core. You provided that for us, allowing Constantine to adapt the process of cancer to counteract the Entity's attack mechanism. We all carry this defence system, now. So, as soon as the Entity breaks down one immune system, another develops."

"We're safe from its claws."

"For now. I also believe Constantine contacted you, through your dreams, to show us that the immersant has worked."

"It was just a dream, Ella."

"No. Your dreams are more like Odorphins' dreams now. You will feel changes in your body. It is the immersants. Your aura is stronger, trust it."

"I do feel different. Why not stay here longer? I have so many more questions I want to ask you. Constantine stayed a hundred years, why not you?"

"I must return to immune my people from the coming dangers. Entities have invaded your home, why not mine? Besides, the person you believe you'll miss, you haven't even met yet. Your true love is of flesh and blood and she lives in your world. Surely you wouldn't give your love to a holograph that seems human, but is not?"

Vincent went to answer but he could not speak. Light waves emanated from the immersant relaxing him. But then his mind's eye soared high into the air to where he floated with Ella some twenty metres above their bodies. Vincent surveyed the Brighton shoreline that was extended by two piers. Then he looked to Ella.

"Brighton looks spectacular from here."

Ella smiled and waved her light web over Vincent. "Look again."

To Vincent's surprise, the shoreline had changed. All was unfamiliar to him except one of the two figures on the beach below. He was sure it was him, but he looked different. He was older. Vincent turned to Ella to ask what he was viewing. But before he could speak, his mind's eye descended to the older Vincent. In an instant he became that older Vincent with many more years of memories. Friendships won and lost, a new teaching tenure, books written and all this activity centred on his one true love. Vincent felt such joy at witnessing a collage of his future life, then an intense calm came over him as he floated down into his future destiny, like an actor to a stage, he became his future self.

DESTINY

THE EARLY MORNING SEA breeze had a crispness to it that took Vincent back. Many years had passed quickly, happily – but the alien events had left a permanent mark on his life. The mental anguish never left him. He remained fearful that the shadows would one day return and take everything he and El had built over these happiest years of his life. He was blessed with two loves, his beautiful wife El and his daughter Connie. He hadn't feared the shadows since the day he survived the collision with the Entity and the disappearance of Constantine.

"Daddy, come to the water," said Connie.

"Soon darling," he said, bringing a sad expression to his young daughter's face.

She looked so like El, with her long strawberry blonde hair and blue eyes that opened wide to a world she was eager to explore. She had a desire to explore from an early age, no doubt inspired by him and her mother, who regularly read to Connie. Tales of travellers were her favourite stories. Small wonder Connie lived to explore the world's delights, often rushing out ahead along the Brighton beach shore line, searching for shells of all colours and shapes to add to her collection.

"Daddy, you promised!"

"One more minute. Okay?"

"Promise?"

"Yes," he said, now quickly finishing the last paragraph of his précis of a forthcoming lecture he had to present. Vincent enjoyed lecturing, even more so since he accepted a part-time position in Melbourne, Australia acting as a tutor and associate lecturer there. He had taken a cut in salary, but didn't mind. It allowed him free time to pursue his passion, researching multiverse theory. He was hired as a theoretical physicist and was gaining a reputation as one the more radical researchers, no doubt due to his experiences with Ella and Constantine. Unbeknown to the world, Vincent had gained insights no other human had faced, which posed a problem - no one would believe such a story. He was also the joint beneficiary of Constantine's business finances, a tidy sum left to he and El to pursue research.

Vincent finished his précis, but realised he had taken a lot longer than the minute he promised Connie. Surprisingly, Connie had not complained about her father's broken promise. Vincent quickly searched the open beach to see what had occupied her mind.

She had walked a fair way down the shoreline, which annoyed him. He had told her repeatedly to remain within calling distance, but Connie always found one excuse or another to wander away. It was "one of her journeys" as she put it. Vincent called out to her, but he was out of her earshot. As he ran toward her, he realised she was talking. At first he thought she was singing to the ocean, which she did often. But she was looking away from the ocean, down the sandy beach, in conversation seemingly with a pretend playmate. Vincent called out, surprising her. She turned swiftly and smiled radiantly.

"Daddy, where were you?" her delight turning to a questioning grimace.

"Sorry darling, daddy was busy," he said, opening his arms out for a hug, but instead Connie held his right hand tight, pulling him back along the beach.

"I have a new friend, daddy. I want you to meet him. Burger..." she said, looking left than right, but only morning shadows danced across the beach shore and the sounds of early morning walkers talking as they strolled the nearby walkway. Connie looked to the distant walkers, believing one may be her new found friend. But then surprise followed by disappointment crossed her face.

"Where are you, Burger? He said he wanted to meet you."

"Never mind darling, perhaps we should go home. Mum will have breakfast ready," said Vincent, believing feelings for her new friend would soon subside. But Connie would not leave. She was convinced Burger was somewhere close. Vincent didn't mind either. The morning was refreshing and it was still early.

"Maybe we should have a swim before we go home," he dared, running into the ocean shallows and splashing Connie with the cold ocean waters.

"Yeahhhhh," cried Connie. She eagerly joined him and started a water fight with the father she adored, all thought of the Burger man lost.

Vincent knew Connie loved to play in the water. From a young age it became clear it was her natural state. It was partly the reason they moved to Brighton, Victoria. It was a coincidence that he should pick 'another Brighton', after his experiences in England's town of the same name. In many ways it felt as if the town had picked him. He'd had a chance meeting with a friend in urgent need of 'house-sitters'. They'd been given short notice for a job posting overseas. No board was required, just a stable family to tend to the daily upkeep and take care of their family cat Scribble. This coincidently occurred not long after Vincent accepted a part-time lecturing tenancy at Melbourne University.

So his little girl could hardly believe her eyes when they moved into the home, a stroll across Brighton Park to the freedom of her own beach and her very first pet. Connie had been taught to swim from an early age and was a capable swimmer by nine. She would spend hours in and around it, seemingly never bored. The ocean was an adventure to Connie, a large water expanse for her to explore, under the watchful eye of her father or mother.

"Race you to the buoy!"

Before Vincent could react, Connie was stroking solidly away from him at a rhythmic rate, determined to be first to the orange mark fifty metres from the shore. Vincent admired her grace in the water. He was proud of his daughter's abilities and encouraged her to improve by often racing her. He dove into the water, finding his rhythm quickly to make it a race. Every race was staged, although over the years Connie had grown in strength, making it harder for him to catch her. Today she opened a ten metre lead, which could be enough for her to win on her own abilities. Competitive himself, Vincent pushed his strokes harder to test how strong she'd become.

Forty metres out and Vincent was actually tired from his efforts to catch Connie. He'd closed to within two metres when a pain surged across his right side. He slowed, fearful that he'd strained a muscle, before stopping to tread water. Connie raced on, still stroking powerfully and unaware he had stopped.

Vincent massaged his right shoulder, attempting to ease the pain when he felt his vision blur. He rubbed his eyes to clear his sight before realising the burning was not of his making. A mist had formed around him and Connie. It was a haze familiar to him. He called to her but she did not hear, as she swam toward the buoy.

The brightness of the day dimmed in the heavy fog, reminding him of England, everything colourless except Connie's bright yellow bathers. Darkness formed above her, hovering, then slowly descending. Before Vincent could raise a warning cry, she swiftly disappeared under the water surface, as if a shark had attacked her.

Vincent ignored the pain surging through his right arm and dived beneath, desperate to find his little girl and bring her to safety. The water was deep and cold as he stroked awkwardly to the depths. At first he could not see her. But he could see a trail of bubbles below signalling a struggle.But from what? Vincent's mind raced as he followed the trail. A full minute had passed. His lungs now burned from the lack of oxygen. He had to surface. All the while, he imagined Connie's lifeless body lying on the bottom of the ocean and her eyes looking up toward him, revealing the terror she had faced. As he approached the surface, Vincent heard a muffled voices above him.

"Daddy, I won," came the joyful sounds of Connie, safely clinging to the buoy. The mist had cleared, allowing him to see his daughter, splashing at the buoy, delighted she had at last beaten her father.

"That's wonderful darling," he said, before he held her close to him.

"Let's head back to shore, now," he said calmly, belying the anguish he really felt.

Had the mist played tricks on his mind, triggering distant memories and signalling the arrival of past demons? Had he returned to a time when he was unable to distinguish reality from imagination? Or was this a warning that another Entity had returned? Even worse, did it seek his daughter? Vincent wanted only to protect her, so he swam close to Connie all the way back to the shore, not once taking his sight from her.

Vincent said little of the experience to El that day, but she knew something disturbed him. He didn't like to keep secrets from El, but he wanted the evening to ponder what had happened that morning. He needed time alone to make sense of the events. Maybe he had become disoriented and imagined it all? But it was unlikely.

Many years had passed. Why would an Entity return now? Or was there a new unknown danger? He sat in his study late that night, searching his memories for a clue. Then a single thought overtook him. Burger.

Vincent turned the study light out and joined El, who was already in bed. He looked lovingly at her as she slept soundly. She'd had a long day of teaching which always left her drained. She loved teaching young children of pre-school age, an interest that started soon after the birth of Connie. It was an all-consuming passion, now. And for good reason. El had a natural gift with children, never tiring of telling them stories. Importantly, it helped El forget her earlier loss. Life had been difficult back then, but after years of coping with her situation, El blossomed with new purpose - teaching and motherhood. Vincent lay back on his pillow, immediately stirring El's light sleep.

"What's the time?"

"Late. Go back to sleep, darling."

El stretched instead and sat up, clearing her eyes and checking the time on the digital clock. She stroked Vincent's hair, occasionally kissing his shoulder.

"It is late. Deadlines to meet?"

Vincent thought to agree, but El had an uncanny ability to see through any dishonesty.

"You don't want to know."

"Yes I do!' El replied, seemingly wide awake now.

"Connie gave me a scare today, that's all."

"Running away on one of her journeys again?"

"No, swimming."

El raised her eyes in exasperation, before falling back on her pillow. "You know she loves the water. The more you discourage her, the more she will want to swim."

"No, she really got into difficulties this time."

El held back her response, but Vincent knew what she was thinking. "I know I should encourage her more, El, but she is sometimes too courageous for her own good," he said, holding her hand.

"Her courage comes from her innate abilities. I sense she will have special powers."

"Like you?"

"Like I was, you mean," replied El, trying to smile, but Vincent knew she never fully got over the changes the Entity inflicted on her. She was always of the view that it was in retaliation for the pain she inflicted on it in their final battle, but Vincent thought otherwise.

"She is the daughter of Ellatine Braccus Max, the bravest woman I ever met," he said, kissing her hand with pride and love. "And yes, she is just like you, Ella."

"I told you, I don't like that name anymore," she said, turning her face away from him. Vincent immediately regretted using her old name, but to him, it was a name he would never forget. But he understood El's reasoning. To her, she was only half of who she once was, stripped of her Odorphin identity and powers. An uneasy silence ensued, before Vincent returned to their unfinished conversation.

"Today, she disappeared from my sight out in deep water. I was sure she got into difficulties. But I could have been disoriented," he said, drawing El's interest.

"Disoriented?"

"I had a pain in my arm and lost some movement. I called to Connie to slow, but she didn't hear me. That's when the mist formed around us."

"El immediately sat up."

"Vincent, you promised you'd tell me straight away of any odd occurrences."

"I know. But the pain in my arm. It could have been a pulled muscle for all I knew. I didn't want to worry you, unnecessarily."

El's expression turned from annoyance to concern as she gazed at Vincent. "It could also have been a stroke or......" Her voice trailed off as she thought of the possibilities. Vincent knew what she feared most. He had to tell everything, now.

"Just before we went swimming, she claimed to have met a new friend."

"Go on."

"There was no one there, when I arrived. I thought it just a figment of her young imagination. She called him Burger. She also said that Burger was looking forward to meeting us."

El jumped out of bed and headed directly to Connie's bedroom.

"She's fine. I checked her just before coming to bed," Vincent cried out, trying to reassure El, but failing. She returned to the bedroom, carrying Connie in her arms. Vincent went to say something, but El signalled him not to wake Connie. She lay her down in the middle of their bed. Connie woke briefly, so El massaged her back until she fell asleep again. Both looked at their sleeping daughter with the pride and love of devoted parents.

"I'm sorry, El. I know I promised you...."

"It's okay," El whispered. "Everything is fine, now. Let's talk about this in the morning with Connie. We'll all have clearer minds, then."

Vincent nodded and smiled, before kissing El and his sleeping daughter. She was right, it could wait until morning.

Vincent woke to the sound of El leaving for her daily, morning swim. Her early ritual had become her passion. Vincent believed it was her time to be who she once was, Ella. She rarely spoke of the past, now, but Vincent believed she retained some small part of her Odorphin qualities. For one, she could remain under the water, without drawing breath for longer than any other human. Vincent learned that one day when he accompanied El for an ocean swim. However, the sight of her disappearing into the depths for extended periods unnerved him, now she was human. Perhaps that fear sparked his vision of Connie disappearing, too? He could have blacked out and imagined the mist and the danger to Connie. The thought did motivate him to check on his daughter. To his relief, Connie slept soundly in her bed, no doubt because El had carried her there before leaving.

Vincent normally slept in on weekends, but he decided to busy himself and prepare a family breakfast. Given the concerns of the previous day's events, he wouldn't have slept anyway. The hour soon passed as he put finishing touches to the table setting and breakfast.

"Something smells good," said El, returning from her swim.

"I couldn't sleep," replied Vincent, kissing El, as she admired his handiwork.

"Is Connie up?"

"Having a shower. She said she would join us in exactly five minutes!"

El laughed with Vincent. Connie was reaching an age when she wanted to regularly remind them that their little girl was growing up and needed her independence. Connie arrived on time, as promised, then all sat down to Vincent's feast. Even Scribble joined them as it pounced onto the breakfast table, delicately avoiding the crockery and cutlery.

"Here Scribble. Your meal is on the floor," said Vincent as he picked Scribble up and lowered him to the bowl of milk.

"I like mummy's breakfast better!" Connie exclaimed, with the honesty of a nine-year-old.

"Well thank you for your vote of confidence, darling daughter," replied Vincent, with a slightly annoyed look on his face.

"You should be grateful, Connie. Eat your eggs please."

"I'm not hungry, mummy. Can't I go swimming now?"

"No. You need your strength to swim in the ocean. So you have to eat all the eggs."

Connie held her head between two clenched fists as she studied her plate.

"I won't say it again, Connie. If you don't eat your food, mummy and daddy won't take you to the beach, today."

Begrudgingly, Connie started the long process of finishing her meal, while Vincent offered the occasional word of encouragement.

"Nearly there darling. You will be able to swim even faster today because you'll be bigger and stronger, won't you."

Connie said little as she forced another scoop of egg down, until she remembered yesterday. "I beat daddy to the buoy, mummy!"

"Yes, I heard about that, darling. And I also heard you made a new friend?"

"Burger!" Connie exclaimed excitedly, suddenly remembering.

"Did Burger play with you?"

"No. He didn't have time, mummy. He just talked. He was funny," said Connie, giggling at the memory.

"What was funny, darling?"

"He made magic tricks, daddy."

"Really. What kind of tricks?"

"He made an empty red box float in the air. Then he asked me to say a magic word to make something appear from the empty box."

"Sounds exciting. What was the magic word?"

"Umm.....it was like my name.....Connie-teen....I think."

Vincent and El looked at each other, before Vincent continued. "Was it Constantine?"

"Yes. That's it! Then he made magic. The box turned to mist and Scribble dropped out of mid-air and ran away! Magic!"

"I didn't see him darling. What did this man, Burger, look like?"

"He looked like a magician. He had a long grey robe and a hood that covered his face. He looked a little bit scary, but he was nice to me," said Connie, with a worried look on her face. "I know you told me never to talk to strangers, but he said he knew you both."

"Yes, you must be careful, Connie. You should have called your father," said El, shooting Vincent a concerned eye. "Did Burger say when he would meet us?"

"Yes. He said he would meet us all on the beach. Maybe we can all go now, mummy?" Connie asked, as she proudly pushed her empty plate forward in front of her.

"Soon, darling. You get ready, while mummy and daddy clean up."

Connie raced from the table excited that they would all be going to the beach, leaving Vincent and El alone and considerably less excited.

"Could it be happening after all these years?" Vincent said, shaking his head in disbelief at what he had just heard.

"Who else could it be?" El responded, equally dumbfounded, before deeper emotions took her over. Tears streamed down her eyes, uncontrolled, surprising Vincent. He put a comforting arm around her, not sure what to say.

"What should we do?"

"I don't know, Vincent." El responded, before standing up and walking to the window. "It could be out there, now. Waiting."

"We have to protect our little girl!" Vincent exclaimed, standing up and joining El at the window."

"How exactly?" Vincent could not answer her. El's tears continued to flow as she tried to tell Vincent something, but could not.

"What is it, darling?"

"I've been a good mother haven't I?"

"You have been wonderful. Connie couldn't have had a better mother, or I a more devoted and loving wife."

"I've tried so hard, Vincent."

"Of course you have. What's wrong my love?"

"When I heard what Connie told me, my first reaction was excitement. I should have been concerned for Connie and you, but all I could think was that I may have a chance to be Ella again. To return to my home. I...." Ella's voice trailed off as she tried to finish what she wanted to tell Vincent, but could not.

Vincent was still too shocked by the events to properly take in El's words. It was like suddenly hearing about the death of a loved one, but in their case, it could be the death of their ten beautiful, loving years together. The shadows were returning to Vincent's life.

Vincent and El sat close to the shoreline as Connie played in the tranquil, ocean waters. Both kept a keen eye on their daughter as she bombarded them with questions, no doubt seeking attention.

"Watch me, Mummy!"

"Did I dive the right way, Daddy?"

Vincent had learned to nod approval, rather than engage her conversation. Connie just wanted her parents' admiration for her water skills. Vincent also kept an eye on the horizon for any tell-tale signs of an un-earthly intruder. It was a pleasant sun-filled spring day that provided warmth against the chilly ocean breeze. What should have been a relaxing weekend on the beach was understandably tense.

"Why after all these years?" Vincent repeatedly asked, seeking answers El did not have.

"With luck, this was a freakish coincidence," El replied unconvincingly. The tense mood magnified as a third voice joined the conversation.

"This is no coincidence," came a calm, controlled voice from behind them.

A man dressed in a full flowing robe stood behind them, just five metres away. His face was covered by a hood, just as the Entity had been, the last time they encountered it. The hooded man stood still as a statue, unnervingly so, not uttering a word, seemingly waiting for questions.

"Who are you?" Vincent asked.

"You already know the answer to that question. But if you're referring to my name, it is David Bergerre. Although I believe you referred to me as the Monk, last time we met?" The Entity replied, as he lifted his hood to reveal the familiar but much older face of David.

"What do you want from us?" Ella demanded.

The Monk flashed a stern gaze toward Ella, revealing the slightest smirk as he spoke. He had a confident but arrogant way about him that unnerved Vincent and seemingly angered El.

"I've come to show you what you are looking for."

"Show who?" Ella probed.

"The three of you, of course."

"And if we decline your generous offer, because we're already happy with our lives and never want to see you again?" Ella continued, her anger building.

"Well, I'll simply take you to the place you do not wish to see." Replied the Monk, calmly but assertively. El cast a nervous glance across to Vincent, before turning her gaze to the Monk.

"Please, just take me. I beg you!" El cried.

"No. It should be me, El." Vincent added.

"I have not come here to barter. What is, is. I suggest you prepare yourselves."

"But Connie is just a child. She won't understand." El implored.

"I'll make it as easy as possible for the young human. Talk to her and prepare for the journey," replied the Monk assertively. Vincent took El's hand and walked with her toward Connie, all the while trying to console her. Tears flowed freely from her as she turned again to plead for the family she loved.

"Do what you want with me, but please leave my child on Earth and let her have her father."

"I have already told you that the fate of you all is already cast. Your lives are like a single molecule of water on the precipice of the largest waterfall. Speak to your child and return to me soon."

Vincent tried to resist the Monk's commands, but it cast a powerful mist around his body, wrapping him in pain.

"Do as I ask or I will inflict great pain on you child," the Monk threatened.

Vincent and El walked away, heads bowed, two powerless humans without immersants to defend themselves. The three returned to the Monk, Vincent and El were quiet and downcast, no doubt shaken by the events, but remaining calm in front of their daughter. On the other hand, Connie was excited to see her friend again.

"Burger! I knew you'd come back!"

"We told Connie you wanted to take us all on a journey."

"Hello again, Connie. I have returned to show you and your parents that I am the greatest magician on Earth. Would you like to see some truly wonderful magic?"

"Yes. Please yes!" Connie replied, barely able to contain her excitement.

The monk flashed his hands in front of Connie in the style of a magician, before he made a red mask appear, seemingly from thin air.

"This is a special mask made just for you."

"Ohh, it's beautiful!" He handed it to Connie.

"Try it on and you'll find it fits the contours of your face perfectly."

"Yes it does. But I can't see."

"I made it just for you, Connie. What I want you to do is count to thirty for me. Can you do that?"

"Yes!" Connie replied, fidgeting with an excitement she could barely contain.

"Good. You must slowly count to thirty. Then and only then, you can take the mask off. And when you do, you will see true magic. Will you do that for me, when I ask you to start counting?"

"Yes. Yes!" She replied, jumping now with excitement and energy.

The Monk gazed toward Vincent and El, readying them for their journey. Both were resigned to their fate as all three held hands in a circle. The Monk waved his right hand in an outward direction, as if casting a spell and instantly all had left the Earth without trace toward their destiny. The four rode a photon wave that travelled from Earth at light speed.

"You're counting, Connie?" The Monk said in a reassuring tone.

"Yes. Three, four, five....."

By six, they had accelerated to a speed beyond the laws of physics, advancing toward a destination Vincent recognised. They rode alongside an infinite number of particles toward a vast light.

"You brought me here when you captured me?" The Monk did not answer.

They were travelling at miraculous speed, yet all was silent around them, bar Connie's voice.

"Fifteen, sixteen, seventeen...."

"Good, Connie. Nearly there," the Monk said.

By twenty seconds, they had crossed a universe and continued to accelerate, reaching the misty expanse that blinded Vincent in a white-out last time he was there. But this time they pierced the field of mist, suddenly gaining sight of their destination.

"Twenty-four, twenty-five...."

Their speed dramatically slowed, almost floating to their final destination. Both Vincent and El could not speak, so surprised were they at where the Monk had taken them. Had they been imprisoned or set free?

15

Miroir d'Eau

THEY HOVERED TO A soft landing on a rectangular shaped, concrete expanse positioned between a river and historic buildings. It had to be Earth or its replica. The coal grey area consisted of many uniformly fitted jets that blew steam half a metre high across it, forming a low lying blanket of steam.

"Twenty-nine, thirty! Connie declared with a mix of pride and excitement.

Vincent and El looked toward their daughter, then to the Monk who nodded his consent for them to remove her mask. El provided her a comforting hug before removing the mask.

"Look my darling. We have travelled half way across the world," she said in as calm a voice as she could manage.

"Ohh mummy! We're in a cloud! Where are we?"

"Your friend is indeed a great magician. We have travelled to Bordeaux in France!" Connie gazed with wide, innocent eyes, before she reacted to her surrounds.

"Can I play?"

El turned to the Monk for a reply. "Of course you can, Connie. Look to your left, beyond the clouds. I prepared a surprise, just for you," he said, pointing in the direction of a long, grassy parkland.

"Look, daddy! Scribble is here with my friends. There's Eva, Claire and Hannah!" Such was her excitement she started to run toward them, but she abruptly stopped, realising her transgression. "Can I, daddy?"

"Yes, darling. Go and play. But don't run too far away," said Vincent reluctantly, knowing he was in no position to protect himself, let alone his family. Better she enjoy herself, he thought, justifying his decision.

Connie rushed through the cloud, arms stretched and reacting to the sounds of her friends playing and calling out to her. She picked up Scribble and hugged him before running to her best friends. All too soon, she was lost in the joy of play, without a care for how the magical events had occurred. Vincent perused his surroundings, shaking his head, not sure what to do next.

"Is this real?"

"What is real," replied the Monk, before extending his arms in the direction of their daughter, inviting them to walk toward the park." It is real enough to suggest that we don't linger on the Miroir d'Eau too much longer."

They all now stood on the green expanse, surrounded by lush, manicured gardens, French architecture and a glorious spring day. Soon after, they witnessed the first un-Earthly event, to remind them that they had just travelled far from their home. The Miroir d'Eau's vapour clouds evaporated, revealing not the dark concrete base that they just stood on, rather a star filled expanse that extended out to what appeared an infinite distance.

"Where are we?" El asked.

"We are at a portal. A very important portal."

"And all this?" She asked, pointing to the city of Bordeaux?

"A canvas, for your convenience," replied the Monk, as a half-smile formed on his face.

"Are we prisoners in your elaborate canvas?" Vincent asked, taking El's hand and looking out to Connie.

"No, quite the opposite. You are free to leave any time," the Monk replied, turning his gaze to the Miroir d'Eau."

"We just walk in to that expanse and we would return to Earth?"

"Yes, that would happen, if you are prepared."

"Then we will take our daughter now and return home," Vincent said, beginning to walk toward his daughter.

"There were a couple of people who are very eager to meet with you, before you leave. They're not far from here. I could take you."

Vincent continued to walk toward Connie, but the Monk's words stopped El in her tracks. She let go of Vincent's hand and turned back.

"No, El. Don't listen to his lies!" Vincent implored.

"Who wants to meet me?"

"Your mentor of course! Well, he's really more like your father, isn't he?"

"El!" Vincent interjected.

"He's close you say?"

"Well, a long walk for a human, but a very short flight for an Odorphin," said the Monk, before with one wave of his hand, he restored El to her Odorphin form.

Ella stood where El once did. She did not move for some time, as if she couldn't remember how an Odorphin interacted with the world. Then suddenly she spanned her arms, igniting her light web into a glorious pattern, not dissimilar to Saturn's glow.

"El, this is not real. Don't do this!" Vincent implored.

Ella turned her head slightly toward the sound of Vincent's voice behind her, seemingly showing doubts, before she suddenly hovered metres above the Bordeaux landscape to peruse her whereabouts.

"Should I take you to him?" The Monk asked.

"El!" Vincent interjected repeatedly, but his wife of ten years did not respond.

"I already know where he is," she replied.

"Of course you do, Ella," the Monk said, turning his gaze to Vincent and smiling. Then in an instant, Ella flew high into the sky to meet with the mentor she had not met in ten years. Vincent stood alone with the Monk in a world seemingly created by the Entity to calm him, but he felt quite the opposite as he faced his demons yet again. He stood before David helpless and unable to stop him tear his family apart.

"Is my life lost forever?" He asked, resignation in his tone.

"Your life is not lost. You will see that, soon enough," replied the Monk as he walked toward him. He extended his hand, inviting Vincent to look eastward toward La Garonne river.

"There is someone here that wants very much to see you again."

Vincent turned east and saw a lone man gazing out to the river, seemingly in contemplation.

"Jean!" Vincent cried out excitedly, rushing toward him and unable to contain his excitement. Jean turned, hearing Vincent's call, also excited.

"My boy!" He said admiringly before holding his nephew in a long embrace. He reluctantly let him go, but only so he could gaze upon him.

"You've aged, but in a good way. You look happy."

"I have been very happy, Jean. These last ten years..." Vincent started saying, before Jean interrupted.

"Ten years? Are you sure?" Jean asked, looking slightly puzzled.

"I know. The time has gone so quickly. But look at you, Jean. You haven't aged a day since we last met," said Vincent, genuinely surprised. "It's been over ten years since you disappeared. We presumed you dead. But this place..." Vincent said, casting his gaze toward the Monk, who held a watchful eye on them and Connie as she played. "Perhaps we are all dead?"

"My boy! As you can see, I'm very much alive!"

"I hope you're right, Jean. So tell me. What happened after the Entity took you? Constantine presumed you dead, but he never gave up hope."

"Ah yes, he tried to help me, as he did you," said Jean, happy about the memory, before his expression changed. "I'm sorry I didn't tell you. All those years. You were young and vulnerable. But I should have done more. I should have...."

Vincent consoled his uncle with an embrace. "You did so much for me. I would never have become professor without your help and guidance."

"Constantine said it was better you didn't know about your situation or the immersants. I was never sure. I always worried about you. But as you found out, we were dealing with exceptional circumstances."

"We were. And we almost won," said Vincent.

"Let's walk along the river. It's beautiful don't you think? Vincent nodded agreement.

"And it takes my mind off all of this. The dark days, I mean."

"Yes. Are you free to walk this beautiful city, Jean?"

"No one has stopped me yet." Jean said proudly, breathing in the Bordeaux air.

"So how long have you been here?"

Jean stopped walking and scanned his surrounds in an agitated fashion as if the answer to Vincent's question lay somewhere between the city and the river.

"I'm not sure I can answer that. Don't get me wrong, my boy, I would tell you if I knew. It's the strangest thing. It's this place. It's disorienting." Jean continued to scan his surrounds, ever quicker, as confusion took him over. So Vincent took Jean's hand and helped him to a nearby bench.

"It's okay, Jean. Don't worry. Let's sit down and take a breath."

"Yes. That will help. Thanks, Vincent," said Jean, smiling at him appreciatively. He struggled to express his feelings, but could not.

His gaze was filled with a mix of confusion and fear before tears revealed his frustration.

"I don't know where I am. Sometimes I feel a wonderful calm, as if I had found my home again. But then this. I can't explain it, my boy. I want to help you but I'm.... I'm lost. Forgive me!"

Vincent consoled his uncle as best he could. But he appeared a broken man, with only confused recollections of his past ten years. They sat quietly on the bench for some time, watching the river flowing south. It all looked so real, but Vincent had to remind himself that they were held captive in a world, not of their universe. Jean breathed deeply, re-gaining his composure.

"Enough of my rantings. Tell me about your life, Vincent. I want to know more."

"Come and I'll show you my life, Jean," he replied, standing and pointing back to where they had come from, toward the field of young play makers.

They quickly joined the children who were playing with an assortment of pets, including Scribble.

"Connie, I'd like you to meet my uncle, Jean."

"A pleasure to meet you, young lady," said Jean, brushing his fingers through her long red hair.

"This is Scribble," replied Connie, holding tight to her pet cat.

"And what a perfect name for your cat, Connie," he said, admiring the scribble-like brown lines that filled his otherwise snow-white fur. He then turned to Vincent.

"You know, I didn't believe you when you said it had been over ten years since we last met. But it seems you have proof," he revealed, admiring Connie.

"I've been very lucky, Jean. A perfect daughter and wife."

"Where is she? I'd very much like to meet her?"

"She went to see Constantine," said Vincent, casting an eye out for the Monk, who had seemingly disappeared.

"And he will want to talk to you, Vincent."

"Have you and Constantine shared this place together, since he disappeared?"

"We only just met, my boy. A few hours before you arrived."

"Was he fine, Jean?"

"He was no different to you."

"What do you mean?"

"He confused me. Like you, he believed we had a long time apart. I was happy to see him, mind you. As he was happy to see me."

Jean turned his attention to Connie, who had started playing with her friends again. The Monk had also reappeared, observing the children as they played from a distance. The scene sparked a memory in Jean.

"A girl. Constantine spoke about a young girl. I remember that, now."

"What girl?"

"Your child, Vincent. He was speaking of Connie. He believed the Monk would bring a girl here. It was important for some reason."

"Do you remember, Uncle? Why was Connie important?"

"I don't know. I mean Constantine didn't know. But he believed it was important to the Hollow People. He also thought it could help us...all of us."

"Are they testing us? Do we have to do something?"

"A test. Yes, there is a test we all must face," said Jean, increasingly becoming agitated as he strained to recall what he wanted to say. Then he stood closer to Vincent and spoke to him in almost a whisper.

"You must leave here, Vincent. All of you must leave. I..."

Jean did not finish what he desperately wanted to share with Vincent. It was as if he'd forgotten the image he had just remembered. Vincent thought to push his uncle further, until he saw the Monk. He was gazing directly at Jean, his eyes wide, revealing his power over him. He said no more, even though he desperately needed to find out the secrets of this place. But he held back, for Jean's sake. The answers it seemed, lay with Constantine. Vincent walked over to the Monk.

"Are we free to go anywhere, or are we your captives?" Vincent questioned. The Monk opened his arms signalling Vincent was free to go where he pleased.

"Do you know where El is?"

"Of course."

"I would like to be with my wife - alone. Can you do that for me?" With a single wave of his hand, Vincent was flying beside Ella, on his way, he was sure, to meet with Constantine.

Vincent and Ella flew high above the pale limestone buildings and narrow lanes that filled the Bordeaux landscape, termed the old city. Vincent had not seen Ella in Odorphin form for a decade. He was happy for her, for he knew the elation she felt when flying. They had experienced a wonderful life together, these last ten years, but Vincent sensed her sadness. She always presented a brave face to both he and Connie, but the loss of her true identity was a painful burden she carried deep inside. He knew she could never stay with him, if she became truly Odorphin again, but seeing her joy flying beside him, he wanted that for her more than anything. But the world they now found themselves in was an illusion, brought on by the Entity. He and all those he loved, from two universes, were in danger, leaving Vincent's hopes with just one, Constantine.

"I'm sorry I left you," she said.

"You did what you thought was right, Ella," Vincent replied, accentuating his reference to Ella.

"I'll do all I can, my love. I hope it's enough." Ella replied, before pointing to their final destination.

The twin buildings of Cathedrale Saint Andre and the Tower Pey-Berland came into clear view. Vincent remembered Constantine's preference for the grand historic buildings of Europe. He often spoke of the cathedrals as calming structures, that reminded him of their home cavern of Titan, much like the ocean reminded him of Titan's lakes.

"I see him," she cried, with the exuberance of a long lost daughter.

She admired him as her mentor and loved him like he was her father. Constantine stood at the base of the tower, the tallest structure in Bordeaux. He opened his light web, revealing violet hues, a welcoming sign for his protege, as did Ella. They held each other in a heartfelt embrace, as vibrant rainbow light surrounded them.

"I feel the changes in you," he said, stroking her long hair.

"You would change, too if..." Emotion welled up in Ella that she could not control.

"You have paid a high price, Ella. I fear you will have to face more, as do we all."

"I don't know what is right or wrong any more. If you have no answers, I fear all is lost," said Ella. Constantine took Ella's hand and surrounded it with a violet hue, before he turned to Vincent.

"You have changed, too. I see more wisdom in you," he said affectionately.

"Can you tell us what the Entity wants from us, Constantine? Why this elaborate hoax?"

Constantine smiled. "Still so many questions," he replied, before signalling for them to enter the tower.

"I think more clearly in these buildings. It's where humans dreamed of lofty aims. Come, let's walk to the top as humans and view this city."

They all stood looking eastward toward the river.

"I see Pont Saint Jean. Our daughter, Connie is playing on the park just near there," said Ella, "I didn't want to leave her, but I had to speak to you, Constantine," she continued, before turning to Vincent with a concerned look.

"She was happily playing with her friends?"

"I don't think the Monk means her any harm and Jean was there as well, watching over her," reassured Vincent, before turning to Constantine.

"Jean appeared confused. Has he been tormented all these years?"

"You're right. Jean is very confused, but I fear it was me who confused him, not the Monk. You see, he doesn't believe he has been here ten years. Your arrival and your daughter, Connie, has further challenged those notions."

"And you, Constantine?" Ella asked.

"I knew more than Jean."

"How?"

"The Entity told me. When I was captured, it took me to a sphere, a portal to everything, he claimed. This is part of that sphere, except the Monk has created this for you, Vincent."

"Actually, I think it was mainly for Connie," said Ella.

"I saw you and the Entity fighting in the sphere. It was in a vivid dream I had, just after you disappeared. Did you communicate with me?" Vincent asked.

"It wasn't me. The Entity allowed you to see us."

"Why?"

"Because you both, somehow hold the key to the future," Constantine replied.

"How can El and I..." Vincent started to say, before he realised, "It's Connie. She holds the key, doesn't she?"

"Yes. Somehow, Connie influences us all in the future - Humans, Odorphins and Hollow People."

"If she holds the fate of all in her hands, will they ever let us leave?"

"That's the strange thing. The Monk keeps telling me all who come here are free to leave."

"Why haven't you, after all this time?"

"Because like you, I have only just arrived. Or that's what I believed until your arrival. The Monk told me you would come soon and you did," said Constantine.

"It's been ten years!" Ella exclaimed.

"So it seems," said Constantine, seemingly struggling to provide an answer for Ella. "Only one person can provide us with answers, the Monk. We must confront him and seek answers, or I'm afraid we may all perish here.

They all returned to the Miroir d'Eau The large expanse of low lying vapour had cleared to reveal a holographic like image of one galaxy after another. It swirled like a merry-go-round of galactic proportions, as a steady low vibration provided a mystical, musical background to the movement. Connie continued to play with her friends, well away from the swirling orchestra of stars, unaware of it or the events that were unfolding. Constantine led Vincent and Ella to where the Monk and Jean stood together, watching the children.

"Ella, Vincent and I have spoken and we all agree that we wish to return to Vincent's universe as soon as possible, so that Connie may return to her normal life," said Constantine, wasting no time.

The Monk gazed at all three, but did not respond.

"Will you keep your promise and allow us to return from where we came?" Constantine demanded.

"I said you were free to leave any time, should you wish to take such a foolhardy risk," replied the Monk.

"Why can't you return with us. You brought us here," Vincent asked.

"I will not do that. You will face the return to the world of Baryon matter alone, or not at all." The Monk stood with stony silence, waiting for a reply, but getting none. Instead, only forlorn looks of defeat. "I will help prepare you for such a journey, though," he added.

"Prepare us? You took us to this place in an instant. Why would it not be equally easy to return? Ella asked.

"You have all returned to the Source. What you once were, has gone."

"We have developed complex avatars that enable us to travel between universes and dimensions. Are you saying our holographic structures no longer exist? We all appear to be standing alongside you. What has changed?" Constantine asked.

"You all have travelled to the source, some for an imperceptible period of time, others for many years. This occurrence has led to fundamental changes to your atomic structure, subtle but definitive."

"You're implying a difference, nonetheless. What has changed?" Constantine pressed.

"It is a stability issue. It's possible that the avatar Higgs particles may not recognise your atomic structure."

"Then"

"You will remain in the Source."

"So our chances of returning to my universe are a risk worth taking or not?" Vincent asked.

"They are roughly equal."

"We have a fifty percent chance of success or failure?"

"Yes, but should you succeed, your real challenge begins. The imbalance in your atomic level will have to be quickly identified and actioned, or your structure will be rejected."

"How much time will we have to rectify that imbalance?" Ella asked.

"The time will vary with each person. As little as a few Earth hours, but no longer than two Earth days. You will all react differently. So your challenge will be to find antidotes that adjusts to the different imbalances in each system."

Constantine looked to Vincent and Ella for approval that they proceed, before responding to the Monk.

"We all want to proceed. But we will need your help," said Constantine.

The Monk looked into the Miroir d'Eau as its centre flashed with a swirling mass of far off galaxies, foreshadowing the ominous challenge they would face.

"I suggest you start with atomic samples of all who will make the voyage."

"We already have the samples," Constantine replied.

"You will need to take more samples. Subtle changes have occurred since your arrival at the source. Join me at Saint Michel church and I will work with you on appropriate orbs that will protect you against the dangers you will encounter."

With that, the Monk vanished before their eyes, followed shortly after by Constantine and Ella, leaving Vincent and Jean at the Miroir d'Eau, not far from Connie, playing at the adjoining park.

"She's an adventurous child," Jean said, admiringly.

"Connie is so much like El. Sometimes I think she'll turn into an Odorphin. She only wants to play and explore. After this experience, she'll want to fly to France."

"All children want to explore, my boy. She will just need a bigger playground."

"Exactly. Connie takes bigger risks than your normal child. I'm sure she'd try to swim to the nearest island, if I let her."

"It may be best, you allow her more than a typical child her age," replied Jean, surveying their surroundings.

"I think we will need your help when we return, Jean," said Vincent, waiting for a reply and receiving none.

"Or perhaps you have other plans when you return?"

Jean appeared evasive, before he met Vincent's gaze. "I'm not returning."

Vincent initially thought it a joke, but Jean maintained a fixed gaze, confirming he was serious.

"You have nothing here, Jean. You're no more than their prisoner."

"It's so hard to explain my, my boy. The Monk would no doubt say that my time in the Source has made subtle shifts to my atomic structure. But I would put it more simply - I don't want to leave. It's the funniest feeling. I never actually remember the Source, yet my instincts tell me it is where I want to be."

Vincent held his uncle's shoulder, showing his concern, as he studied his face. He hadn't appeared to age a day since their last meeting, but his demeanour was of someone much older. His inquisitive nature had left him, as if experiences in this half-way house between life and the time before time had drained him.

"I need you, Jean."

Jean's volatile emotions resurfaced as sadness overtook him.

"I wish I could better explain why I feel this way, Vincent. It's as if Alzheimer's has attacked a certain part of my brain. I remember every special day we have shared, as if it were yesterday. Yet this other life that consumes me is as vague as a lighthouse's spotlight in a fog. Even worse, it feels as if there is a Medusa hidden in the thick fog, whispering to me to head for the light. I know I go there at my peril and yet I feel I must join her."

Vincent turned toward Connie, more to hide his sadness from Jean. "If not for me, think of Connie. I know she would grow to love you dearly."

Jean studied Connie, seemingly seeing someone more than a child happily playing.

"She will do great things, Vincent. She appears to have an insatiable thirst for knowledge and a fearlessness to pursue it. You will need to show courage as her father and a willingness to let go of the ones you love."

"What do you see?" Vincent asked, hiding his fears for his daughter. He had shown courage a decade earlier, facing the Entity, but the thought that he may lose Connie to it would be too much to endure.

"It's impossible to see the future clearly. Past, present and future swirl together in a dance of life and death in this world the Monk calls the Source. It feels more like a vivid dream that can only be interpreted not understood."

"Do you see Connie in the Source?"

Jean reacted to Vincent's question, as if he suddenly remembered what he had seen.

"Remember that life and death are not real, rather two sides of the same coin. Stay strong when you face the darkest of challenges, for they will eventually bring times you will cherish." Jean held Vincent close to him. "Do that for me, my boy. Won't you? Promise me?" He said, almost pleading.

"Yes, Jean. I promise."

"Look high above you, Daddy. What is that?" Connie asked as she raced toward him. Two Odorphins hovered high above them.

"Wow! Aren't they beautiful creatures, my darling? They hover like seagulls don't they?"

"Yeah, they're beautiful. They won't hurt us, will they?"

"No, Connie," Vincent replied, holding her close.

"I told you I'd show you magic, didn't I?" Said the Monk, suddenly appearing behind them.

"Where's mummy? I want her to see them, too!"

Vincent cast a questioning glance toward the Monk, searching for an answer.

"She is in the city, teaching some of the children. But they flew over her class as well."

"Oh good! Will she be long?"

"Not long, but she will have to miss this new journey that I want to show you and your father. It's to another fantastic world that I think you will enjoy," said the Monk. Connie immediately pulled on her father's arm, seeking permission.

"Yes, we are both going on this journey," replied Vincent, firmly holding his daughter's hand.

"You and your father will be accompanied by the two magical creatures and your mother will join you soon after. Will that be alright, Connie?" The Monk asked.

She jumped up and down excitedly at the thought of a new adventure, before turning her eyes to her father, who nodded his head in the affirmative, before speaking.

"Go and play with your friends a little longer and I'll call you when we are ready."

As Connie raced back to her friends, Ella hovered down to the Miroir d'Eau. Vincent waited for her to transform into her human form, as he walked toward her, but she remained Odorphin. The sight of her alien features drew mixed feelings in Vincent. He was happy that Ella could again be her true self, but anxious about what it would mean for their life together. And what would it mean for Connie? He greeted her nervously, unsure what to say, almost as if they were strangers.

"Connie wanted to see her mother," he said, immediately regretting his veiled accusation, but hoping she would react to it by changing to her human identity, but Ella held her gaze out to the Miroir d'Eau.

"The journey through the portal will be dangerous. It will be safer for Constantine and I to remain in our Odorphin form," she replied, turning to him and holding two rainbow-lit orbs on the palm of her two out-stretched hands.

"One each, for you and Connie."

Vincent held the two orbs close, like two long-lost friends. "These bring back memories, my love," he said, touching her face and studying the violet coloured beams that emanated from her light web.

"More than memories, Vincent. Once lived, always lived. Don't let time confuse you."

"I remember when you told me that on the Brighton pier all those years ago. I hope that's true as I always want to be with you, my darling."

Ella fanned her light web around Vincent, warming his body with its gentle vibrations. "Whatever happens on this journey, know that I truly love you. Promise me you will never lose faith in what we have shared."

Vincent drew Ella's inner body close to his, feeling the emotions her alien face could not reveal. "What wrong, El? It's as if you know what is going to happen."

"Promise me."

"Yes I promise. You will always be my one true love."

Ella's body relaxed, as her light web changed to a darker maroon hue. "Did we scare Connie?"

"She thought you were both beautiful bird-like creatures. She wanted to fly with you."

"That's good. I don't want to speak with her on this journey. She must not know my true identity. The shock would be too unsettling for her."

"Don't worry. I will keep her close. The Monk told her that you would follow us later."

"Good," she said, before turning her gaze to the sky, where Constantine hovered high.

"It's nearly time. You must bring Connie to the edge of the portal. Use the orbs, then put her mask back on, before you step into the portal. We will follow."

Vincent wished El was in human form so that he could hold his wife of ten happy years. But she appeared aloof and unsettled. His instincts were telling him that whether they succeeded or not, all their lives were about to permanently change.

Vincent and Connie returned to the edge of the Miroir d'Eau with the Monk and Jean by their side. Its surface was of calm shallow waters that reflected postcard-like mirror images of the nineteenth century Gothic building of La Bourse. The serenity of the scene belied the pending storm that they were about to step into.

"I love this place, Daddy," said Connie.

"If you keep studying French grammar daily, I will bring you back to Bordeaux."

"Oh yes, I will. My friends taught me so many new words. Je t'aime ma pere et mere."

"Very good, my darling. And we both love you very much, too."

"When can we return?"

"We will take you every summer vacation, if you study hard. Now, let Jean help you with your special mask, so the Monk can show us more magic."

As Jean fitted the mask on Connie, Vincent approached the Monk who stood by the portal's edge.

"If we succeed, will this be the last time I or my family see you?"

The Monk reacted slightly bemused by Vincent's question. "Define success?"

"If we all arrive home safely."

"Yes, I can assure you that you will not see me again if that occurs. Your life and that of others would return to normal, as you see it."

"And Ella?"

"That will be her choice. Not mine."

"No offence, but I hope I never see your kind again," said Vincent, forthrightly.

"None taken. But that, I cannot promise you. You and your uncle have started a complex process that can never be unravelled. What you are yet to realise is that these shared, unfolding events will have profound effects that go well beyond your limited view of success. What I find ironic, is that you are gifted with the vision to see it, but you choose not to."

"I will not search for answers, if they risk the lives of my family."

"That I'm afraid, you have no control over," said the Monk with a confidence that unnerved Vincent. In truth, he knew he could never escape the clutches of the Hollow people, should they wished to pursue him. He just hoped that he could remove Connie from their viper web.

"Send us home," he said, wanting to say no more to the Monk.

Connie joined him and held his hand as firmly as the mask had been wrapped around her young face. Vincent cast a final look at the Bordeaux cityscape, before it began to change in shape. Buildings twisted and folded as if he viewed it through the rim of a wine glass as wine swirled around its edges. Van Gogh-like images encircled the portal as it swirled around them into the pitch black pit that filled the Miroir d'Eau.

On the Monk's signal, he held Connie firmly and stepped into the portal that would return them to their world of matter. Both vanished at the speed of light from the Monk's half-way world, closely followed by two Odorphins. All four fell toward the familiar dense fog that Vincent presumed would rebuild their structures into baryon matter. Vincent expected their journey through the fog to be as quick as their last encounter, but this time everything slowed, allowing him time to see the fog with greater clarity. It wasn't a fog, but more the grandest of oceans that stretched out, encompassing what initially looked like giant stars. But as they drew closer, he could see that the many stars were made up of an infinite number of stars. He was looking at galaxies, or perhaps universes, spread out to infinity and surrounded by a vast ocean that encircled them like a colossal winding river. Briefly, he could see the multiverse, but then they fell into the grand swirling ocean that shaped and held the universes in place. They struck the coal coloured sea at light speed, plunging into their uncertain futures. Vincent felt as if he would drown in the eternal ocean, but there was nothing he could do, except hold his daughter close to him and hope they would survive the journey through the bottomless deep. He thought he caught a glimpse of Ella's light web, before a shimmering light directly below him diffused the smaller light. They slowed as strange shaped ripples weaved alien patterns around them, lit he believed by the light of universes. Vincent held Connie closer to him, fearing one of the myriad of ripples may part them. Connie lay still in his arms, apparently in deep slumber. Vincent guessed the orb protected her from the gravitational forces, just as all the orbs he had used had protected him, except this one. Perhaps Constantine wanted him to experience these sensations?

"Yes, I wanted you to feel this very special ocean, both its depths and its surface," said Constantine, telepathically. "You are about to surf the multiverse' galactic rim."

Vincent first saw the approaching storm well before feeling its force. It was not unlike rapidly breaking waves. The maelstrom came into clear focus, looking more like an entanglement of a thousand breaking waves, creating a cylindrical weave of energy unlike anything he could have imagined. The sight of its force terrified him.

"This energy field will re-build our mass. We must all ride through it," said Ella reassuringly, seemingly observing the fear in Vincent's eyes.

"Join us, El. We need you with us," said Vincent, as he looked in all directions to locate her, but Ella didn't reply, leaving Constantine to respond.

"Each one of us must travel through this field alone, Vincent. You must let go of Connie, now."

"Never! El, where are you?"

"None of us can travel together, Vincent. If you don't let go of Connie, you will both perish. Quickly do as Constantine asked," she replied.

Vincent did not want to let his little girl go, but reluctantly, he did as asked. The energy was bursting around them as if a dozen whirlpools of water approached them from every direction.

Reluctantly, he let go of Connie, immediately regretting his decision as Connie quickly fell toward the ferocity of the whirlpool. Vincent instinctively reached out to her, all too late, as she vanished into its epicentre.

"Ella. Help her," he cried, willing himself to follow her, but unable to move. Vincent was held by an invisible force as he floated helplessly above the unfolding violence. Constantine followed Connie into the field, then finally Ella disappeared into the portal to Vincent's universe. To Vincent's frustration, time appeared to stand still as he floated above a storm that was rapidly pulling itself apart. Had he missed his only chance to return home to his family? Was he doomed to an eternity in this never world?

"Please let me go, too," he pleaded into the screaming gales, hoping someone was listening.

"Do you accept your future?" Came the voice of the Monk. Vincent looked in every direction, hoping the Monk had joined him to guide him through the storm.

"Please, I have to be there for my daughter. I will do anything, but let me be with her."

"You told the Entity that you saw your purpose. Do you remember?" The Monk asked.

"Yes. Yes, I remember."

"And what is your purpose?"

"To teach my world to understand and help my daughter do the same."

"Then why do you continue to turn your back on that life?"

"I value my daughter's life ahead of my own. That's why I must be with her, now."

"You cannot control her destiny. Stop fearing death and follow your destiny. Then you will be released from your self-imposed chains."

Vincent ignored the Monk's words as he continued to struggle free from the invisible force that held him, but the more he struggled, the tighter he was gripped. Vincent screamed, frustration overwhelming him, but no amount of anger could break the Monks hold. An equal mix of sweat and tears rolled down his face as Vincent accepted his fate.

"I will follow my true course." He called out, reluctantly.

"Is there death?"

"No." Vincent replied, his head bowed.

"Will you face your fears?"

"Yes. Release me now and let me be with my family."

Vincent fell toward the storm, knowing what would follow would change his life and the lives of everyone he loved.

Vincent woke in a sea of foam, his last memory was of a wave of white energy striking and blinding him in a whiteout. All sensation ceased in the whirlpool as did time. He initially thought he remained in the multiverse field, until he sighted the familiar rusted pier of Brighton, three hundred metres to his right. Constantine and Ella flew low to the sea, halfway to the pier. They looked like two giant seagulls searching for food as they hovered then dived toward the water. But instead of breaking water, small flashes of light erupted, seemingly stopping them from entering the ocean. They continued swooping frantically, each time their descent was met with the same electrical resistance. Vincent initially wondered what they were searching for, before a single thought chilled him to his core.

"Connie!" He cried, before running from the foam into the crashing waves that had formed the shore-lined foam. He swam fifty metres before encountering the force field that had likely stopped Ella and Constantine. Then, to his horror, he saw Connie. Her body lay face up and still in the choppy waters, as if she were sleeping. Vincent hoped that to be the case, daring not to consider the alternatives. He desperately searched for a way past the force field, by swimming and diving along its edge, but it appeared to be surrounding Connie in all directions, in a fifty metre rectangular based dome. He swam fully around the field and repeated his circumnavigation until too exhausted. Between deep breaths he cried out to the Monk.

"You said I would fulfil my destiny and yet you take all that matters in my life from me. Please, let her go!" He begged, as he looked skyward. He repeated his pleas, unable to contain his growing fears for his daughter's safety, as he angrily hit the force field with increasing intensity. Then, Ella flew to him, changing to her human form as she tried to console him.

"Is there no way through, El?"

"We've circumnavigated it many times. It's completely sealed."

"Why? What is it?"

El touched the force field, lighting up its opaque surface with her light web.

"Its shape is exactly that of the Miroir d'Eau," she said, reluctantly.

"No, it can't be!" Vincent screamed.

They held their gaze toward Connie, who remained unmoved in the centre of the expanse.

"She could be sleeping from the orb," said Vincent.

But as they watched on helplessly, they noticed that Connie's body was becoming increasingly translucent.

"Please! No! Take me, not our daughter!" Vincent pleaded. But in the next instant, Connie's ghost-like silhouette disappeared, along with the force field that held her captive. Ella took Vincent's hand and flew to the empty space of water that their daughter had occupied. Ella scanned the area for any trace of her daughter, before turning skyward toward Constantine. He fanned his light web a dark hue, seemingly signalling bad news. Vincent did not dare ask Ella what had happened. His gaze was directed past the water where Connie had been, to the rusted old pier. He recalled the time when he had nearly lost his life to the Entity. And now, ten years later, the life of his little girl had been lost, seemingly to the Monk. Vincent felt numb with pain, unable to speak, even to El, who he knew must feel the same. Then bitterness and anger filled him.

"Why do they play with us, El? They hold great powers, yet they act like cruel gods. Why would observers of the multiverse act in such a grotesque manner?"

"This special time we shared was unforgettable, but none of it was real. It was a life shared on a dream-like plane."

"So our love wasn't real?"

"I loved you, knowing that this was always likely to be our fate," said Ella. She caressed Vincent's face, before he moved back from her, unwilling to accept her affection.

"We did all that was possible to make them see what we shared, Vincent."

"We shouldn't have left the Monk's world. I shouldn't have pressed..." said Vincent, before guilt stopped him from saying more.

"We were ready. Delaying our return would have made no difference. Connie was missing one important element."

"What?"

"She was not born in your world. She was born in another place. You could say we were granted a glimpse of her potential life. That life is where your real future lies, Vincent."

"You're leaving me, aren't you?"

"We're all returning to our real lives." Ella replied, extending her hand to Vincent, only to be ignored.

"You never loved me. You don't even show remorse for the loss of our child!" Said Vincent, walking away from Ella, toward the pier.

"I loved you with all my heart. If there was any way of returning to our family....to the life we shared, I'd return to it in an instant. But all of this life was pre-destined. It can't be changed." She replied, following Vincent, then grasping his arm to stop him.

"What possible reason could drive them to create this cruel world?"

"They were learning, just as we need to learn."

"Learn what? How to tear people's lives apart?"

"They saw our future destiny. We were the first to travel the multiverse, as we were also the first to travel through the Higgs Field and back."

"So we are no more than some twisted experiment?"

"They believed there was no other way. Remember, Jean was the first and he failed to return back to your universe. You, Constantine and I were the second to attempt to return and we succeeded where Jean failed."

Vincent gazed at Ella, anger building in him. "Connie didn't return, which makes them murderers!" Vincent cried, unable to contain his pain.

"Many have lost their lives, to further the cause of science."

"Science? You speak of science when you have lost your daughter. I'll show you what I think of science!"

Vincent removed his trusted notebook from his coat pocket and held it high in the air for a time.

"I have sacrificed so much to show you my love. I wonder if it was ever returned? Am I no more than a science experiment to you? I have lost the daughter I cherish. It seems I have lost you and the love you never had for me."

Vincent threw his notebook into the Brighton waters and walked away from Ella, towards the end of the pier. Ella immediately followed, holding him tight, ignoring his efforts to break loose.

"I loved you with all my heart. We have shared ten beautiful years. But this was always going to end, if Connie failed to return through the Higgs Field. That was our destiny. That was her destiny. Connie failed to return where in the future, the real daughter you conceive in your universe will not."

"They took our ten years, El. Do you think I'd want to live that again without you?"

"Those ten years were lived in another place, constructed by the Hollow People. You have loved a holographic image of me, probably in a digitally constructed world. What we experienced was no more than an experiment carried out by a race with no empathy for our concept of time. They perceive all time and all possible futures as a misconception. The value we put on our life is little more than a trick of the mind."

"Then why bother?"

"My guess is that Connie will play an important role in shaping a future that leads to a higher consciousness to the multiverse. We have our part to play, but it is still to happen."

"And that role is?"

"You already know that."

"Enlighten me?"

"We both have to return to our real lives to fulfil our own destinies. We must go home, Vincent," said Ella, her sadness spilling into tears.

"Ten years, El. A beautiful daughter. You may be able to let it go, but I can't."

"Then hold on to these memories and honour what we shared by living the life you were meant to have. Remember what the Monk told you. There is no death. I believe Connie lives in the Monk's world, with Jean."

"I hope you're right, El"

Both reached out and embraced, trying to quell their loss with affection, sharing their grief in the long silence. Vincent thought what El said was true, but raw, painful thoughts remained with the daughter he had just lost. No amount of logic would ever make that feel right.

That was Vincent's last vision of his future life before Ella extended her hand to him, jolting him from their ten years together, back to the moment before the Entity took them to its world. She held his hand as they walked back toward the shoreline of Brighton beach. They passed by the 'eastern toll house', one of twin toll houses at the shoreline entry to the pier. They stopped at a viewing platform for a final glimpse of the calm ocean waters. Vincent stood in silence with Ella until the fog lifted, revealing calm blue waters and the slow rhythm of gentle waves. The pier they had just walked on together had gone, leaving only the burnt out remnants, the same dark rusted shell on which he fought the Entity.

"I don't know what is real or imagined anymore," said Vincent.

"Everything you just experienced was from your real future."

"I will have another daughter," said Vincent.

"Yes, she shall bring you great happiness."

"But she will see the shadows too, like I did in my youth. There must be a way to stop that from ever happening to her!" Vincent almost pleaded with Ella for an answer, but he knew there was none.

"This is why you must learn as much as you can about the multiverse." Ella looked out to the ocean, before continuing.

"Every world you visited was real. But now you are back in your dimension. This is the world you know and believe to be real. This is where I first arrived on your Earth," she said, pointing to the rusted shell of the once grand pier.

Vincent had experienced a range of emotions there, joy, grief, loss and terror. It was a dark shadowy world in that place, yet mystical as well.

"Why here?"

A knowing glance formed across Ella's sea blue eyes.

You'll find out in good time."

"But I must return. I have lost too much in this shadowy place. My life is back home."

"As I recall, you contracted your labour to us until the end of the month," she said light heartedly, taking his hand, before continuing.

"Stay until then. Explore these shores, particularly around the piers. Do this for me and for Constantine. And for Connie. Promise me."

Ella gazed deep into his eyes, her light heartedness replaced with serious intent.

"I will. I could do with the rest!" Vincent replied, bringing a small feeling of happiness between their tears.

Both laughed. A brief feeling of joy returned after the darkness. A small window of light had re-emerged lifting their spirits. Hope.

"I keep my promises. But everyone will think I'm mad!" Vincent exclaimed.

"Then I'll keep my promise."

Ella spread her light web wide and wrapped it around Vincent. It glowed like a pulsar. Radiant light poured from her, filling Vincent with intense joy.

"It feels so beautiful. I never want it to end."

Radiant light surrounded him and poured through his willing body. Ella's beautiful form vanished in the blinding light, but then he felt the new immersant flowing through him. His initial blindness transformed to sight so radiant, that he felt he'd spent a lifetime blind. Colours danced before him, textures so rich he could not name them. Even a perfect rainbow would look more a grey fog in this light. A shimmering of violet danced around the infinite textures as if he saw other universes - whole universes so close he could touch them.

And in that world bathed in radiant light he first saw Ella clearly. She whispered a melody of sounds to him.

"Now you see through Odorphin eyes and hear through Odorphin ears."

Vincent cried tears of joy. "For the first time in my life I can see."

And the sight of Ella's Odorphin form had a clarity and a symphony of colour that danced around her body. Her skeletal form, normally blurred by the textures of her light web was now fully revealed. She stood before him, her body vulnerable, unprotected. Ella's frame was thinner than any human could be, but her shape and skin was unmistakably of human origin. Her face radiated white as frost, where her sea blue eyes shone like a morning ocean. Her light web too was a shimmering mass of psychedelic light that surged around her, a symphony of colour. Vincent felt an invisible current draw him to her hypnotic eyes like an inlet to an ocean.

They were more powerful than any addiction he had ever experienced. He wanted to immerse his soul into her shimmering eyes as he let go his inhibitions. Then he saw his reflection in her eyes. A green hue surrounded him. He believed it was his aura, for he saw the misty hue stream from his body toward Ella's light. Vincent could not draw his gaze from her, drawing ever closer, until he felt he was looking through Ella's eyes. He bathed in its warmth and new textures for what felt a lifetime. Every sight, sound and taste in his body became a feast of sensual pleasure. He would have surrendered the core of his soul to Ella so that he could remain in that sweet expanse.

His body erupted in sensual pleasures as he stood close to Ella in a lovers' embrace. His skin tingled to the sensations that unfolded layer upon layer, until one final shuddering delight; and then one last kiss. He felt Ella's soft breath on his lips as he held a last gaze into her alien eyes. Then she stepped away. He knew Ella was leaving. He would never again feel her sweet sensual joy. But before leaving his universe, Ella slipped an orb of star light on to Vincent's open palms.

"Our bond is forged."

"Is this for me?"

"No. It's for Connie. So that she will be prepared next time she voyages to the world of the Hollow People. With this orb, she will return to you and she will be able to live the life she is destined to lead."

MICHAEL LEON

Ella caressed Vincent's face for the last time, before she held her light web high and flew quickly to the rusted canopy of the West Pier. There the light web intensified to rich colours. Pulsating rays emanated from her, bathing the old pier scaffold in rose red. Sound followed the light, an intense high pitched noise, making Vincent shield his ears but not his gaze. A flash of white light charged up from the ocean depths, engulfing Ella, before she vanished without trace. He had never felt so alone.

Vincent slowly settled back into a normal life. He walked the shores of Brighton every morning, passing the early morning joggers and the walkers, many with dogs, all sharing the wide expanse of the esplanade as they commenced their day invigorated by the sea's fresh breezes.

Every day for a fortnight he stopped at the old shell that was once the West Pier. Sometimes he stood staring at its ghostly features for over an hour, willing Ella's return. But he had to accept that would never happen. By the third week he preferred to walk the Brighton Pier. The pier was filled with the aromas and activities of everyday life. Fish and chips fried in the many small food stalls as children rushed to the assortment of games and rides that were on offer. Proud parents shared their children's delight, no doubt re-living their own youthful experiences on the pier a generation earlier.

It was there that Vincent first saw her. She had long red hair flowing across her bare shoulders, glistening in the warm sun, as she gazed westward past the old pier. Vincent rushed toward her, his hopes high.

"Ella. You've returned," he said excitedly.

"I'm sorry, do I know you?"

Vincent knew then it was not Ella. Her appearance was identical, but her voice differed in tone and accent.

"Oh, I'm sorry. It's just you look so much like someone I knew. Please forgive me."

"That's alright. Are you a local here? You don't sound it," she said, her accent filled with deep European tones.

"No, I've been here for a few weeks, visiting from Australia, spending some time with old friends. But they had to leave."

"Me too."

"Your friends left too?" said Vincent confused.

"No, I'm visiting England on my own. I meant that I'm from Australia too. I've been here for a few weeks. I'm El," she said, extending her hand.

They both laughed, with a familiarity that belied their just meeting.

"I'm Vincent, I hope you don't think me too forward, but would you care to join me for a coffee."

"I think I'd enjoy that," she replied, before they set off for the nearest cafe, happily mingling amongst the lunch time crowd as they shared many stories with each other.

RENEWING
The Soul

SOULS OF CHICAGO #4

ANNABELLA
MICHAELS

Renewing the Soul
Souls of Chicago Series #4

Copyright © 2017 Annabella Michaels

ISBN: 978-0-9989888-3-2

annabellamichaels.blogspot.com/

Cover art provided by Jay Aheer of Simply Defined Art – www.jayscoversbydesign.com

Editing provided by Pam Ebeler of Undivided Editing – www.undividedediting.com

Proofreading provided by Judy Zweifel of Judy's Proofreading – www.judysproofreading.com

Interior Design and Formatting provided by Stacey Blake of Champagne Formats – www.champagneformats.com

Copyright and Trademark Acknowledgments

The author acknowledges the copyright and trademarked status and trademark owners of the following trademarks and copyrights mentioned in this work of fiction:

Cadillac Escalade- General Motors
Royal Air Force
U.S Navy SEALs
Bambi- Walt Disney Productions
Grant Park. Chicago, Illinois
Buckingham Fountain. Chicago, Illinois
"Pour Some Sugar On Me"- Def Leppard: Mercury
"Tangled Up In You"- Aaron Lewis: Stroudavarious Records
The Walking Dead: AMC Networks, Inc.
Netflix: Netflix, Inc.
Mario, Luigi, Donkey Kong-Nintendo: Nintendo of America, Inc.
Queer As Folk: Sowtime, Showcase
The Twilight Zone: Rod Serling
X-Men: Marvel Comics
Koenigsegg- Supercar
Uber- Uber Technologies, Inc.
Ford Shelby Mustang- Ford Performance Shelby
The Palazzo- The Palazzo Las Vegas